A Time For The Wicked

(The Secrets Within)

By Howard Keiser

D1319250

Table of Contents

When evil was hailed and justice had failed.

When the watchmen slept,

And their lights grew dim.

That's when the wicked darkness crept in.

Chapter One: Research For the Greater Good of Mankind

Have the global dangers of modern-technologies out-grown the morals and common sense of modern mankind? Doctor Robert Jennings was deep in thought, contemplating this very question in his office, which was located inside a 14 billion-dollar laboratory. The privately funded, Nano cell-biotech research lab was built inside of a mountain in a remote area of the Blue Ridge Mountains in western Virginia. The property Globocorp purchased to build the lab had become another project for their branch company - Globotech. The project was to convert an abandoned coalmine into one of the most high-tech research laboratories in the world.

The old coalmine came with one thousand acres of land that was level enough to build on without major excavation. The coalmine and the property were a perfect fit for a top-secret research laboratory. In the early 1900s, there was a small mining town built three miles away from the coalmine where the miners and their families lived. They named the town Little Falls after the waterfall that fed into a small river that the town was built around. The water was clean and the people had easy access to it. There was an old dirt road that the townspeople used to descend from the mountain to the main road. Trains wound their way down the worn path to the coal yard where the coal was distributed to railroad companies, cities, and people's homes. However, the coalmine closed after a horrific accident. Twelve coalminers were caught in the mine when it caved in and fell through into an underground cavern.

Unfortunately, back then the technology and money it would cost to retrieve their remains prevented the families of the dead to do so. From that day on, the coalmine remained closed. Nobody would go near it because of the ghost stories, and superstitions that the mountain people believed, back in the day. Many still believe the area is cursed. All of this was favorable for Globocorp to buy the land dirt-cheap.

The laboratory was three stories deep inside the mountain. It was finally completed; now it was time to man the lab and begin the research. Globotech had been scouring colleges and research laboratories around the world for the brightest minds and the most promising recruits. Part of one of the biggest corporations in the world, Globotech offered all potential employees four times the money that they could make anywhere else. They were also promised enormous incentive bonuses for any new discoveries in biological and Nano cell technology. The reason for the large paychecks, and bonus incentives were they had to sign a non-disclosure agreement, and agree to not leave the premises for ten years. 'Ten years' sounds like a long time to be removed from society, but these young scientists had everything they could possibly need, and more, all on the premises. It really wasn't a tough decision to make.

Globotech had done their homework picking out their researchers. They made sure to get the smartest, top-in-their-class, candidates. Most of them were offered the opportunity straight out of college in their respective fields of research. Many of them jumped at the opportunity. They would be doing research with Doctor Robert Jennings. Great things were expected to come from the revered doctor. Throughout the scientific community, it was thought he would be the next Edison or Tesla. They dreamed of making history, and improving the world and humanity. Then, after ten years, they would not only be famous accredited scientists, but also very rich. The sacrifice of censored communication with loved ones, and a secluded social life was hard, but a chance like this was something most of them knew they would never get again in three lifetimes.

The second floor had a nice restaurant-bar, a state-of-the-art gymnasium, with a quarter-mile running track made of vulcanized rubber. The other half of the second floor housed the maintenance crews, secretaries, clerical people and janitors. There was a secure storage area for all the needed chemical cleaners and parts for equipment, in case they were needed. The third floor, which was the top floor, consisted of research laboratories divided up by specific fields of research. Every lab had a main conference room and an office. The facility was enormous.

Each of the three floors was the size of two football fields. There were four large service elevators and four elevators for the staff, with emergency staircases connected to each of the three floors. The doctors and research scientists were all housed on the first and bottom floor. It was elegant living with hot tubs, steam rooms, and luxury apartments. The design and lighting made the first floor seem like you were at ground level, out in the open, and not deep in the bottom of a cavern. The exterior grounds were beautiful; there was a man-made filtered pond with a waterfall that was built to look natural, flowing from ten feet high. Numerous, comfortable screened-in gazebos and picnic areas were scattered about, many with paths leading to the pond. A person working for Globotech always got the best money could buy. Outside, surrounding the compound was a high-voltage electric fence with razor wire and guard dogs. There were also armed security shacks every two hundred yards, with patrols along the fence line that checked in every thirty minutes.

Security had been stepped up when Doctor Jennings successfully advanced Nano cell technology by decades during his seventh year of research. There was one road in and out of the thousand-acre grounds. The security changed shifts every eight hours. With the security office building on the grounds near the private airport, that accommodated any size airplane or commercial jet. Most of the guards were put up in Little Falls, where Globotech built housing for them, and their families. The security guards were told that they were protecting a top-secret American facility. The security employees also signed a non-disclosure agreement contract. They understood that if it were proven they told anyone any procedural details of their assignments, no matter how miniscule, they would be sued, terminated, and possibly face felony charges. The front and only way in or out of the lab was big enough for a tractor-trailer truck to back in and unload all supplies that were needed.

Only two roads came to the massive six-inch-thick titanium-coated vapor-proof doors. One road came from the private airfield on the grounds, and one from the security employee parking lot. Doctor Jennings understood the extra security; after all the money Globotech invested in his research, if someone stole their discoveries, they would get billions of dollars of research; plus countless man-hours of work, for almost nothing. He was grateful for the extra security, one less thing he needed to worry about.

The doctor was so relieved when he figured out a way to design a Nano cell, smaller and amazingly more powerful, just by figuring out how to have it not need its own power source. Looking back now, it seemed like a simple idea. It always amazed him how people over-complicate things. KISS – keep it simple, stupid – was his motto and wow, did it prove to be true. In hindsight, he couldn't believe a simple idea had been ignored for six years, and it only took a little over a year to make it happen.

Globotech was sending their corporate supervisor out more frequently and he started putting the pressure on Doctor Jennings. He knew Doctor Spears from Globocorp was due for a visit soon, and he was in for some amazing results. How could he say, "Oh, gee... I'm sorry I couldn't come up with much of anything..." especially after Globotech dumped billions of dollars into this project, based on his reputation.

As his head rushed back to the beginning of his professional life, Doctor Jennings ruminated on how he chose this specialized field of scientific research. He had first heard of Nano cell technology from one of his college buddies, Jim Dunn, who was very intrigued with the fairly new Nano cell technology. Jim said, "Imagine a man-made electronic device so small it can only be seen with a microscope! Some studies have said this technology will someday help people with nerve damage. Those who are paralyzed will be able to walk again."

Doctor Jennings wasn't buying Jim's prediction. "Jim, how can you bypass the nerves that carry the subconscious and conscious signals to work, coordinate, and control every muscle, and organ in your body, not to mention every other function?" he asked. "I'm not as optimistic as you."

"Robert, I don't know all about it, just the theoretical goals. The article explained that when computers get faster, and if we can make these Nano cells send and receive enough data to communicate with each other, they could be implanted in the brain and the muscle that no longer gets any signal. As long as the muscle is not damaged, it can be signaled by the Nano cells communicating from the part of the brain whose function was to signal these areas." Jim paused to let that sink in. "In essence, you're bypassing the dead nerves, kind of like changing from a hard-wired computer system to a wireless one. It was just something I read, I thought you might find interesting. I don't think we will see this happen in our lifetime, but it's a cool theory."

Jim old buddy, Doctor Jennings thought, it's no longer a theory. Not only have we done it, but we have also surpassed that technology by leaps and bounds. The Nano cell Doctor Jennings invented is actually so small that it can infiltrate the skin and will head toward a prepro- grammed area anywhere in the body. Being on the exact same bioelectrical frequency, the Nano cell moves toward the same magnetic flux or field that its intended host is on, just like the opposite poles of a magnet attract each oth- er. They could actually drop them from an airplane like a crop duster that drops invisible dust. They would find ev- ery mammal in the area. The Nano cell would then get in- side the blood stream, and travel to the areas where they are programmed to go. The Nano cell could then override any natural signals from the brain. If they needed to, they could have the animals move in any direction. For now, they could control all mammals, except mankind.

Doctor Jennings couldn't wait, his Nano cell had already taught them so much about how the biological electrical network inside the brain works in coordina- tion to the bodily functions. This was just the tip of the iceberg. The scientific knowledge and the discoveries that will be made due to these accomplishments may soon be able to cure every disease known to mankind.

"Thank goodness we came through," he laughed. His best people were nicknamed "The Magnificent Sev- en", because there were six staff members, plus the doc- tor. They came through big time. Now all they needed to do was find all the applications this could be used for to help solve so many problems in this world.

Doctor Jennings was proud of one particular sci- entist in "The Magnificent Seven" and the outstanding research he had done. He found a way to use a mam- mal's electrical current to power the Nano cell. Then he was able to figure out an ionic algorithm that could duplicate or replace subconscious orders from the brain to nerves in any part of the body. These signals would override any conscious signals such as decision-making.

While the team was working on that, as happens often in research, discoveries were made accidentally. As they were testing the Nano cell, feeding it different electrical, ionic algorithms, an audio biologist accidentally bumped a switch on a subsonic frequency transmitter, and the test raccoon reacted immediately. The test subject went into a rage, slightly injuring itself trying to get out and attack them, which the team found peculiar. Doctor Jennings decided to test the raccoon for levels of adrenaline and every glandular reaction it could have.

Doctor Stein, their bioelectrical specialist, and Doctor Hogan, their audio specialist, spent the next week going over the data and comparing sonic and electrical frequencies. From their experiments and the test readouts, they figured out how to control an animal's instinctual reactions and moods. While they were working on which combination of ionic algorithms caused certain reactions, the young technician, Nancy, came into the lab while the raccoon-test subject, was in a rage state. The raccoon's adrenaline levels spiked off the charts, as soon as Nancy entered the lab. The raccoon literally broke its teeth and claws, trying to get at her. Once Doctor Jennings shut down the ionic algorithms, the test raccoon relaxed, as if it was in a state of shock.

"What just happened here, people?" Doctor Jennings said to his staff.

Nancy spoke first. "Excuse me Doctor, I hope it wasn't my fault, but I have an important message from Globocorp."

He took a minute to size her up. "Nancy, would you be willing to give us some assistance with an experiment right now?"

"Yes Sir. It would be an honor," she replied.

"Okay, go out into the hall and wait there for someone to get you."

After she left, Doctor Jennings told his staff to start it up, just like it was before Nancy came in. There was no surprise that the raccoon became very violent, but not off the charts like when Nancy was there.

"People, I am going to ask Nancy to come back in. Be ready to shut it down quickly, just in case the test subject breaks the cage open, otherwise, keep it going. This test subject is already too damaged to be useful much longer. I would like to know how long this animal could survive at this hyper-accelerated rage state."

When Nancy came through the door, the same thing happened. The raccoon transformed from violent to an ultra-violent rage, something no one there had ever seen or even imagined before, including Dr. Jennings. He decided to see what a prolonged exposure would do. He anticipated acute brain damage from his subject, so he let it run its course. Eight minutes later, the raccoon's eyes bulged out. Blood hemorrhaged out of its nose, ears, and eyes; and then it died.

"Everybody - in my office," Dr. Jennings announced. "Nancy, you also, please."

He told two techs to get the test subject prepped for an autopsy. The doctor, his staff, and Nancy all walked in silence toward the office conference room. There was a spectrum of feelings: from elation in witnessing an

9

amazing discovery, to a sickening feeling of watching a disturbing unnatural act. All the scientists believed that it was the most savage thing they had ever witnessed. It was like watching the girl in the "Exorcist" movie on steroids...something no one would think was a possibility.

Once inside the office conference room, Doctor Jennings motioned for everyone to take a seat.

As they all sat down, there was an eerie silence, as if no one could believe what they saw with their own eyes. Dr. Jennings could see the look of shock on everyone's face, especially Nancy. She seemed to be dazed. The doctor asked the conference room attendant to take orders for coffee, tea, or water for everyone.

"Okay, people, what the hell just happened in that lab? And what caused it?" Heads turned to look at Nancy.

"Hey, I sometimes work with animals, and their heads don't usually explode when they see me. Just saying..." That received some laughs because it wasn't meant as a joke; but, ironically, it was true.

"Nancy, do you wear cologne or perfume? Are you menstruating right now? Did you shower today?" The questions came at her hard and fast. "What about your activity today? What and who have you been in contact with since you woke up this morning?"

Doctor Jennings stopped the barrage of questions. "Calm down, people. Let's do this scientifically. This is being recorded, but let's also take notes and see what we come up with."

At that moment, Pete, the janitor, who had been in the conference room emptying the trashcans said, "Excuse me, Doctor Jennings."

Everyone looked at him; unaware he was there until he spoke. Pete Miller worked for Globotech and had been cleared to be anywhere in the compound unless he was asked to leave by any doctor or tech. Doctor Jennings liked Pete. He was full of great stories about mountain living.

"I have an idea of what could have made that critter wild."

Sharp laughter from a couple of doctors split the air. One turned to Doctor Jennings and said, "Come on, Doctor Jennings. Dismiss this man. He can empty the trash later. We have serious work to do."

A hint of red flushed Pete's face as he turned away, bowed his head, and started toward the door.

"Pete, wait. Don't go. I want to hear your idea," said Doctor Jennings. "Tell us what you are thinking."

"When I was a youngen' and used to trap critters like beavers and muskrats and such, we would always have to put the smell-scent down. Boy, it smelt something awful!" You could hear a chuckle or two from the team. Then he turned to Nancy and said, "Miss Nancy, no offense ma'am, you smell just fine."

She smiled back.

"One day me, my paps and grandpaps was out checkin' and a-settin' up traps and I asked my pap, 'Hey, Pap, why do these critters come a-runnin' to something that smells so dang nasty?' My Pap said, 'Well, son, I don't rightly knows. Ask your granpaps.' So, I says, 'Grandpaps, why do these critters come a-runnin' to something that smells so dang nasty?'"

Pete paused a minute, not sure if he should continue.

"Keep going, Pete. It sounds interesting," Doctor Jennings said with a raised eyebrow.

Pete nodded. "Well, my Granpaps says, 'Son, it's not just smell. Boy, I am going to learn you some valuable lessons today. Mind what I'm a-goin' to tell you, Son. This here is a deep secret that's been a-passed down from granpappies to sons and grandsons since before our oldest kin came up to these here mountains.'"

Someone among the group let out an impatient sigh. Doctor Jennings locked eyes with Pete and said, "I'm sorry, Pete. Please continue."

Pete gave him a wink and said, "Now, where was I?" It was obvious that he was just busting the rude doctor's balls. "Oh, yeah. Granpaps says, 'you and your paps come a-closer. You never know who could be a-hearin' us the way the wind carries a man's talkin' voice up in these here hills'. Well, in all my born days, granpaps had never taught me no secret that my paps didn't already know. Well, you can just imagine how excited we was, me especially. Well, we threw down our rifles and run over to granpaps. He said, 'Now you boys hear me now, hear me real good. If'n you don't, you ain't goin' to git no scent when the good Lord takes me. The secret of the scent will go with me if'n you don't listen real hard.'"

"Yes Sir, we both said at the same time. 'Okay, now you boys know how I ask you to bring me all what's left of the critters when you're done-a-skinnin'? We both nodded and he said, 'Inside all critters' bodies, there are things called glands. Now one 'a' them, their glands has what's a-known to a wise man as a pheromone.' So I says, 'a what?' And he slapped the back of my head a-might and says, 'Boy, I ain't funnin' here. You best be a-hearin' me this time. I ain't about to start a-yellin' family secrets out! You take out that there pheromone gland and ya squeeze it a-real nice and a-slow into a mason jar. Then ya keep on a-doin' it cause there ain't a-might in it. Now don't go a-mixin' different critter pheromones together or it won't a-work as good. Beaver with beaver; muskrat with muskrat, and such'. "Then Grandpaps told us the secret. He says his grandpaps told him that these here pheromones, is what a-makes the critters come a-runnin'. They's invisible and get into the critter's brain and they can't help but go to it.'"

Doctor Jennings was sitting there with his mouth open, thinking out loud.

"My God, that's it! That sounds like the highest probability!" He shifted his eyes to each member of his team and realized that just about all of them showed signs of not paying attention. They were not really listening to Pete's story!

He jumped up out of his chair, ran over to Pete, shook his hand and said, "Pete, you're a genius! You just might have saved us months' worth of work!" By now everyone was paying attention as Doctor Jennings patted Pete on the back with a sense of pride. "Come on by my place later on tonight, around 8:00. We can have a fine glass of scotch to celebrate. I will open my best bottle!"

Pete smiled wide and said, "Thanks, Doctor Jennings."

"Pete, you can call me Robert please, and thank you. If you're right, I give you my word you will get a nice big money bonus from Globotech - on my recommendation."

Pete's face lit up and he presented his widest smile. "Well, thank ya, Robert. That sounds just fine. I'll be seeing ya tonight, Robert." Then he winked at Nancy and slipped out the conference room door. He didn't see her, when she smiled back.

Confused, the staff shot quizzical looks at their boss as if he had two heads coming out of his neck. They wondered if the doctor had finally cracked under pressure.

"Nobody leave!" Doctor Jennings ordered. "I need to explain a few things to you people." *People,* was not what he wanted to say: *Assholes,* was more fitting, except for Nancy.

Before he continued, Doctor Jennings stopped to read the message Nancy delivered to him that started this wild frenzy leading to a plausible discovery. He learned from the message that Doctor Spears would be arriving in six days to personally check out the team's developments. The message also expressed Globocorps' profound gratitude for their hard work. It was signed Mr. Atlas Grey, CEO, Globocorp.

As Doctor Jennings placed the letter back into the envelope, he turned to the team, "Did anyone get anything out of my friend Pete's, idea?" No one said a word.

"Did you all take notes like I instructed you to?" Again, no one answered.

But now the clock was ticking. The Doctor Spears from Globocorp would be there in less than a week. Doctor Jennings and his team had to move fast to test Pete's theory. None of the geniuses sitting at the table came up with a better theory than Pete.

Doctor Jennings was careful with his words when he asked Nancy if she would be willing to participate in a series of tests to see why the raccoon reacted so fiercely, only to her. The raccoon's hyper-aggression toward Nancy was an amazing, singularity; it had to be addressed immediately! Doctor Jennings assured her the tests would not be dangerous, or more painful than blood work.

"Anything for the cause," She answered with a shrug. She was also told she would receive a nice bonus for her help.

Doctor Jennings then got tough with his staff. "While all of you sat there, dripping with arrogance and your heads up your pompous Asses, the janitor made the most sense. I believe he arrived at a promising theory."

You could've heard a pin drop.

"To make up for your bad manners, arrogance, and not listening to your boss, I am assigning all of you to work an extra shift tonight." He stopped to let that sink in.

"I, on the other hand, will enjoy an evening of cocktails and intellectual discussions with Pete, our janitor, who ten minutes ago was actually the smartest man in the room." By now he had everyone's attention. He then explained what he had learned from Pete.

He concluded by saying to his team, "Now, before you go, please try to learn from this. Science is a very unpredictable thing. It's easy to overlook a simple answer because you are looking so hard for a complicated one. Nancy, would you accompany the team? It is time for us to figure out where we go from here."

The next morning while Doctor Jennings sat behind his desk in his office, Doctor Nickels rushed through the door with great news. "Doctor Jennings, we have not only isolated Nancy's pheromone, but we were able to synthetically make five gallons of an enhanced version!" He spoke rapidly and at times was incomprehensible. "The only reason for enhancing it is because we knew we were in a time crunch, with Doctor Spears' arrival," he explained. "I... um, was also supposed to tell you how sorry we are about our behavior yesterday."

Doctor Jennings' eyes softened and he patted him on the back. "Doctor Nickels, that is fantastic news, and apology accepted. Let's test it today. Oh, wait... never mind. I forgot that you just put in two shifts in a row. Get some sleep and I will wait for you before we test it." Doctor Jennings then said, "As a matter of fact, tell the rest of the staff what I said, and we can test it at the beginning of the next shift."

"Thank you, Sir," Dr. Nickels answered. "But we are ready right now, if you are."

Thirty minutes later Doctor Jennings and Doctor Nickels were in the chemistry lab, preparing for the test. Doctor Jennings was filling up a spray bottle from a beaker of the synthetically enhanced pheromone liquid while Doctor Nickels looked on.

Doctor Peters came in to announce that everything was ready for testing. He was holding a yardstick in his hand and Doctor Nickels sprayed one end of it with the synthetic pheromones.

"Where are the others?" Doctor Jennings asked.

"Actually, they were exhausted. Some of them just got to sleep," Doctor Peters declared. "I can wake them Sir, but I don't think we will need anyone else for this test. They all felt terrible about yesterday and wanted to have you wake up to good news."

Doctor Jennings was proud of his team. "Well, all of you - my best people - came through for me, and learned a valuable lesson in the process. Even an uneducated person can have a good theory. Sometimes people with real life experience learn things that a book-smart person, never will!" He quietly chuckled then said, "It's going to be a wonderful day! Thank you Doctor Peters. What kind of test subject did you choose?"

A lab rat Sir. Easier to control and clean up," the doctor answered.

"That's just what I would have suggested," exclaimed Doctor Jennings, rapidly nodding his head.

Doctor Peters was pleased by Doctor Jennings' reaction. "Well, then, what are we waiting for?"

The three doctors walked to the test lab, with Doctor Peters firmly clutching the yardstick sprayed with the enhanced pheromone near the rat's cage. He then asked Doctor Nickels to turn on the subsonic-electrical algorithm for rage. The reaction was instant. The lab rat turned uncontrollably violent, off the charts. Doctor Jennings called to shut it down. The test rat stopped all movement and relaxed his body as he shifted into a peaceful and calm position.

"Fantastic, gentlemen! Now, let's remove the pheromone stick, grab some coffee, and see what happens without the pheromones."

They approached the test lab in high spirits. So far, the experiment was successful. Doctor Jennings gave the signal and Doctor Peters turned it on. Once the rage algorithm was activated, the same off the charts violence and rage returned.

"Shut it down Doctor Peters!" Doctor Jennings ordered. Once the machine was shut off, the rat, once again, became relaxed and calm.

"We must have some of the pheromone on us," Doctor Nickels concluded. "We have to scrub up good and change our clothes."

They came back clean with new clothes and tried again, and got the same results.

"Is it possible that we still have the pheromone on us?"

"No Sir. Not a trace on us. The cleaner we used would have definitely removed it," Doctor Nickels responded to Doctor Jennings.

"I wonder if somehow we have ingested the enhanced pheromone?" Doctor Jennings questioned.

"I am sorry, Sir. I should have thought of that." There was a pause before his next comment. "We may actually be sending out the enhanced pheromone through our own bodies."

"Okay," Doctor Jennings said. He was willing to believe this hypothesis. "Time to wake up someone who hasn't been near the pheromone."

Twenty minutes later, two more people from Doctor Jennings' staff entered the lab. While the three doctors with possibly ingested synthetic pheromones watched from a television monitor in his office, the experiment offered another layer of information. The test lab rat reacted to them at an elevated rage level, but it was by no means off the charts. It was concluded that they were, in fact, infected.

"I believe our bodies will filter the enhanced pheromone out," Dr. Nickels offered. "I can run tests on us and find out if our bodies will filter it out, and how long that will take."

As it turned out, the tests proved that Doctor Nickels was right. The three men were back to normal in three days, one day before Doctor Spears' arrival.

Chapter Two: The Four Witnesses

Mary Wilson was going to school to be an interior decorator. She thought it was a classy, cool job, and she loved decorating. Her classes were during the day, so she worked nights in the bar part of a sports club. She would party on weekends and had her share of one-night stands, but she always took the pill, and almost always made whoever her partner was for the night use a condom. Two months ago, she went to a college party. She was wasted, and she knew she had sex with a cute guy, but couldn't remember his name or even what he looked like. She got caught up in the moment and asking about a condom was not one of the questions asked that night.

She had a doctor's appointment at 10:15 a.m. The five at-home pregnancy tests she took had to be wrong. She was nervous as hell sitting by herself in the doctor's office, waiting for the results.

"Miss Wilson, you tested positive," said the doctor standing over her in the waiting room. "You are approximately six weeks pregnant."

"What? How could that have possibly happened?" she complained.

"Excuse me?"

"I *never* miss taking the pill and I always practice safe sex."

"Well Miss Wilson, you are definitely pregnant."

She didn't know what to say. She grabbed her purse and jacket and stormed out of the office without saying another word. As she sat in her car, hands on the steering wheel and head bowed toward her belly, it finally sunk in.

"I'm pregnant. What the hell am I going to do? How can I go to school if I have a baby?" She liked her job and life was going along sort of okay for the moment. She was working in a bar restaurant making good money, mostly because she was very pretty and had a nice body. I won't be able to work there pregnant, and if I have the baby, I don't even know who the father is. All of a sudden everything hit her; it was real. Her mind was racing. I can't get help from a guy I don't remember. I can't get help from Mom. After she left Dad and me four years ago for some obscenely rich, old, and death-bed-looking guy, she's been out of the loop. I don't even know how to get hold of her; she doesn't give a shit about me anyway.

"Shit! What am I going to do? God, I wish Dad was alive. He would know what to do."

That night in her dorm room, she prayed. She cried, she got angry, and she felt sorry for herself. She wanted to go to sleep and wake up like nothing ever happened.

"Please help me, God, please. I don't know what to do. Please, God, help me." That night Mary whimpered herself to sleep.

The next day, she calmed down enough to get her head together. "I'm making an appointment to talk about an abortion. What kind of life could I have? I would have to quit school. I wouldn't be able to work a good-paying job while pregnant. I wouldn't be able to support a baby and a full-time nanny so I could work. There's no way. It's not fair to a baby or for me. I can't believe I am even having this conversation with myself." She called the abortion clinic and made an appointment to visit Planned Parenthood the following Monday.

Mary stood there a minute with the phone in her hand and the realization that she plans to abort her baby. She took a deep breath, then slowly exhaled, trying to settle her nerves. "Okay, that's settled." Having made the appointment and feeling like she had a plan, she started thinking about what her father would say.

"I know I am doing the right thing," she whispered to herself. "But why do I have that guilty feeling?"

Mary knew her dad would strongly counsel her to carry her baby full term and have the baby. But that is not what she wants to do right now. She wants to get rid of her problem. Besides, she would lose her job if she decided that.

"Honey," he used to say, "If God blesses you with a child there is a reason. People are going to do what they want. I'm not judging them, that's between them and God." He was careful to say the right thing, and paused a minute to collect his thoughts. "I only tell you things like this because I want you to see the truth. **Truth,** that's a strong word, baby girl. Some people can't see the truth, even about themselves. They twist it and lie to ease their own heavy conscience. The only one-hundred percent way to see the truth is through the eyes of the Lord."

"Dad, can I ask you something?"

"Sure, anything honey."

"What are you talking about?"

"Sorry, I'm talking too much again," he would say. "I just want you to be happy, and the only way I've been happy is when I accepted Jesus in my heart for real."

Mary didn't want to hear that. "Dad, please. That's my choice. Don't push God on me again."

Her father gave a subtle frown. "Sorry, baby girl. You're right. It's a personal choice... Let's talk about something else."

Mary wished her father were still around. He could always cheer her up; help lighten the mood, even when he was dying in the hospital. When they got to the question of dying, she asked him if he was afraid to die.

He said, "No, I know where I'm going. I'm just worried about you, Honey. When I'm gone if you need some help or advice, what are you going to do?"

"Oh Daddy, I wish you could stay with me forever. I have nobody else I can trust, and nobody to love me as much as you do."

As his eyes welled up with so much love for his only daughter, he softened his voice and said, "Sweetheart, I'll be checking in on you, and you have someone better than me to love and trust."

"Who?"

With his eyes wide and his smile wider, Mary's father said, "Jesus. Trust Him little girl, He will take care of you for me until we're together again."

"Okay Daddy. I'll come by after work." Mary gave her father a big hug and gathered her stuff to go.

"Okay Honey, I love you."

"Love you too, Dad."

That was the last time she saw him alive. Tomorrow marks the anniversary of his passing three years ago. It still hurt so badly when she thought of him, especially when she needed him, or when his birthday came around, any holidays, and the day he died from cancer.

She parked her car, went into the restaurant, and punched her timecard. Then she started folding napkins. She thought, Love you Dad. It will be three years tomorrow, still no Jesus. I sure could use some help right now. Jesus, if you're really there, how come you're not helping me out like Daddy said you would?

They opened the doors to the restaurant at 11:00 a.m. Most people sauntered in after 11:30, but every now and then the early birds would be waiting for the doors to open. She liked when it was busy because it took her mind off her problems and the time went faster, plus she got more tips. They weren't as good as the night shift, but it was still worth coming in. There were twelve tables and fourteen counter seats. Mary had the six booths along the back wall, a busy section, and her boss knew she could handle it. She was, by far, his best and smartest employee, not to mention the most beautiful; and boy, could she attract the people in the bar at night!

No one paid attention to the two young construction workers who came into the bar sweaty and dirty, except Mary. They were patching potholes with hot asphalt in the parking lot outside and came in to cool down. One looked to be about 20, the other about 25 or 26. The young one was cute, but the older one was so handsome, even as dirty and sweaty as he was. She thought he was probably gay if he didn't have a girlfriend. Wait, what the hell am I thinking? She was so used to giving guys the "once over," that for a minute she forgot the mess she was in. That's it! I've got to stop that! No men until I figure out what I'm going to do with my baby'. That was the first time she thought of the growing fetus in her belly as 'her' baby and not just something that would become a baby in nine months.

The two guys sat at one of her booths, and she walked over to take their order. "Can I help you?"

They both looked at her and smiled. The cute, younger-looking one said, "Yes, ma'am. Anytime."

The older, handsome one said, "Yes, please. We would love some water and sweet tea."

My God, he's hot, she thought. "Sorry, what was that again?"

"Um, water and sweet tea, please."

Mary fumbled a bit and said, "Okay, I'll be right back."

"Thank you, Miss," he replied.

Wow. That guy had her hypnotized. What the hell is wrong with me? Am I some kind of crazy person that can't control herself? Screw that! She walked up with a tray, carrying two large waters, and two sweet teas. As she set the drinks down, the younger one spoke first.

"You're very pretty for a waitress." She really didn't want to deal with his flirty words.

"Excuse me, Miss," the older guy interjected. "Please don't mind him. He was dropped on his head as a child."

"No problem." She flashed a grin at Handsome and their eyes locked solid.

"I'm sure Billy meant to say you would be beautiful in any environment." He turned a little red in the face and said, "My name is Robert James, but you can call me Bobby." He held out his hand to her.

She took it and said, "Mary." She didn't want to let go, still locking eyes with him. She felt like he was a good man, honest and trustworthy. 'My God, I would love to have this guy all for myself'.

Billy coughed, and it broke up whatever insanity Mary was thinking in her crazy-ass brain. It must be hormones, Mary reasoned, I'm an emotional, crazy person today.

Mary turned to Billy. "What can I get you?"

"I'll have two cheeseburgers with lettuce, tomato and large fries."

After jotting down his order, Mary looked over at Handsome. "How about you, Bobby?" Just saying his name gave her goose bumps. This is crazy; I've never felt like this before, ever. It must be the baby. There's that word again. It's not a baby yet, just a bunch of cells or something.

Bobby tried to read her expression. "Mary, are you okay? You look like you have a lot on your mind."

Flustered, Mary said, "Yes, Bobby. I'm fine." It took everything she had to remain steady on her feet and not melt right there in his lap. "What can I get you?"

Bobby smiled and said, "I'll have the tuna melt and French fries, extra crispy."

"Okay. I'll get that right out."

"Thanks Mary." By now his steel blue eyes were smiling as wide as his smile.

When she walked away, she heard Billy say, "I think I'm going to be sick. Why do all the pretty girls fall for you?"

Bobby laughed. "I don't know, but that one is really special and so, so beautiful."

Did she really hear that? Mary had another table to wait on.

Sitting at the table was a beautiful woman in her 30s. She was with a girl, maybe 17 or 18, and also very pretty. Both had dark hair and beautiful sky blue eyes. Mary was sure they were mother and daughter. She liked guessing ages and relations. She made a game of it. It took away some of the monotony from her job and made it more fun.

"Hello, sweetie. My name is Helen McClain, and this is my daughter, Jane."

"Hi, Helen. Hello Jane. My name is Mary."

"Wow," Helen stated. "Not too many Marys' around these days."

Jane said, "You know, I don't think I've ever personally met a young person named Mary before."

Helen remarked, "Now that you mention it, I don't know any Marys' either."

Helen and Jane seemed like really sincere, nice people.

"Okay ladies, what can I get for you?"

Helen replied, "I'll have a coffee please."

Jane said, "I'll have a large Coke please. Oh, and Mary?"

"Yes, Jane?"

"Thank you."

"You're very welcome, Jane." They all laughed.

Helen said, "Thank you Mary," and they laughed again. "I wasn't trying to joke."

Jane replied, "Mom, that's why it was funny."

"Oh," Helen laughed. "Thank you, sweetie."

Mary said, "I'll be right back."

Mary came back with the drinks for the ladies and said she would return shortly to take their orders.

"Take your time honey, no rush," Helen replied.

Mary delivered the food to Bobby and his friend. She first set Billy's plate in front of him, then gave Bobby his. She didn't want to look at him for fear of embarrassing herself, so once she put both plates down, she started to leave.

Bobby said, "Excuse me Mary." She stopped and turned around.

"Yes Bobby?"

"Um... Mary, would it be okay if I took you out to a movie or dinner?" She stopped in her tracks.

"Yes Bobby, I would like that." What am I saying? "But I will have to call you. I don't give out my number until I know someone's not a stalker." She smiled and giggled as the butterflies acted up in her stomach.

"I'll give you my cell phone number." He wrote it on a small note pad, ripped it out, and handed it to her. She held it along with his hand, and they stared at each other until Billy started to audibly gag. She took the paper and walked over to Helen and Jane's table.

"Hi, sorry about the wait."

Helen said, "No problem, honey. It looked like you were a little faint over there."

Mary blushed, "Oh no, I'm fine." She flashed Bobby's phone number in front of Helen.

"Bobby's number? Is he cute?" Jane asked. "I can't see him from here."

"My God," Mary spoke softly. "He is incredibly handsome. I don't know why, but I like melt when I look at him. I can hardly pull my eyes away from his when we look at each other. This has never happened to me before, and I can't believe I'm telling you all this."

Jane said, "Not to worry, mom gets people to spill things you wouldn't believe, but this is a cool story. I'd like to get a look." She started to turn around.

Helen snarled, "Jane, you can't see him, but his friend is visible and looking this way. Let's not embarrass Mary, honey."

Jane replied, "Sorry, I'll play it on the down-low."

Helen laughed and said, "I'll have a salad with broiled chicken and vinaigrette dressing."

Mary turned to Jane. "I'll have a grilled cheese on rye with bacon and tomato, and fries, extra crispy. Thanks Mary."

"You're welcome Jane." They both smiled at each other.

As Mary walked away to put in their order she thought, those two are so cool. I feel like we're good friends already. What a weird day.

Back at the boys' table, Mary put on her professional smile and asked, "Hello, guys, is everything okay?" She stared at Bobby and smiled.

Bobby said, "Yes it's great! Thanks, Mary!" He couldn't help but stare back.

Billy just grunted with his mouth full of fries.

Once Helen and Jane's food was ready, Mary brought it to their table. She noticed how much they loved being together, and how happy they seemed. They were talking to each other like best friends do. 'I wish I had a relationship like that with my mom', she thought. 'I have no one. Eh... so what? I'll tough it out'.

"Hi Helen, Hi Jane. Here you go - grilled cheese, fries, and a salad with broiled chicken."

"Thanks Mary," Jane said.

"You're welcome Jane," Mary said with a grin.

Helen said, "Mary what's your last name? I feel like I know you."

Mary replied, "That's so weird, I feel like you guys are old friends that I just met. It's been a strange day all around. My last name is Wilson."

Helen asked, "Are you by any chance Thomas Wilson's daughter?"

Mary was taken aback for a moment. "Yes, I am," she stuttered.

"Oh! It's so nice to meet you Mary. God bless you, honey. Tom and I were good friends."

Mary stammered, "I don't know if you know this, but it will be three years tomorrow since he died."

"I know dear," Helen said.

Mary just couldn't help it. She lost it and tears flowed. "He's gone and I've got nobody, I'm all alone."

Helen and Jane got up and hugged her, also crying. "Mary honey, your dad told me he prayed with his whole heart that the Lord would watch over you. I have never been in here before, but while we were driving by something told me to come in for an early lunch."

Jane wiping away a tear said, "Yes that's strange. Usually we don't eat until at least 1:00 p.m. I don't know how you do it, Mom."

"Honey, after a while you know when the Lord's nudging you for His purpose. Why don't you come to church with us tomorrow Mary? After church we're having a barbeque at my house. How does that sound?"

"It sounds nice, but I'm not into church," Mary said stiffly. "I'm mad. God has done nothing but make me suffer." Mary's smile twisted into a knot.

"Oh Mary, God loves you. He loved your dad, and your dad loved Him. Tomorrow they are going to mention your dad at the church service. They do it every year. Everyone loved him. Please come, for me," Helen urged.

"For me, too," Jane said. "Please?"

Swallowing a bit of pride, Mary gave in. "Okay, but don't expect me to shout 'I'm saved and praise the Lord', because it's not going to happen."

"Honey you can believe or not," Helen assured. "That's your choice. Your dad used to say, that's between you and God."

"Okay, I'll be there," Mary, decided. She quickly walked to the restroom to fix her tear-streaked face. When she looked in the mirror, she almost laughed. 'Thank God I went light on the makeup. Okay, not bad. Maybe I'll scare Bobby away. That would be great, since I apparently can't even control myself. She forced herself to relax and take some deep breaths. When she came out, Billy was signaling her to come over. It had taken her a second to remember his name.

"Hi Billy, can I get you anything else?"

"No, but could you tell me why you instantly liked him over me?"

"Really?" Mary asked. "I didn't and I don't want to like anyone," she said, perhaps a little louder than she wanted to. Then she turned to walk away and Bobby grabbed her arm.

"Mary, are you okay? Is there anything I can do?"

She twisted a little sideways and was going to say no thank you, but again, she melted into his eyes.

"Bobby… I'm just going through a lot of stuff right now." And then she pulled away. "Sorry."

"Mary, wait. You don't need to apologize. I have never felt like this; like I do right now looking at you."

She hesitated, and then walked away thinking, I want to call him so badly it hurts…but I am not going to bring any man into my screwed-up life right now. She threw his number in the trash on the way to the kitchen. For a brief moment, she wondered if she had made a mistake and considered digging through the waste to find that piece of paper, but she didn't.

As Bobby and Billy were leaving, Bobby walked over to Mary. "Mary, you look like the type of girl who could conquer anything. I am praying to God that you will call me."

She said goodbye and smiled a smile that lit up the room, but when Bobby walked out the door, Mary almost broke down again. *Damn hormones!* Why is this baby making me so emotional? She went to see if Helen and Jane were okay.

"Hi, how are you guys doing? Can I get you anything else?"

Helen said, "We're fine, but can I ask you a question?"

"Sure," Mary replied.

"You don't have to answer if you think I'm being a nosy old busy-body." Helen's eyes made contact with Mary. "Is there something more than your dad being gone that is bothering you? I feel like you're in trouble and need help."

"Mom!" Jane exclaimed.

"What? It's just that I have a very strong feeling about you, Mary."

Mary sighed. "No Helen, I'm just so emotional today. I just met you guys and it feels like I've known you for a long time. That never happens to me. I'm just having a very weird day."

"Call it a hunch Mary, but are you pregnant?"

The color in Mary's face flushed away. "How could you possibly know? I just found out this morning." She looked at them both with such a sad, pitiful face and started crying. "I don't know what to do." They both got up like before and hugged her again. "Don't you think I'm a sinner now and will go to hell?"

Helen stroked Mary's hair. "Mary, honey, now I know why I'm here. I promised your dad that I would look out for you if God put you in my path, and if He didn't, then my name isn't Helen."

"Well, I made an appointment for an abortion. It's still only cells right now, right? It's not a baby yet."

Helen spoke softly, "Honey, have you ever heard people say, blessed with a child?"

Mary felt another rush of tears, "That's what my dad used to say. Oh, my God, what am I going to do?"

Helen replied, "I am here now honey. We will pick you up tomorrow morning at 8:00. Church isn't until 11:00. We will have time to discuss all your options. Just remember, you are not alone! You found me and I found you. I made a promise to a very good friend and I always keep my word."

"Besides," Jane said. "You can never have enough Marys' around." She hugged her and laughed. That made Mary smile.

"All right," Mary replied. "You have my address and I'll be ready at 8:00. Oh, what should I wear?"

"It's pretty casual, I usually wear pants, and even jeans are okay. Some people wear nice dresses, like my mom," Jane explained.

"Yes," cried Helen, "That's because I rock in a tight-fitting dress!" They laughed at that one.

Mary said, "I bet you do Helen. Both of you are so beautiful." They hugged her and left. What a day, Mary thought. Maybe there is a God.

Chapter Three: Reaping the Rewards

Doctor Jennings was told that Doctor Spears was now on the premises, and that he would be in his office in twenty minutes to go over the latest discoveries. Doctor Spears wanted copies of all data, every piece of information on everything that had been done in the lab for the last seven and a half years. Doctor Jennings already knew this and was fully prepared. He wanted to show Doctor Spears the recording of their latest discovery, as gruesome as it was. One never knew what any discovery could be used for in real world applications, or how it could be adapted for any number of other uses. He also knew that being a fellow scientist, Doctor Spears would appreciate their amazing discovery, despite the horrific nature of it. Doctor Spears knocked and walked into Doctor Jennings' office. Both doctors shook hands. Doctor Spears spoke first.

"How are you, Doctor Jennings?"

"Excellent Doctor Spears. I have prepared a film for you of our latest discovery. I think you will find it spectacular, but be prepared - it's quite gruesome."

"Doctor Jennings, after all the top-notch, high level work you have done, there is still more? And you say it will amaze me? I am actually excited. You have certainly piqued my interest."

"Well, thank you Doctor Spears. Please take a seat. Would you like a drink or anything else?"

"No thank you," Doctor Spears replied. "Maybe after the film. I can't wait to see what you have come up with."

Doctor Jennings turned on the recording of the experiment with the raccoon. Doctor Spears was flabbergasted. He got up and shook Doctor Jennings' hand.

"Doctor Jennings it takes a lot to surprise me, let alone impress me. Sir you have gone far beyond both. Congratulations and well done! How did you accomplish this?"

After his full and detailed explanation, Doctor Spears suggested another experiment, one where he would personally be in charge. He also told Doctor Jennings that he would be announcing fantastic news from Globocorp tomorrow after the experiment. For now, Doctor Spears wanted to see how a test subject-animal, exposed to only synthetically enhanced pheromones, would react being attacked by a weaker, related species with Nano cell technology set on a full-rage signal. Could a weaker related species with Nano cell technology defeat a stronger, bigger, related species exposed to the enhanced pheromones?

For the first test, Doctor Spears would use a healthy full-grown lab-rat ingested with the synthetic pheromone, pitted against a healthy full-grown field mouse that had absorbed the mind- controlling Nano cell technology. Both would be placed in a cage with a removable barrier between them. The field mouse of course, would have the Nano cell technology already in its brain, while the rat wouldn't. They would then use the subsonic, bioelectrical, algorithm for kill or rage, at full power. It would be a way to see if a weaker, similar species mammal could survive against a stronger one, five times its size. If that happens, he knew it could be duplicated without the enhanced pheromone, with only Nano cell tech in both rodents. He was interested to know how long the smaller test subject would last in comparison to one five times larger. It sounded like a good start.

"Unfortunately," Doctor Spears stated. "Sometimes you have to break some eggs to make an omelet."

He then presented a gift to Doctor Jennings from Mr. Atlas Grey, himself.

"This might possibly be the best scotch in the world. It certainly was the most expensive!" He uncorked a very old bottle of scotch and poured three fingers into both glasses, one for each of them.

"Doctor Jennings, I would like to propose a toast to a genius of a man who has even surpassed Mr. Grey's expectations, something that no one has ever done before! Again, very well done!"

They drank the scotch, and agreed that it probably was the best in the world. Doctor Spears scheduled the test for ten o'clock the next morning. He asked Doctor Jennings if that would give him enough time to prepare the experiment. Doctor Jennings explained that it was a simple process and would only take thirty minutes or so to set it up.

"Could we meet in the lab at 8:00 a.m.? I would like you walk me through all the procedures?"

"Certainly, Doctor Spears."

When he left, Doctor Jennings poured another glass of that fine scotch. He was curious to know about the news from Globocorp. He woke early the next morning, eager to get down to the lab before Doctor Spears arrived. He had explained the situation to his staff the night before so everyone was ready. He was clear that Doctor Spears from Globocorp would be in charge of the experiment. They were to wait until his arrival so they could walk him through the various procedures.

Doctor Spears arrived right on time and was introduced to the staff as they explained each procedure in detail. He learned how the equipment was controlled and operated. Doctor Spears already had all the data on the subsonic, bioelectric, and ionic algorithms.

The pheromone-infected lab rat was placed into the cage. The common field mouse with the Nano cell technology was placed on the other side of the removable barrier of the cage.

"Whenever you're ready, Doctor Spears."

"Ready, turn on the signal!" Doctor Spears ordered.

The tech turned it on and the mouse went into super-hyper, attack mode. The lab rat was in attack mode as well, but nowhere near as erratic and super aggressive as the mouse.

"Remove the cage divider!" ordered Doctor Spears.

Before the technician could move the divider even an inch, the crazed field mouse squeezed through the gap and attacked the lab rat so fast that it was hard to follow with the naked eye. The lab rat bit off a large chunk of flesh from the test mouse, but that did nothing to slow it down. Within thirty seconds, the mouse had gotten to the lab rat's throat and ripped it out, killing it. The mouse continued to tear the rat to pieces for nine minutes and eleven seconds until its eyes bulged out, and blood streamed from its ears, nose, and eyes. The mouse died in exactly nine minutes and forty-one seconds from the moment the signal was turned on.

Doctor Jennings kept his eye on Doctor Spears for a reaction. It looked like he was enjoying the bloody, gory details of the experiment. He had a strange smirky smile on his face and his eyes were wide open, he looked like a kid who was surprised with a new puppy.

Doctor Spears finally spoke. "Doctor Jennings, in all my years working with researchers and scientists, I have never seen anything like this. It's absolutely astounding. I also think now would be a good time to tell you that Globocorp has placed me in charge of running tests on all the mammals in the lab."

Before Doctor Jennings had a chance to react, Doctor Spears put his hand up for silence. He reached into his pocket and took out a folded piece of paper, and began reading.

"To Doctor Robert Jennings, Congratulations! You have exceeded my expectations and came through for Globotech, Globocorp, and the world. Doctor Jennings, you and your staff shall go down in history as some of the greatest scientists in the world. My private jet is waiting for you right now. I would like you to come to our main office so I can thank you personally. I am also offering you a position as president in charge of Globotech Worldwide. I would like to explain to you the importance of this job for Globocorp, and to the people of the world. You are the right man for the job. A job that is so vital to a world in turmoil. A job that, as far as I am concerned, you were destined for. You're a brilliant, one-of-a-kind genius. You have unrivaled scientific research skills and exhibit highly sought-after leadership qualities. You have really come through for Globocorp. I think it's time for you to come and see what a man of your abilities can achieve on a global scale. I am truly hoping you will consider this position for the greater good of the people of the world. Sincerely, Mr. Atlas Grey, C.E.O. Globocorp."

Everyone in the room was on there feet, clapping. Doctor Jennings' face blushed red and he put up his hands. "But Doctor Spears, what about my work here? I still have to figure out all of the applications for every one of our discoveries and inventions. All of them can be used worldwide, for the good of mankind."

"Don't you see, Doctor Jennings? You will be in charge of all of it - this place too. You can work on all these things and more. Imagine the financial and political resources you will have at your disposal. The possibilities of what you could accomplish working with thousands of top-notch researchers, with unlimited resources." Doctor Spears put his hand on his colleague's shoulder. "You and your team have just begun to change the world for the better. Let's magnify it with a global team effort. Maybe, just maybe, we can save this planet. What do you say, Doctor? Your chariot awaits."

For that split second, Doctor Jennings paused to consider the implications. How could anyone say no to that? It's my duty as a scientist and a human being.

"I accept Doctor Spears!" The group cheered.

Three hours later Doctor Jennings was airborne, headed for Rome, Italy. Doctor Spears told everyone to take the next week off, in appreciation of their successful work. He boasted that there would be the finest food with the best wines, bourbons, and liquors that money could buy every day – it was a full week of celebration.

"The weather is beautiful outside. Get out and enjoy the grounds. Cheers for all your work! And now it's time to celebrate! After your well-earned break, we can get back to work on finding even greater applications for these great accomplishments you have all helped to create. My team and I will be studying all the data, so we will be on the same page. When your week of well-earned rest and reward is over. I will be down at the bar tonight to toast to your success and our future successes!"

Employees that worked there appreciated the break, especially because they were able to go outside. As the doors opened, you would think vampires were emerging from a dark night of sleep. Experiencing daylight hours was a rare occurrence, as seen on the pasty white faces from working inside for so many years without the glorious sun beating down on their bodies. There were a few exceptions, like those who worked the night shift. The freedom of basking in the sun was invigorating. With two more years left on their contracts, they got a healthy dose of "life on the outside," not to mention that this scientific miracle elevated their status into the history books.

Pete, the janitor, would be proud to tell his grandson that he was there when these historic events took place, and that he personally knew Doctor Robert Jennings. Doctor Jennings always said he could never have succeeded without them, including Pete – for sure.

The staff knew that once they finished their stint with Doctor Jennings, they would be sought after in the scientific community; they could write their own ticket. Their renewed excitement about working on this project's applications was infectious. Their goals exceeded their wildest dreams. Their personal sacrifice was almost over. The light at the end of the tunnel was finally visible, and it looked stunning.

Doctor Spears had not been seen since his toast to the team's success. Everyone assumed that he and his team of technicians and fellow doctors were putting in as many hours as possible to get up to speed when work convened.

This was true; he was working overtime to make sure every recorded piece of information, and all data from every day of the seven-plus-years' of meticulously documented work in this laboratory was delivered to Globocorp headquarters. He also had the subsonic, bioelectric algorithms' encrypted code adapted to all their corporation's satellite uplinks. In 24 hours' time, he would be able to send the signal anywhere in the world at any time from Globotech or his own encrypted laptop. He made sure every detail of the Nano cell technology was hand-delivered to Mr. Grey. Doctor Spears also kept an encrypted copy of it all on his highly advanced laptop. What's more, it was stored on multiple encoded thumb drives that were flown to his laboratory at Globocorp headquarters. He was waiting for conformation that all this information had been received.

Doctor Spears had an experiment in mind that made him smile like an impatient child waiting on line at Disneyland. He hadn't been this excited in years. His right-hand man wasn't a doctor; he was a six-foot, four-inch brute of a man with dark eyes and a terribly scarred face. He was the only person Doctor Spears would listen to, besides Mr. Grey. Tony Colonia was a hired ex-military mercenary, and he was in charge of keeping Doctor Spears safe at all costs. Tony was personally assigned to this position by Mr. Grey himself.

Doctor Spears looked up when Tony walked into his office. "Did the confirmation come yet?"

Tony smiled, which unfortunately made him look even more frightening. "Oh yes, Doc. It sure did."

"Is everything ready, Tony?"

"Yep. We just have to get everyone outside and lock the titanium doors."

"Tony, did you make sure our cameras are covering it all in high definition?"

"Yes, Doc. Everything is ready, all of Doctor Jennings' people have been told that we are conducting a dangerous experiment, and they will have to remain outside of the compound until it is done."

Doctor Spears then asked, "How did they react, Tony?"

"Most of them were okay with it, but Doctor Jennings' staff wanted to be in on the experiment. I told them what you told me to tell them, that you felt they deserved this break and they were going to get it. I told them not to worry and that as soon as their break was over they could go over all the data. They were fine with that."

Doctor Spears was grinning from ear to ear. "Fantastic, Tony. This experiment is going to dwarf any experiment Doctor Jennings could have ever conducted!" He took a heavy sigh and changed his demeanor. "Tony, are our people ready? Are you sure all of our people are safe and locked out of the experiment area." "Yes Doc." Lets do this Tony.

Chapter Four: The Dining and Dance Party.

The day of the big outdoor dining and dance party had finally arrived. Doctor Spears brought in a high-end catering service and spared no expense in throwing a spectacular soiree. He said it was the least he could do for making them all stay outside during his experiment. However, Doctor Nickels and Doctor Peters expressed their disappointment to Tony about not being involved in the experiment. But after seeing all the extravagance, with the soft decorative lighting that lit up the area like an exotic fantasyland, they were no longer insulted about not being included in the experiment. The grounds took on the appearance of a beautiful country celebration with an elegant surreal charm, and they were glad they didn't miss this party.

Pete Miller, the janitor, and Nancy Peterson, the technician, had been seeing each other since the night they both helped to discover the pheromone theory with Doctor Jennings. That was the same night they also discovered their attraction for each other. Nancy loved everything about Pete. He was an amazing person; like no other man she had dated. He was ruggedly handsome with a gentle spirit. His unsophisticated charm was one of politeness and kindness to everyone, even when they didn't reciprocate. He had a way of talking that was never loud or boisterous, a humble man with enough confidence in himself to be who he was, without pretense. Pete used stories to get his point across and he could tell some fantastic stories!

Nancy loved to listen as he spoke about his life and times. His words took her to exotic places and on exciting adventures within her private imagination. What an amazing talent, she thought. Nancy was aware that Pete never went to college and although at one point in her life it would have mattered, not anymore. She viewed Pete's stories as his education, like he had grown up in an earlier time in history, but he didn't. Pete and Nancy were the same age. Pete had grown up in the Appalachian Mountain Range in an area not far from the Smokey Mountain Range. When he was young, his family had no modern indoor plumbing except a hand-pumped kitchen sink. Once a week his mom would heat water on the coal-burning cooking stove so everyone could take a bath. They also had an outhouse for a toilet.

Pete attended the only school in town that taught students from kindergarten all the way to the 12th grade. He grew up in a very poor area and seemed to have only fond memories of his life growing up in the mountains. Pete told Nancy that there is nothing as good as the simple life. He said it was a rewarding way to live; and yet, it amazed Nancy how different their childhood experiences were. She believed that if Pete lived with all of the advantages she had, with his intelligence he could have become an icon in society. But, truly, she liked Pete just the way he was. And then it hit her, oh my goodness, I'm in love with Pete! What would my parents think of him? She laughed to herself imagining how awkward that would be, but deep down she knew that if any man in the world could win her parents over it was definitely Pete.

Pete was as smitten with Nancy as she was with him. He was baffled that a wealthy girl from Boston with a fancy college degree could have him feeling like a love crazed youngen'. Miss Nancy wasn't conceited or spoiled; she was a very beautiful and special lady, and in Pete's eyes the most beautiful lady that ever-graced God's green earth. Pete hoped Nancy loved him like he did her because he couldn't imagine not having her in his life. Miss Nancy had given him happiness like he had never known before.

That night he planned to ask her to marry him. He brought a promise ring and he was ready to pop the question. Pete had to know one way or the other, even though it was far too soon in their relationship. If his feelings for Nancy got any stronger, and she didn't love him back, he knew his heart would be broken. But he needed to know, and tonight was the night to find out.

Pete walked up to Nancy and hugged her like he had never hugged her before. He stepped back and stared into her eyes, lingering on the beauty she emanated when she was with him. But that night she was worried. She had never seen Pete act like this before; he seemed nervous and very serious about something.

"Pete, is everything all right?"

"Yes Nancy, everything is just fine." Then he leaned forward to kiss her. "Nancy, I have something really important to ask you."

People began talking all at once and things got a bit chaotic. Right above the doors the emergency strobe light was still flashing. It made everyone wonder what happened during the experiment. They all hoped Doctor Spears and his people were all right.

"Nancy what's going on?" Pete asked.

"I don't know Pete, maybe we should head over there and see if one of the doctors knows anything." When they got to the doors, Doctor Nickels was addressing the large crowd of worried people.

"People, let's calm down!" he shouted. "We need to find out why the emergency lights are on. Doctor Peters is calling Doctor Spears right now." The crowd was bursting with fear of not knowing what was happening.

"People, please! Let's have some quiet so he can communicate with Doctor Spears, and find out what happened!"

"Oh, Pete, I hope no one is hurt!" Nancy whispered as she held on to his hand.

"Don't worry, Nancy I'm sure everything is okay." He held her tight, comforting her. He knew she could be right; Doctor Spears may have tried something dangerously stupid. Pete never really talked to him, but he just got the feeling that the doctor was not a totally sane man. He always had a strange look behind his polite demeanor.

Once Doctors Nickels and Peters conferred, Doctor Nickels walked to the front of the group. He put his hands up to call for quiet.

"Listen up, everyone! Doctor Peters has just been informed by Doctor Spears himself, that a test subject had gotten loose from the experiment enclosure. He said everyone was fine and it will be about five or ten minutes until he can open the doors and let us in." He could hear the murmur in the crowd before he continued. "Doctor Spears also asked me to extend his invitation to anyone who wants a night cap at the inside bar. It's on him."

The crowd breathed a collective sigh of relief. Thank God no one is hurt or injured.

"I wonder what kind of experiment Doctor Spears was conducting," Pete said, as if asking Nancy.

"Funny you should wonder that Pete, I was just wracking my brain wondering the same thing," Nancy answered. "I can't think of anything, but don't forget, I'm only a technician and I don't get to see all the data."

As Nancy spoke her last word, the red emergency lights stopped and everyone started to calm down. Pete and Nancy were in no hurry, and waited away from the crowd. They were happy just to be with each other. Nancy looked into Pete's eyes after a few minutes of kissing and softly whispered in his ear that she would like to stay in his room tonight.

Pete smirked. "But Nancy, we're not married yet," he teased. Nancy blushed with embarrassment. He didn't mean to embarrass her, so he picked her up and spun her around. He put her down and stared into her eyes. "Nancy I was just teasing you, I'm sorry. I would love to spend the night with you. It would be the perfect end to a perfect night."

But without warning, Nancy pushed Pete's shoulders back.

"Pete, I feel strange, and I can't really explain it."

"What's wrong? Was it my teasing?"

"No Pete, it's not you. I'm scared, but I don't know why. I can feel an adrenaline rush coming on."

Nancy took Pete's hand and placed it on her heart. She saw his expression change to one of worry.

"Nancy," Pete began. "I have a strange feeling like something isn't right. I feel like--"

Before he had time to react, the love of his life was ripped from his grasp so quickly it was a blur. A growling wind had taken her from his arms. Pete almost fell down, but managed to remain standing, dumbfounded.

A large mountain lion had Nancy by her neck and she was reaching for Pete when the beast ripped her throat out. Pete stood there, watching the life leave Nancy's eyes as she breathed her last breath. The mountain lion tore Nancy to shreds faster and more violently than Pete thought possible of any living creature on earth. He was splattered with the blood and flesh from his beautiful Nancy. That snapped him back into reality.

Pete yelled a battle cry in a rage and started to launch himself at the killer cat on top of what was left of his Nancy. Instead of going forward he fell to his knees in pain. He turned and looked at his feet, ankles, and calves and saw at least fifty vermin attacking him as if they had rose up from hell with superpowers and were tasked with ripping all the flesh from his body.

In a matter of twenty seconds Pete's skeleton was visible up to his knees. He was bleeding out. A puddle of blood was growing rapidly and he started to go into shock. He knew at that moment that the chipmunks and squirrels and mice attacking him were demons. He never thought he would be so afraid of small vermin like these, but he had never been more terrified in his life. As Pete's tendons, muscles and ligaments were torn from the bone, he fell backwards, his legs now just skeletal, bent completely in half.

"I'll be with my beautiful Nancy," he gurgled.

Doctors Nickels and Peters were in the middle of the crowd. They had just witnessed what happened to Pete and Nancy, who were about twenty yards away from them. Doctor Peters looked at Doctor Nickels, and both had panic in their eyes. Doctor Nickels shouted, "Spears, you son of a bitch!"

Then the unthinkable happened. Every single mammal in the area came charging at the crowd. They were surrounded with no chance to escape. Technicians, doctors, and everyone who was there were screaming in terror. The only mercy, if any, was that it was over quickly. Tony and Doctor Spears certainly enjoyed the show. While they watched the horrific outdoor carnage on a huge television monitor, they were both riveted to the screen. Tony was moaning and giggling with pleasure. Doctor Spears would blurt out "incredible" every once in a while, with a broad smile on his face and a hungry look in his eyes.

When it was over. Tony cried, "Doc, that was the best show I have ever seen!"

"Me too, Tony! What an incredible success!"

"I even liked the part when the animal's eyes bugged out because their brains exploded inside their heads," Tony added, while laughing and snorting like a pig.

"I did too!" Doctor Spears cackled with his high-pitched, screech of a laugh.

After they both calmed down Tony said, "We've got to do this again, Doc."

"You're right about that! I'm going to be in charge of this globally, to reduce the undesirable populace, and help save the world from being over-populated."

"Fantastic Doc!" Tony replied.

"So, is our second experiment ready?" Doctor Spears asked.

"All set Doc." Tony uttered with a gleefully twisted look on his face.

"Now, Tony, it's imperative that the satellite system is working and sending the signal, we have to fly back to Rome now. I have an important meeting with Mr. Grey, our Lord. Set it to go off at 11:15 a.m. The place should be full by then."

"No problem Doc. I can time it from here on your encrypted laptop."

"Thank you Tony. Besides Mr. Grey, you're the only one I can really trust.

Chapter Five: A Beautiful Sunday

Mary's shift was over; it was a long and crazy day. When she stepped foot into her house, she went straight to bed, and slept right through until morning. She woke up happy and felt like she had no right to be, but what the heck? She hadn't been happy for a long, long time and it felt good. She thought, maybe happy hormones are on the menu today. As she dressed, she thought about how she would act inside a church, where she had never really visited as an adult. I hope they don't think I'm going to embarrass myself and start praising Jesus. Maybe this is a bad idea. But I really like those two more than I've liked anyone since my dad. If I have to endure church so be it. Maybe I'm not all alone like Helen said.

When the car horn beeped outside, she was ready.

"Coming!" she hollered, as she closed the front door and walked to the car. Helen pointed to the front passenger seat. Jane was in the back seat. She smiled at Mary, and Mary smiled back.

Helen had a big smile and was feeling playful.

"Mary," she started. "You're going to have to get naked and allow the preacher to dunk you into an ice-cold pool of water. Are you okay with that?"

The look on their new friend's face made Helen and Jane almost pee their pants with fits of laughter. "Sorry Mary, I just couldn't help it," Helen said through tears of laughter. "You know I was just kidding, right?"

Mary couldn't help her own laughter. "Helen, you are so unpredictable! Like a magician not announcing his next trick!" They all laughed as Helen put the car in drive.

Helen wasted no time in finding out more about her new friend. "Mary, what was your life plan before you were blessed?"

"Helen, I was never blessed. God has done nothing for me, except allow me to suffer."

"Mary honey, by blessed I mean pregnant," Helen clarified. "Sorry about that. It has become a habit to say it that way."

"Oh," said Mary. "I should have known what you meant. My dad would also say it like that." Mary paused before she answered. "Why do you want to know? I'm not trying to be rude, just curious."

"Because I'm going to help you."

"Why? Because I'm going to church?"

"Mary, even if you don't go to church, I want to help you. I feel that your dad knew somehow that I would be in your life and I believe God wants me to help. I love God, so I'm helping you. I also think you're a beautiful person inside and out."

"God wants to help me, Helen?"

"Yes Mary. God loves you."

"Why would God love me? Nobody ever loved me but my dad, and if God loved me so much, why did he take him away from me?" Mary's voice was shaking and she was barely holding herself together. *Damn hormones,* she thought.

"I don't know why," Helen lamented, "But can't you see all the strange coincidences that have been happening to you, and to us, for that matter? Can't you feel an emotional change in your life?"

Mary thought about it for a second. "I do feel very emotional, but I'm sure that's just all the hormones from being pregnant."

"Honey, my daughter and I are not pregnant. We don't normally cry our eyes out and hug waitresses we've just met, in a place I would normally never go, especially when neither one of us was even hungry. God is doing this."

"But why, Helen?" Mary asked with a slightly raised tone.

"Because God loves you. And He chose you. Your dad asked Him to watch over you, and so did I, and so did my Jane," Helen replied.

Mary had a hard time accepting these words. "Why did you guys ask? You didn't even know me."

"Because we loved your dad," Helen said. 'But most of all, when God gives you a job to do and you choose to do it, you are blessed. On a personal note, the minute I saw you, I knew we would become family." Both Jane and Mary smiled at each other with tears in their eyes. "So, besides working at the diner, what else do you do?"

Mary replied, "I'm in college on a scholarship studying to be an interior decorator. I doubt I can finish now if I have this baby. My job at the club is usually at night bartending and waiting tables, since that's where the money is. I won't be able to work there for too much longer. I'm sure they will find a reason to fire me when they see I'm pregnant. They only hire cute girls with nice figures."

"Maybe I can get a job there!" Jane cried.

"They would hire you in a minute, even with no experience."

"Thanks Mary."

"Welcome Jane." They both giggled.

Helen interjected their silliness. "Okay Mary, here is what we do. You stay in school and keep your job until you decide it's time to quit, and then move in with us. We have plenty of room. When the baby comes, Jane and I can help watch your blessing from God while you're in school."

Mary didn't know what to say. "How do you know I'm not a serial killer?"

"The chances of three serial killers being in the same car would be astronomical!" Helen laughed. "You set yourself up for that one Mary!" she added.

Mary felt a bit awkward and surprised by this offer. "I would like to think about your offer, Helen. It's just...these past two days have been so overwhelming."

Helen agreed. She knew it was a lot for Mary to take in. "Let's just forget about our problems for a while and enjoy this beautiful day."

After stopping for breakfast, they headed to church. When they came up to a gravel road, Helen took a right and drove down the bumpy path. Mary's face lit up with wonder when she saw the beautiful field of wildflowers to the left of her. On the right, a small grove of perfectly spaced apple trees graced the property. There was a well-maintained white picket fence all around the property. It was all so beautiful. For a moment, Mary gave a sigh of relief. I love this feeling, she thought to herself.

As if she knew what Mary was thinking, Helen exclaimed, "I love this place, it has a special kind of peace to it."

Jane, on the other hand, was impatient with her mother's slow driving. "Mom, we are running late. Do you think you can pick up the pace a little?"

Helen spotted an open parking space and pulled right in. The beautiful white church with a steeple and church bell was impressive, but it made Mary nervous. She had never been to church to pray on a Sunday. The only times she found herself in such a sacred place was for weddings and her dad's funeral. As they started walking toward this beautiful house of worship, a voice called out Mary's name and they all turned around.

Jane whispered to Mary, "I don't know him, but I wish I did."

"Mary," Helen announced. "That's the same guy that gave you his phone number at lunch yesterday!"

Mildly amused, Mary scoffed. "Come on guys, this is getting weird. Did you set this up?"

"The Lord works in mysterious ways," Helen answered. By now she had a mischievous look on her face, as if to imply that she was not at all surprised.

Bobby walked over to Mary trying to hide his surprise and awkwardness. "Hi, Mary!"

"Hello Bobby. What a coincidence!"

"Yeah, it's incredible!" Bobby answered back. "This is my first time here. I just moved here two weeks ago for work and needed to find a church. I asked around and my neighbor mentioned this one. She said it's great and that the people are friendly here."

Their eyes locked, and it was just like the meeting at the restaurant. Breaking the silence, Jane coughed, as if to say they weren't alone.

Mary took the cue. "Oh, Bobby this is Helen and Jane."

"Pleased to meet you." Bobby said.

"It's Mary's first time here too," Jane interjected. "Are you sure you're not stalking her?" Bobby blushed and became a little defensive. "No! I'm not like that at all." That made Jane laugh, as her face lit up and her eyes twinkled with a playful menace.

Mary assured Bobby that Jane just had a funny sense of humor. The girls laughed and Bobby said, "Oh okay, I confess. I really have been stalking her." He smiled at Mary and asked, "I hope you don't mind."

Mary smiled back and melted into his eyes again.

But just then, something weird happened. Bobby quickly changed his tone and ordered the women to act quickly. "Come on ladies, we have to leave here now... Fast!" He was taking command of a situation that was about to happen. "Helen, we'll take your car! I'll drive. Come on!"

Without hesitation, Helen grabbed Jane and Bobby grabbed Mary. As they piled into the car, they heard the desperate screams and saw men, women and kids running from the church. Animals from all over were attacking them. They were recklessly savage with super speed.

"Helen, the keys!" Bobby yelled. She threw him the keys and he backed up the car, and slammed it into drive. He gave it just enough gas to rip out of there without skidding on the gravel. The rearview mirror showed the chaos. Some of the animals were giving chase. Others were lunging at the car, coming at them from the fields and the apple orchard.

A large black bear shot out from the orchard and was gaining on them. Bobby slammed on the gas pedal as his knuckles turned white gripping the wheel, and trying not to veer off the road. Bobby looked at the path in front of them, then at the bear. If he hit that bear they would all be killed. He was almost at the paved road where he knew he could pick up the speed, but there was a hard right turn ahead and the bear was closing in.

"Shit! This is going to be close!" he yelled. "Hold on, ladies!" He slowed and cut the wheel, sliding sideways a bit, but still in control. The huge black bear slammed into the right rear panel of the car, then bounced off and rolled onto the paved road. The force of the hit almost made them spin out. He thought they were safe, but as he looked in the rearview mirror, he could see the bear was up and barreling after them. Within minutes, he finally gained some distance between the bear and the car. Bobby saw the bear drop down and it looked motionless.

"Is everyone okay?" he shouted.

Helen answered first. "I think so. Nice driving Bobby, how did you know we had to leave so quickly?"

"The same way you knew to do as I asked. It's a gift from God. I've always had it. I sense danger before it comes, usually with just enough time to avoid it."

His words brought some comfort to Helen and Jane, but the carnage they witnessed aroused their fear again, they held each other tight, unable to comprehend what happened.

While Bobby and Mary were looking at the bear, Helen and Jane saw many of their friends ripped to pieces by squirrels, foxes, cats, dogs, and even rabbits. Bobby asked Mary if she had her cell phone, and she handed it to him without a word.

He dialed 911.

"Little Falls Police, you have called 911. What is your emergency?"

Bobby spoke with a steady voice. "We are on our way into town from the church at 51 Forest Road. There has been a massacre there. Savage animals attacked the congregation!"

"Sir, it is a crime to prank 911."

Her words irritated him. "Lady, I don't know why I even called. You people couldn't stop it anyway. The only thing that could have stopped what I just saw is a bomb."

"Hello? Sir?"

"Yes, we are on our way to you!" Bobby shouted. "We'll be there in twenty minutes." He hung up the phone and turned to Mary.

"Mary, I can't believe what I just saw. I have been all over the world, mostly outdoors. I've studied animals and I know that what we just saw is supposed to be impossible, but it happened. It is like something out of a sci-fi movie." Mary leaned into Bobby and thanked him for saving their lives.

Chapter Six: The Important Recruit

Doctor Ivory Black was looking through an electron microscope, examining brain cells from a rabid raccoon and comparing them to the brain cells of a non-rabid raccoon. She heard a knock at the door and a man came in. She guessed him to be in his mid-thirties; he was very attractive. Standing a little over 6 feet tall, he looked to be in great physical condition. And those eyes! They were beautiful: blue; but not light blue. In fact, they were an oddly dark blue, with a distinct black circle around each iris. *Soulful eyes*, she thought.

"Hello Doctor. I'm Agent John White from the National Security Agency. I have been sent here to ask for your help on an unusual and difficult case."

"Really? Agent White, have the animals been spying on our government again?"

"Not quite Doctor. You can call me John."

"Okay, John. You can call me Doctor Black."

"Well, Doctor Black your work in Nano cell technology, biology, and your books on mammals' actions and reactions have made you one of the top scientists in your field, quite possibly in the world. You were also a Captain in the Air Force for four years, and that Doctor Black, puts you at the top of our list." John couldn't believe how beautiful this exotic-looking lady was. She had big, almond-shaped eyes that lit up a room with their emerald green color. And her body! Wow, who knew that a female scientist could look so voluptuous in a lab coat? Agent White could see that she was gifted in all the right places.

She rolled her eyes and said, "Okay. I hope you can make it quick. I'm in the middle of some important work."

"I'm sure you are, Doctor, but you will definitely want to check this out. A group of animals in a mountainous area in Western Virginia, all different species, got together, and ripped to shreds about a hundred people. Apparently, they didn't eat them or fight with one another...they just attacked the humans. Then, while they were still ripping and tearing, they all died, one right after the other. The report stated that it seemed that their brains exploded."

Doctor Black laughed hysterically. "Okay. Where is the camera? Am I being punked? Did Doctor Jones put you up to this? You're not one of those Strip-O-Gram people, are you?" She laughed again. "Okay, you got me. Good one, Agent White! But if you don't mind, I really have work to do." She smiled while trying to hold back her laughs.

"Doctor Black, I am not joking," John said. "If I have to strip for you to come along with me, I am willing to do it, for my country." He smirked.

She looked at him and said, "Seriously John, this painted scenario is impossible on so many levels. There is just no way that nature would behave that way.

"Doctor, who said it happened naturally?" John responded.

Doctor Black thought for a second, then flatly replied, "Okay, let's take a look. I need an hour to get my gear together."

"Your gear is waiting on the helicopter. I had your assistant get it together while we were talking."

"You did what?"

"Doctor, this is a direct order from the President of the United States of America. This may turn out to be a national emergency. Now, if you're going to help us, let's move. Time is critical."

Ivory wanted to help, and something in his voice made her do exactly what he said.

"Yes Sir," she replied.

They both sat in the back seat on the ride over to the chopper. Doctor Black spoke first. "So, Agent White, I suppose you have an entire report on me?"

"Yes Doctor, I do," he said, as he took out a folder from his briefcase. "Your full name is Ivory Ebony Black."

"Crazy, right? But it grew on me. It made me stronger."

John smiled. "This is pretty funny. I'm not trying to insult you, but it's so ironic."

"Oh? And why is that, Agent White?" Ivory was trying to remain polite.

"Well, your dad was white, and his last name was Black. Your mom's maiden name was White, and she was Black. Hey, maybe we're distantly related."

"Not a chance, John!" Ivory shot back. Now he was just pissing her off.

"Your name is Ivory Ebony Black." He couldn't stop laughing.

"Hey, jackass, what's so funny?" Ivory's deep green eyes glared at him.

"Sorry, I was just thinking, when we get to the scene and I say, 'Hi, I'm Agent White, and this is Doctor Black'...the looks we're going to get. This is funny. It's a little bit like that Abbott and Costello skit, the 'Who's on First' joke they do, but this is for real."

"Jerk," she sneered, but she was actually smiling. She knew the Abbott and Costello skit and it was funny. Then they both laughed for a minute.

"Okay John. What nationality are you?"

"What's that, Doctor?" John questioned.

"What race are you, or what combination of races are you?"

"Oh! I'm human," John answered, dodging the question.

"What part of the human race, though? As in, the nationality of your ancestors?"

"I don't really care, although they are funny," John pitched back.

"John, I bet you're one of those people who believes Polish people are stupid and Irish, and Germans are drunk all the time."

"Hold it Doctor. I *am* Polish, Irish, German, and African-American."

She looked embarrassed. "Oh, I'm sorry. Well, I don't believe in that stuff either. I was just trying to make a point."

"That's okay," he said with a smirk. "I do believe in one thing about African Americans, though."

"Oh, really? What's that?"

"I do believe…" he said as he pointed to his private area, "I do believe…that Mr. Johnson is of African-American descent." They both tried to keep a straight face, but ended up laughing at his insinuation.

"That's what they all say!" Ivory replied.

"Do I have to prove it, Doctor? Just say the word."

"No! Keep it in your pants, John, or you might lose it!"

"Yes ma'am!" He was polite about it.

"Don't call me ma'am! It's Doctor Black or Ivory," she snarled. What is it about this guy? Normally she would have slapped someone who had joked around with her like that, but he also seemed to be more than meets the eye. Then she laughed because of his joke about Mr. Johnson. John was what she called a sleeper, something that seemed less than it really was.

She was thirty-five years old and hadn't dated much or been with a steady guy since college. She knew her work required sacrifice; a steady guy wasn't her thing. John was making it really hard to not want to get to know him. This had never happened to her before. He also felt the vibe. His work was vital to the safety of the people of the United States, and a relationship was out of the question.

The car had stopped, and the helicopter was waiting.

"John, I think you're a very nice person and very attractive, but my work makes it impossible for me to become involved with another person, so let's keep this strictly business."

"Me too, Doctor. My job makes it pretty much impossible for me to have an exclusive relationship, and sometimes that does bother me. I don't usually flirt with anyone either. Maybe I can't help myself around beautiful vixens. I'll keep it professional from now on."

Ivory turned her head and walked toward the chopper, smiling. Did he just call me a beautiful vixen?

The chopper landed in a parking lot near a twenty-foot wide asphalt path leading into a wooded area. Ivory instructed Agent White to put on a biohazard protection suit.

"It will fit right over your clothing. If this is an airborne, biological contaminant, we should be okay. Anyone who has been to the scene should be found by someone with a suit and quarantined in a vapor-proof room with electronic bio-filters."

"I called in the troops Doctor Black. Our detainment and mobile laboratories should be here any minute."

"Good thinking, John – I mean – Agent White."

"Thank you, Ivory – I mean – Doctor Black." They both chuckled.

"Oh, man. This is crazy."

John sighed. "Tell me about it."

There was a sheriff at the beginning of the path, and John walked up and introduced them. "Sheriff, I'm Agent White with the NSA, and this is Doctor Black." The sheriff smiled at that and Ivory rolled her eyes when John gave her the "I told you so" look. "Sheriff, we will be taking over as of now. I'm going to need your complete cooperation."

"Yes Sir, Agent White," the sheriff replied.

"Sheriff, I want anyone who has gone closer to the scene than you are right now to remain here and stay at least fifteen feet away from everyone else."

"That might be a problem." He lifts his finger and points. "Right over there is, as far as I know, the only person who has been at the scene. He has been really close to all my guys for a couple of hours while we waited for you all here."

"How about you Sheriff? Have you been in close contact with him?"

"Well, yes Sir, I have."

"Okay Sheriff," John said, "Here's what we do. No one leaves, and there is most likely nothing to worry about, but we do things by the book. "Doctor Black, do we still need the suits?"

She said, "Yes. We are going to be in contact with the physical evidence, and we should also be concerned with the thought that it might be airborne." She stopped to let that sink in. "Agent White, we could also be infected from physical contact with biological-contagions."

Agent White nodded. "Sheriff, I see you have a SWAT team down there. Since they have already been exposed, please have them come here. Nobody leaves until I give the okay. I hope that is clear, Sheriff."

"Yes Sir." The sheriff walked toward the SWAT team. Ivory was thinking, there is that voice again. Like when he used it, there was no choice but to obey... and fast.

The captain of the SWAT team walked up to John.

"I'm Agent White, NSA," John announced. "I need you and your team to back us up. I doubt that there will be any problems, but you never know. You and your team will be under my direct command."

"Yes Sir."

"Okay then. Let's move!" John ordered.

As they walked up the one lane road, Ivory thought that it was amazing how John takes command so easily. As they walked through an unlocked security gate, the road started to widen into an open area where they came upon all the carnage. In all her studies and years of dealing with animals, mostly mammals, Doctor Black had never even imagined a scene like this. Something unnatural had occurred here. This scene made no natural scientific sense. It had to be man-made; a man-made disease, only something that a human being created, could cause a scene like this. She noticed that even some of the SWAT guys were barely holding it together. She told John to inform the SWAT team to stay at least six feet from any carnage or evidence.

"The SWAT team can wait outside the circle of evidence. I need to take as many samples of as many different types of evidence as possible, and get it quickly to a lab for analysis," Ivory said.

John ordered, "Captain, you and your men will remain no closer than seven feet outside of the perimeter, away from any evidence or carnage. Keep your eyes open and facing toward the wooded area, if anything hostile approaches, blow it away. Copy?"

"Yes Sir!" the Captain replied.

"Doctor Black, our mobile laboratory is set up and working. They have informed me they are testing the security guard that discovered the scene," John informed her.

"Great. Agent White, please have someone bring these samples down to the lab for testing."

"Captain," John ordered, "Have one of your men bring these down to the mobile lab for testing."

Ivory was careful to put the test samples in canisters, then into biohazard bags so that they wouldn't allow whoever was in contact with them to get infected by what was inside. Ivory kept circling from outside the evidence. Then she made smaller circles as she headed toward the center of the evidence. That's when she noticed a very wide opening built into the side of the mountain. She shouted, "Agent White, you need to see this!" He was by her side in seconds. Just then, they got a call from the lab and it was confirmed that it was not, in fact, a contagious disease.

John and Ivory took off their bio suits. John told her he was going to go inside and check it out. Ivory demanded that she go with him.

"Doctor, I was going to ask the SWAT Captain to accompany me. There could still be some crazy wild animals inside...or who knows what."

"John, I was a captain for four years in the Air Force, and I am probably a better shot than you. I shoot almost every day." John gave her a surprised look.

"What can I say? It relaxes me." Ivory gave a deadpan grin.

"Okay, Doc." John pulled out a Colt .45 pistol and another handgun.

Ivory asked, "What the hell is *that*?"

"The Judge. It shoots either .45 caliber or 28-gauge shotgun rounds."

"Give me the Colt .45, please." He handed her the Colt. She pulled back the slide and turned off the safety.

"Okay. Here's how this is going to work. I go first; you cover my six. You need to tell me right now that you will follow my orders immediately or you don't go."

"At least your manners are better than your common sense." What is it about traumatic situations that make not funny things funny? She contemplated.

When their chopper landed and they got out, she followed John toward a man standing with three beautiful women. Two were still in their early twenties; one was mid-to-late thirties, but definitely a knockout.

"Could you introduce yourself to those people? They are the only witnesses to the church massacre," John asked Ivory.

"Oh, those poor people. What should I tell them?"

"Tell them...for their own safety, they have to come with us, and that these attacks are the work of an evil mass murderer. Tell them we are trying to stop the murders and so far, they are the only survivors. Tell them they are in extreme danger. Then I'll meet you guys at those two jets. I need to instruct the pilots."

Ivory smiled at him. He actually got goose bumps. What the hell? Am I twelve years old again? Things are getting weird, John thought. Ivory walked toward the three women and a very handsome young man.

"Hello, I'm Doctor Ivory Black. I'm so sorry for what you have gone through. The person I was just with is in charge of this battle against a man-made technology that someone is using to kill in large quantities. I am the scientist that is in charge of figuring out what kind of mind control they are using, and how to stop it. We are making progress and time is of the essence. Please follow me. We are headed to Washington D.C. to a Nano cell Biotech research lab to talk to my colleagues."

Jane was taken aback. "Doctor, you are so exotically beautiful, and your eyes are so mysterious."

Ivory laughed nervously. "Please, all of you call me Ivory."

Helen said, "I have a good feeling about you, Ivory."

Doctor Black didn't know why, but Helen's words made her feel better and more relaxed than she had been. When they reached the jets where John was waiting for them, he told Ivory and Bobby to fly with him, and for Helen, Jane, and Mary to fly in the other jet. John had these two special jets made with more room for passengers. They weren't really Harrier jets, but had the same technology to hover and land in places that most jets couldn't. He called them phantoms.

"Ladies and gentleman don't worry. These jets have been converted for us to travel where we need to go. They are a little more spacious, and the pilots won't make you lose your lunch. Let's go!"

They all said, "Yes Sir," except Helen; she just grinned.

"Nice ride," Bobby said. John chuckled at his remark. Bobby reminded him of himself at that age. They landed in less than 30 minutes. They all walked through security after John showed his credentials and said the group was with him.

Unbelievable, Ivory thought. When she worked here, she had a harder time getting people in, and she was the boss. Ivory spotted someone in the distance; she ran up and hugged an older man.

He said, "Ivory we miss you around here. I have to tell you, the samples you sent us an hour ago are decades ahead of anything I have ever done, and even surpass your work, which is hard to believe."

"Jerry, I need to see everything you've found out," Doctor Black demanded.

"Yes. Get on your clean suit, and let's go into the lab."

"Doctor Jerry Jones, my name is General John White. We are in a national state of emergency and our entire nation is under an imminent threat. At any moment, thousands or possibly millions of American lives could be lost from the very technology that you are going to look at. Please keep in mind that time is our worst enemy. The time for pleasantries has passed."

"Yes, General."

"Doctor, I'm going to leave my lieutenant here. He will get you transportation and more security. Everything goes through him. Here is an encrypted cell phone. Call Doctor Black with any new discoveries as soon as you find out anything at all. She will be leaving very soon with my team. Doctor Jones, the security of our country is in your hands now. Do not speak to anyone else about this. Tell your team to collect samples and don't tell them why. If you have to let someone in on any top-secret information, clear it with me, and me only. Is that clear, Sir?"

Doctor Jones said, "Yes Sir! Of course. This is quite scary General."

"Doctor Jones, you have my complete confidence. Just follow procedure, and you will do fine. If you need to talk to someone and are in any way panicked, don't hesitate to confer with Doctor Black."

"Yes Sir," Doctor Jones said.

Ivory confirmed. "Yes Jerry. Call me any time, day or night." That seemed to calm him down. Helen giggled.

Ivory noticed that there is something different about her. Helen knew when John used that voice-command thing. Maybe that's what made Helen laugh. I hope she is taking this seriously.

Chapter Seven: The Strange Team

While the doctors were conferring in the laboratory, John decided to fill them in on what was happening. He felt an obligation to do so; he knew that if he set them free, that would be the end of them. He decided that as strange as this was becoming, what the hell? They were all on his new mission team until he could find a safe place for them. It seemed like fate. Who knows?

Maybe his new team was hand picked by God. He laughed at such a thought.

John gave them the top-secret information that pertained to this case. They might all soon be dead anyway. He knew that more than half the government was on enemy payroll. General White had no idea who he could trust.

Helen gave him a look like she knew what he was thinking. "General, don't worry so much. If God is with us, who can stand against us? Remember this about your new team: The Lord works in mysterious ways." And then she smiled a silly grin.

"Helen, thank you. I don't know how you did it, but I feel a peace I haven't felt since this all began."

"General, I didn't do anything, but you're welcome anyway."

Then John filled them in on everything he knew. Ivory and Doctor Jones came toward him.

Ivory said, "John...we need to talk to you A-SAP."

From the look on her face, this didn't look like it would be good news. John told the lieutenant to take the witnesses to get some coffee in the cafeteria. He looked at Helen and said he would talk with them more later if they had any questions. John went into Doctor Jones' office.

"Well, what did you guys find out?"

"John, this is worse than it looks," Ivory began. "I'll explain it in the least technical way I can, because its high tech. Like, next-generation high tech," Ivory said. "Someone has invented a Nano cell smaller and more powerful than anything Doctor Jones or I have ever seen. This Nano cell is a man-made microscopic electronic device that is being researched by some of the best scientific minds in the world. The stuff we just saw is at least ten to twenty *years* more advanced than the stuff I invented; and that was considered the most advanced Nano cell tech in the world. This Nano cell tech was done secretly, and has not been patented yet, or is patent-pending."

John cut her off. "Okay. I get it, but what can it do?"

"Well, it has a ton of great possibilities for doing good things, like making physically disabled people walk; or curing incurable sicknesses. However, the people who developed this are using it to murder innocent people! Those sick assholes!" By now, Ivory's eyes were open wide and her voice was rising.

"Ivory, try to calm down," John said.

"Sorry. It's just... all the good that this Nano cell can do is unprecedented, but some deranged assholes are using it for serial killings!" Now she was shouting.

"Ivory, calm down." John used *the voice*. She calmed down. "I need you guys to drop everything else you're doing and figure out a way to gain control of this technology."

Both Doctor Jones and Ivory sneered at his remark. "You're kidding, right?"

"Look," John grumbled, "Whether you know it or not, you may be our only hope in stopping this."

Ivory sighed. "John, it gets worse."

"How much worse?"

"Well, they are able to control animals...just mammals, so far."

"Shit," John exclaimed.

"You see the problem? She asked.

He nodded.

"We are also mammals," Ivory stated. "The human brain is much more complex than all other mammals. I don't think they have succeeded on controlling humans, *yet*; but it's just a matter of time before they will succeed at human mind control!"

"We only have part of the equation, General," Doctor Jones indicated. "There is more to this than just the Nano cell technology."

John thought for a second. "All right, here's what we're going to do. Doctor Jones, get your best researchers to both murder scenes and go through everything with a fine-tooth comb. Bring whatever you need. If you don't have what you need, we will get it for you, A-SAP! Check every blade of grass and every leaf on every tree if you have to. Find something we can use to help us counterpunch this evil!"

"Yes Sir," Doctor Jones replied.

"Also, only talk to Ivory or me about anything you find, and no one else. Do you understand, Doctor?"

"Yes General."

Chapter Eight: Temptation and Special Treatment

Doctor Jennings was thinking how quickly things could change. One minute I'm in charge of a reclusive, secret research lab, for over seven years. Then, a day after Doctor Spears arrives, I'm flying in a helicopter en route to a private jet to meet possibly the richest, most powerful man in the world! I haven't even had time to think about what I am doing. It has been so long since I have been out in the real world. I hope people still wear suits and shake hands when they meet. I suppose I should have expected this. Maybe I'm more of a recluse than I thought.

Doctor Jennings' chopper landed, and he could see a beautiful private jet about fifty yards away. He felt a panic attack coming on. Just then, a gorgeous young lady in a Globocorp uniform greeted him.

"Hello Doctor Jennings." She was seductive in her delivery, with a sexy Italian accent. "My name is Annett. I will be your guide, and if you need anything at all, please ask. I was told to treat you like a king." She winked, hugged him, and kissed him on both cheeks.

Like they do in Italy, he thought. "Thank you, Annett. You can call me Robert."

She smiled. Man, was she pretty! Though he didn't get out much, he laughed at himself. Annett was about five-feet, six-inches tall. Her jet-black hair flowed past her shoulders and her beautiful golden-brown eyes reminded him of dark honey. Annett put her arm through his and led him toward the jet. She was wearing a tiny and wispy mini skirt. Doctor Jennings remembered they were called that in the 1970s, anyway. Maybe they were back in style, he thought.

When they reached the stairs to the private jet, Annett turned to the doctor. "Follow me, Robert." She let out a giggle as she walked up the steps and turned around to catch Doctor Jennings checking out her legs. When he realized he was caught, he bowed his head and blushed a deep red from embarrassment. "Robert, it's all right. If I did not want you to look, I would have let you go first. You like?" She wiggled her butt for him.

Doctor Jennings thought that maybe this was how society now acted. He guessed that it was polite to look and compliment, but not to touch without permission. "Yes," he said nervously. "I like it very much, Annett. Quite lovely." Annett laughed with a wink and a smile.

They boarded the jet and Doctor Jennings was pleasantly surprised by its elegant interior. Just the artwork alone was worth millions – that is, if they were originals – and they sure looked like they were.

"Robert," Annett purred in his ear, "I have a surprise gift for you from Mr. Grey. Please sit right here, and I will be right back." He watched her saunter away with a swing in her hips. When she returned, she was holding a very old bottle of scotch. It looked to be at least a hundred years old.

"Robert, Mr. Grey shares your appreciation for fine scotch and has given you a case of these. It is one of, or maybe even the best scotch in the world. It certainly is very costly, to say the least."

"That is very nice of Mr. Grey. This bottle looks older than the bottle Doctor Spears brought me." He noticed that when he mentioned Doctor Spears, Annett's eyes glowered with contempt, but it could have just been his imagination.

"Let's open it. You be the judge of which one is the best. Don't worry Robert. You have 23 more bottles." She thought that was very funny and they both laughed – he, out of politeness, she, because it was her joke. He knew humor was slightly different across cultures. Perhaps Annett's joke was funny in her culture. That made him laugh; which made her laugh, harder, thinking he thought she was funny.

Robert wondered, is she one of the most beautiful women in the world, or have I been living in a cave too long? I wonder if this is how men who get out of prison after ten years feel. He watched Annett uncork the ancient bottle of scotch. She was very coordinated and quite well balanced. He would have stumbled because the jet had started to taxi to the take off point. Annett held two short scotch glasses in one hand and poured with the other. Then she placed the bottle in such a way that it wouldn't tip when the plane got going. She handed him three fingers of what was supposedly the finest scotch in the world. Doctor Jennings gladly accepted, but thought right now - as bizarre as this day was turning out - he would have settled for Johnny Walker Red.

"To your sacrifice, Robert. Congratulations! As you Americans say, down the hatch!" She drank a small, one-finger drink. Robert downed his three fingers.

"Well, Robert. What do you think?"

"Annett, I do believe that was the smoothest and best-tasting scotch I have ever had, and that's saying something."

She smiled and said, "You cannot fly with only one wing Robert. You must be sure about your judgment." She laughed and poured him three more fingers, and another small one for herself.

The scotch was working. Doctor Jennings perked up. "I would like to propose a toast to a very lovely young lady who knows where to find some fantastic scotch; the best in the world."

She thought that was hilarious. "Thank you, Robert."

The Captain announced that they were taking off in a few minutes. He ordered them to fasten their seat belts, and then he said, "Greetings, Doctor Jennings! It is an honor to have such a distinguished guest on board. Enjoy your flight Sir."

Annett came over with a big, sultry smile and buckled up Doctor Jennings. He noticed that she had unbuttoned the top of her blouse and was not wearing a bra. While she buckled him in, she smashed her breasts right onto his face then backed away. "You like, Robert?"

"I like, Annett."

She giggled and poured one more round of scotch before they took off, then buckled in right across from him. It's either the scotch, or she really is looking at me like she wants to ravish me, Doctor Jennings mused. I'd better take it easy on the drinks or I might make an ass of myself.

The Captain informed them that they were free to remove their seatbelts. Annett smiled at Doctor Jennings. "I have been ordered to help you relax and get used to living in society again Robert. I have another surprise for you. Please follow me." She got up and took the scotch with her. Curious, he followed. Annett led him into a large massage and shower room. She told him to take a shower and then have some hors d'oeuvres and another scotch. She would be back in twenty minutes."

Steaming with anticipation, he did as he was told. When she came back in, Annett had a blue silk robe on. Her hair was in a ponytail and she told him to lie down on his stomach, and place his towel over his buttocks. She took off her robe, and displayed her naked body. Laughing at his expression, Annett teased, "Robert, you are a doctor! Haven't you ever seen a grown woman naked before? I will be using oils and I don't want to stain any clothing. Besides, it is exciting, no?"

"Quite exciting Annett," he said, stumbling over his words. She smiled warmly at him. "Lay down. I want you to relax." He plopped down on his stomach, the towel covering as he had been instructed. Annett yanked off the towel and spanked him lightly. "Don't be so shy Robert. You have a nice butt, and I want to see it."

"Fine with me Annett," he said nervously. This sexy woman started massaging his shoulders before working her way down. Robert was so relaxed he almost fell asleep.

As she was massaging him, she became curiously aroused. "Robert, when was the last time you have been with a woman?"

"To be totally honest, it's been over ten years An-nett. I don't even know if my plumbing still works, if you catch my drift."

"Oh, such a sacrifice is so noble Robert, but not fair. Turn over." He flipped over on the massage table. "It seems that the pipes work very well. Yes. Nice plumbing, Robert. Let's relieve the plumbing pressure," she giggled. When they were done, Robert had to admit that he felt fantastic. Annett then bathed him and shaved him before she left the room. She came back with scissors and an electric hair trimmer. "Robert, I'm going to cut your hair. Okay?"

Feeling like a new man already, Doctor Jennings said, "Sure. Go right ahead, Annett. You are a woman of many talents."

"Thank you, Robert. You are quite a talent, as well." She gave him a wanting, sexy look. She left the room after she finished his haircut, then came back in with a very expensive suit and helped him dress.

I could get used to this he thought, but he knew it was just her job. He would like to think that she fell for him, but she was out of his league as far as looks and age were concerned. But he wanted to believe that maybe this could be for real. As she handed him another scotch, she smiled and kissed him.

"Robert you are a nice man, and so important to the world. I just want you to know this is the first time I have ever done any servicing for a passenger, and I really like you."

"I really like you too, Annett."

"Really?"

"Yes. I think you are the most beautiful and kind-est woman I have ever met."

Annett had a tear flow from her eye. She kissed him sensually. "I think your plumbing needs to be fixed again. We have time, Robert, and my plumbing needs it too," she chuckled.

Later, Robert fell asleep after they were told to buckle up due to minor turbulence fifteen minutes before they were scheduled to land. Annett woke him with a soft kiss and said, "Robert, we have landed." Annett seemed very excited and kept smiling at him like she knew something he didn't know. Please he thought, no more surprises. Don't these people understand I have lived in a cave for seven and a half years? Is this what they call culture shock?

She noticed something was wrong with him. "Are you feeling okay?"

"To be honest, I'm feeling kind of panicky. I've just come out of my cave for the first time in over seven years."

"Of course Robert. Do not worry; I will take you to a place right away where we can talk alone. Is this good?"

"Thank you Annett, very good."

When they landed, a Rolls Royce limo was waiting for them. The driver introduced himself in English as Pauli, and if Doctor Jennings needed anything, he could just ask.

"Pauli I would love to get to my room and take a short nap. That would be fantastic."

"Right away Doctor Jennings. It is an honor to meet you, Sir."

What the hell is going on? Robert wondered. I feel like the president getting off Air Force One. I haven't even applied my invention or our discoveries to good use yet, and it seems I'm some kind of celebrity.

Pauli stopped in front of a large separate house on the grounds. "Here we are, Doctor Jennings. This is where you will be staying while you are here."

"Wow," Doctor Jennings exclaimed. "It's beautiful!" Annett wrapped her arm in his and they headed for the front door, following Pauli.

Annett whispered, "It is more fun to follow me, no?" She laughed.

"Definitely," Doctor Jennings replied enthusiastically.

Pauli stopped at the door and turned around. "Doctor Jennings, this ring has been sized for the index finger of your left hand, and the only way the door will open is if you have it on that finger and touch the doorknob."

Robert touched the doorknob with the ring and the door opened. Pauli smiled and brought in the luggage. "Doctor, shall I bring your luggage to any specific room, or rooms?"

Annett said, "Pauli, can you bring them to the master bedroom please."

"Yes certainly," Pauli said.

Robert asked if he should tip Pauli and if so, how much. Annett got a big laugh out of that one; tears were splashing out of her eyes. Doctor Jennings laughed at Annett, which made them both laugh harder. They managed to bring it down to a small giggle by the time Pauli came back and said goodbye.

"Pauli, we will call you if we need you, and grazie," Annett said.

"Yes, thank you Pauli," Doctor Jennings added.

"Please, Doctor Jennings," Pauli beamed. "Just driving you in my car was an honor I will never forget, thank *you*."

When Pauli closed the door, Doctor Jennings looked at Annett. "What? Did I just become Elvis Presley without knowing it?"

That got her going again. "Robert, please," she cried. "No more jokes! My stomach is hurting. I cannot laugh much more." That made Robert laugh, even harder. As to why, he had no idea, but he couldn't stop. When they both calmed down Annett whispered, "Can I take a nap with you? I'm very tired, and a nap sounds good."

"Yes, please. Where is the bed in this place? I would love to take a nap with you, Annett." She led him to the bedroom.

He didn't remember drifting off to sleep, but when he woke, Annett was softly kissing him.

"Robert we must get ready for your meeting with Mr. Grey. It is in an hour and a half."

"That seems rather quick," he scoffed. "I would have liked to have one day to assimilate into this socially impulsive environment."

"I don't understand. My English is good, but not very good like yours."

"Sorry, Annett. What I meant is, I would have liked at least a day to get used to being out of my cave."

"I keep forgetting. It must be very strange for you, the sudden change. Yes?"

"Annett, sometimes I feel like I'm going to pass out from panic. Thank God you are with me, or I would."

"Thank you my pretty man. You make me feel so important."

"Thank you Annett. But for men, we say handsome, not pretty. That would be a compliment for a lady or a girl."

"Oh! Sorry," she laughed. "You are *definitely* not a lady or a girl." She laughed again. "Now, come into the shower with me. We can save time if we do it together," she teased. "My handsome man."

After a particularly hot and steamy shower, Annett and Doctor Jennings were dressed and ready to meet Mr. Grey. She gave him two drinks. "I know you have anxiety, but when you feel it, look at me, I will ease you. I will share my calmness with you." She kissed him softly then wiped some of her lipstick off his lips.

Pauli rang the doorbell and a screen in every room showed a live video of him waiting at the front door. Doctor Jennings looked at Annett. She shrugged. "This place is very high tech, Robert. Take three deep breaths, and relax." She came up to him and lifted her skirt so she could sit on his lap. She softly grabbed each side of his face and said, "Look in my eyes."

He obeyed. She assured him, "Everything will be fine. If you feel any panic, just squeeze my hand and I will help, all right? Be careful not to drink too much scotch. You must be able to walk a straight line. Let me decide for you, only tonight, because it is an important night. Yes?"

Desperate to ease some tension, he agreed. "Yes, fine."

Annett opened the door and told Pauli they would be out in in a minute.

She closed the door, adjusted his tie, and grinned, "Let's rock and roll, Robert." That made him laugh, which made her laugh more, as they both came out and got into the limo.

Pauli said, "This way please," as he opened the limo door for them.

"I think you deserve to drink with me; a toast." Annett poured them both a glass of scotch. "I would like to say I am having so much fun with a very handsome and sexy man. To Doctor Robert Jennings."

They drank it down and Doctor Jennings said, "I would like to make a toast as well." Annett smiled and poured them another. "To Annett, the beautiful lady with the prettiest eyes I have ever seen. Annett, without you by my side, I don't think I could get through all of this. I want to thank you, from my heart." One quick gulp and he drained his glass.

She pulled out a handkerchief. "Robert, that was so nice. It makes me cry happy tears. I will look like a mess if I keep crying!"

"Drink your scotch. That will help."

So she did.

Before long, the limo stopped and Pauli opened the door. "Good luck tonight, Doctor Jennings."

"Thank you Pauli," he said.

Annett and Doctor Jennings walked through the front doors into a Gothic-designed gigantic castle. The castle, or at least small parts of the castle, at one time was a royal building from the Constantinian Era. Constantine was the Roman emperor who had decided to stop the persecution of Christians in the Empire of Rome. Historians knew this action as "The Triumph of the Church," or "The Peace of the Church," and even "The Constantinian Shift." No matter which way you looked at it, the Constantinian Era became the beginning of the Roman Catholic Church.

Mr. Grey was a direct descendant of Constantine and had royal blood in his veins. Atlas Grey was his legally changed name. His birth name was Lucifer Judas Santino. Mr. Grey was also an English Earl. He was able to buy the land and title from an older Earl who had no living relatives. The old Earl knew that Mr. Grey could trace his ancestry back to Constantine. The amount of money that Mr. Grey paid – much more than its value – may have had a little to do with it. Mr. Grey was an Earl referred to as Lord, and it turned out he was the last living descendant of Constantine who had laid the foundation for what became Roman Catholicism. This fantastic combination of ancient and modern technology reflected his heritage.

There were Roman coats of arms of Constantine in every room. The bathrooms were a combination of modern facilities and old Roman bathhouses. Gold faucets and handles, including the toilet flushers, were everywhere.

Doctor Jennings thought it was pompous to show off your money in such a way. He knew that many people disagreed with him, but he imagined what good this ten-thousand-dollar sink faucet could do if the money was used instead for research, or to feed the starving. Just enjoy the ride, he assured himself. You can't change the whole world's point of view. He took three deep breaths, turned on the sink water with the golden faucet handles, washed his hands, and went out to meet Annett. She was standing about ten feet from the bathroom door.

Annett waved when she saw him. She led him to their table in an enormous, elegant room that looked like it could comfortably seat five hundred. Their table was front and center.

"How come we are the only people here?" Doctor Jennings asked.

"It was Mr. Grey's idea that we come early and have some hors d'oeuvres and drinks, so you are more comfortable. He is a very smart man. He probably knows how hard it is to do what you're doing. You know, adjusting to being out of your cave." They both laughed.

"You have a beautiful laugh," Doctor Jennings offered.

She gave him that flirtatious smile and said, "Maybe we can sneak off and check the plumbing pipes a little later, Robert."

"You are going to wear me out," he chuckled.

She feigned a frown, "Well, if you don't want to, I understand."

"Oh, I want to all right, just teasing you a little."

"Robert, you should never tease a lady."

Just then the waiter came to their table, "Hello, Doctor Jennings, hello, Miss."

"You can call me Miss Annett."

"It is an honor to meet you both. I'll be your servant tonight on personal orders from Mr. Grey. Anything you want, anything at all, just ask and it is yours." He took their orders for caviar and lobster tails, already unshelled and buttered.

Annett leaned over to Doctor Jennings, "Why is he honored to meet *me*?"

"Now you know how I feel Annett."

She looked at him, surprised by his answer. "What are you talking about? You have given most of your life to discovering ways to help the world and have come up with many things, I hear. I am just a pretty face that will fade with age. Really Robert, I am a nobody."

"Don't forget about your body. You're not just a pretty face, but you're also smoking hot."

She grinned at that.

"Annett, I believe we are all equal. I was gifted with a high IQ and an ambition to use it for the good of mankind. You were gifted with empathy and beauty. You have compassion – that is a definite gift. You are a genuine treasure. Just being around you makes me happy."

Her eyes started to water again. "Oh Robert, that is so beautiful, what you just said. Nobody has ever talked to me like that before. *You* are the treasure."

Robert looked into Annett's beautiful brown eyes. "I would like to be around you, sweet, beautiful, Annett, for a long, long time."

Looking at him with love and adoration, she whispered softly, "Robert you make me so happy. I have never felt such feelings of love. You have made me cry with joy and laughter since I laid my eyes on you." She paused a minute to let her words sink in. "You are beautiful, kind, and I love being near you Robert. I would love to be around you forever."

Chapter Nine: Strange Meetings

General John White and his strange new team landed on a natural ledge on the side of a mountain. The ledge stuck out about forty yards and the ground below sloped from two feet at the top of the ledge to twelve feet at the bottom, on this side of the mountain. The ledge was the only place flat enough to land in the area. They rolled under a camouflage roof so as not to be seen by any possible spy drones or satellites. John was quite sure the government knew about this place, and there were more enemies in the government than patriots right now. At least the new president was an American and a patriot, not like the last enemy-fraud planted by globalists to destroy the country by every socialist trick in the book. This is what they were fighting for now. The last president, planted by power and money, appointed over one hundred terrorists and enemies of the state in all areas of the government. The corrupt old-time, money-grubbing senators, congressmen, and congresswomen allowed it - as long as they got their cut.

Such greed. Where will your children live, or your grandchildren, when our country becomes a third-world country? Only the filthy-rich elite will rule, the hundreds of billionaires, and the few trillion Aires will rule.

Millionaires will be stripped of money to make the elite look good, and they will become the scapegoats. Well, he thought, we fight evil as long as we can. John never really thought he would still be able to fight. If the female communist won, it would have been over. Thank God for the reprieve. The silent majority finally came out and voted. John thought it wasn't just that. God's people humbled themselves and prayed because they knew if they didn't, the country was lost.

Now was the time for all good people to fight, because if they didn't, evil would win. Evil could not be allowed to continue to escalate. It was becoming too powerful. John knew he was fighting just until God's church was raptured. In Revelations, God's church was only mentioned in heaven. Not once was it mentioned as being on Earth during the last seven years of the worst suffering in the entire history of the world. The only way for the enemy to win is for God's church to be gone. He had a feeling that wasn't too far in the future. Too many prophecies had come true that pointed to that time getting closer. He struggled with these ideas, but ultimately thought, I'm not going to worry about that. I'm just going to do my job to the best of my abilities.

Growing tired of the formalities, he told his new team to call him John unless they were not alone and among other people. He gathered the group and said, "Follow me."

They walked down a hallway about 20 feet and stopped. John felt around the wall that looked like the rest of wall they had already passed. He then pushed his hand into a certain spot and part of the wall slid sideways to reveal a stainless-steel door. He put his face in a certain spot and an electronic voice announced, "Prepare for eye scan." A retinal L.E.D. identifier scanned his eye, and the door slid open. He then ordered everyone to follow and explained that this was one of many bunkers he used for his work. He described how it was fully stocked with food and had a nice kitchen if anyone wanted to cook dinner or have a snack.

"Right now, I need to talk to some military people, and I need Ivory to accompany me. We shouldn't be longer than an hour. Please make yourself comfortable." John turned and walked away. Ivory smiled at them in an assuring manner as she followed him. He walked over to another wall and duplicated the same eye-scan procedure that he used to get into the bunker from the hall. They both walked into his office, which was spacious and high-tech. John looked a bit concerned.

"Ivory, those people out there are probably thinking they somehow got zapped into a "James Bond movie" or a "Stephen King novel." I need your help with them. I'm pretty funny when I'm with a person who has the same kind of sense of humor as mine...or someone who has the hot's for me like you do."

"Excuse *me*, John, but I believe it's you who has the hot's for me!" Ivory countered.

"Really Ivory? If I remember correctly, you asked me to strip naked when we first met."

"Look, John. I'm already insanely angry with the crazy, evil people who are torturing, controlling, and killing beautiful animals, in order to kill poor innocent people. I can't believe I'm even saying this, but I think if I definitely knew who the guilty party was, I could actually kill them. That is something that

I would never have believed possible of myself. Do yourself a favor right now, and don't piss me off more than I already am."

"So...you're denying the fact that you wanted to see me naked?"

"Have you lost what little brains you have?"

John doubled over with laughter. He couldn't stop, especially when he looked up and saw her face. Ivory finally realized he was messing with her, and she started to laugh too. Finally, when they both calmed down enough to talk, Ivory asked, "How do you do that?"

"What's that?" John asked.

"You can get me from extremely pissed off to laughing hysterically. I have never met anyone like you."

John moved in closer, as if he was going to tell her a secret. She looked in his eyes, and he grabbed both sides of her face and kissed her hard. What surprised Ivory the most was that she kissed back, just as hard.

"Wow," they both said after John pulled away. At first, there was an awkward silence. "Should I strip now?" John joked. The timing was perfect. "Ivory, when you're in an extremely stressful, hate-filled situation, you can't just stay pissed off or angry all the time or else you will burn out. You're our super genius, so we can't have you burn out! Without your brains, to put it bluntly, we're screwed. I know a few tricks to calm combatants down in stressful situations such as this one."

"So John, do you stick your tongue in all your stressed-out soldiers' mouths? Or just the females?"

"That kiss...I will never forget it for as long as I live. And the answer is no. I've never kissed to help a highly stressed out or angry person, before. I just couldn't help it and, frankly, that scares the hell out of me."

"Oh. Maybe you should use that tactic, because it really worked on me."

"That's a good point. Maybe that *would* work," he said with a serious face. They both started laughing again. Ivory hugged him and kissed him again, this time longer.

John broke it up. "As fantastic as this is – and it has never been more fantastic for me, those people in the other room have to be dealt with. They are probably thinking we left and someone is going to come in and execute them, or something along those lines."

"You're right John. You're the expert. What should we tell them?"

"The truth. Reassure them that we are the good guys, and we are a team."

"Do you think they need any of your cool tricks to calm them down?" she giggled.

"Hey, Ivory, float like a butterfly sting like a bee. Do you know what that really means?"

"Yes, I do, Muhammad Ali would bounce around the ring, floating like a butterfly, then punch his opponent, stinging like a bee."

"Wrong, but don't feel bad, that's what most people think. What it really means is something that is much harder to do than it sounds."

"Oh yeah? What's that, smart guy?"

"Well, Ali lost his first couple of fights because he stayed mad for the whole time he was fighting. If you're as angry as you can be, no matter what kind of shape you're in, you won't last three rounds unless you knock out your opponent. Most likely, you will be exhausted by the second or third round and lose. Ali learned to relax, even when he was being hit, and he learned to get extremely pissed off when he punched, which made him hit harder. Then he would calm down and relax right away."

"That sounds impossible," Ivory scoffed.

"I can do it. With time and training, most people can."

"Who are you? If we're going to have a relationship, which it sure looks that way because you can't control yourself around me, I want to know your story. You're so cool," Ivory smirked. "I'm serious!"

"All right," John said, "I will tell you my whole life story if you tell me yours."

"Deal, buddy," She felt like a teenager again.

"Let's check on our team Doctor. When we have time, I'll tell you all about me."

When they opened the door, he realized that there was cooking going on. Most people would be sitting in fear or in shock, from witnessing the massacre. Helen turned to John and Ivory, and said, "Wash up, you two! We all whipped up a great dinner." John looked at Ivory, and she shrugged.

"Float like a butterfly, John." Ivory smiled. It was the kind of smile that gave him butterflies in his stomach. Then she moved closer and softly kissed his lips.

"Wow. What a sexy vixen you are, Ivory."

"Right back at you, stud," she whispered.

'This is going to be interesting. He mused.

Helen had all the food on the table and asked everyone to take a seat. John was impressed with these people. They were acting like they were just getting together for a dinner party. Something surreal was going on here. And yet, he felt something peaceful, a kind of presence.

John sat at the head of the table with Doctor Ivory Black on his right and Helen on his left. Jane was sitting next to her mom. Mary was sitting between Ivory and Bobby; Bobby was sitting at the other end of the table across from John.

John spoke first. "I'm amazed that you guys were able to get this delicious dinner together so fast. It smells great. Let's eat, and then I want to hear about all of you, and a summary of your life stories, because this whole entire scenario is, for lack of a better word, crazy."

Helen laughed and the rest joined in, but they were all nervous. She said, "John, would you like to say grace, or should I?"

"I will, Helen. Father we thank You for this food and thank You for Your blessings. Thank You Lord, for bringing us together to do Your will. In Jesus' name, Amen."

"I knew you were with God the minute I saw you General," Helen giggled. "I mean, John."

As they were eating, John turned to Bobby. "Have you been in combat before?"

Bobby looked at John like he had read his mind. "How did you know? It's something I really don't like to talk about. Yes Sir, General White. I was a lieutenant in the Navy SEALs. I guess now is the time to tell my story, since you need to know your team." Mary looked at Bobby; she was surprised by what he revealed. Everyone knew about Navy SEALs and how they were some of the deadliest people on Earth. Bobby noticed the look she gave him and turned away, almost shamefully. Mary grabbed his hand and squeezed it. When he looked at her, she smiled, and it seemed to brighten up the room. Mary just couldn't believe someone as nice and gentle as Bobby could hurt a fly, but it didn't change her opinion of him.

"Okay, here's my story General White, I was leading my team on a mission. The details of the mission were classified. We had just finished setting our demo-charges when I got a gut feeling that we were in imminent danger. I told my men to scramble. I found a reed - just like in those old movies. I used it to breathe underwater as I floated away from the bridge we were demolishing. Bright lights came on and .50 caliber tracer-rounds were flying all around me. One nicked my thigh underwater. I put pressure on it so the blood wouldn't show my position. I thought to myself, we've been compromised. Someone sold us out. I swore I would find out who did it. I would find them, and kill them with extreme prejudice!"

"Sorry ladies, but the General needs to know. I knew my brothers were all dead; I had the detonator so I blew up the bridge. Mission accomplished. I was able to get out of there and back to the states. When I reported to my captain what went down and that we had been compromised, he said, 'I'm sorry son, this man's army is not what it was. Politicians are involved, and good men are dying from treason and for campaign donations.'"

"It was my time to re-enlist; I just couldn't do it. I had my own mission, and that was to find the traitors who killed my team, my brothers; they killed for money. I had to positively identify the traitorous filth, and terminate them from their evil existence. This is what I lived for! A year later, I found out how many people were involved and how high up the ladder it went. Right up to the very top. I was furious and ready to die for justice."

"I rented a small one-bedroom shack from a sweet, older lady named Mrs. Fields. She knew a paving outfit that was looking for help. I had been paving since I was a young boy. I needed money and supplies for my planned vigilante justice. She set up a meeting with the owner of the asphalt paving company and me. We all met at her house, which was an old farmhouse about fifty yards from the renovated chicken coop I was renting from her. Mrs. Fields made us a fried chicken dinner with all the fixings. The owner of the paving company, Mr. Johnson, showed up at the same time I did."

"He introduced himself to me. 'You must be Bobby', he said.

"Yes Sir. It's a pleasure to meet you."

'It's a pleasure to meet you too Bobby, best not keep a lady waiting'. He knocked on the door and Mrs. Fields said, 'Come on in, boys.' General, I know what I'm saying right now doesn't sound important, but it turned out to be the most important day of my life. Well, we all sat down to eat.'"

"Mrs. Fields said, 'Would you say grace, Bobby?' I told her that I didn't know how. She said she would teach me. I'll never forget the words she used. 'Dear Father God, we have been blessed with a new guest – a wonderful, kind young man. Lord, please, I ask this through my love of Jesus Christ, I know this young man has been going through a very hard and troubling time, I feel it Father. What I feel is an urgency to have this boy feel Your peace and forgiveness. I ask as a personal favor that You send Your Holy Spirit here tonight to prepare this young person to be forgiven and to forgive. I know You have plans for him, and I feel that those plans are going to happen very soon.'"

"Well, you might think I'm crazy," said Bobby, "But I felt a peace I had never known or felt before. Then she told me that the Lord does not force His blessings on us, and that I had to choose to accept them. 'Bobby she said, 'will you freely accept the Father's blessing, and will you accept forgiveness for your sins from Jesus Christ, the Lamb of God, who suffered and died willingly so He could pay for your sins'? Well, I had a feeling come over me that I can't even explain. I got on my knees right then and there, and said, yes, ma'am, I do. She told me to say it out loud, so I did. I said, Lord Jesus, I accept You and am truly sorry for my sins. As I was saying this, tears of joy were coming out of my eyes. I jumped up and hugged Mrs. Fields. I thanked her for helping me to know God.'"

"Mr. Johnson came over and it looked like he had tears of joy in his eyes, too. He said, 'You're hired', and we all laughed and cried joyful tears at the same time. I had been working for him for a little less than a week when I met Mary and fell for her the minute I saw her.'"

He looked at Mary, and soft tears were streaming down her face.

"The next day was the day at the church," he continued. "General, if you don't think I'm crazy by now, what I'm about to tell you probably will make you think I'm nuts. Ever since I can remember, I have been able to get a warning when I am in danger, and so far have had just enough time to avoid it...sometimes I barely avoided it. That's my story, and I did my best to be totally honest about it."

Helen nodded her head in agreement. "John, you know if Bobby hadn't warned us and made us move so fast away from the church, we wouldn't be here today."

"That is God's honest truth," Jane stated.

Mary trembled, and asked quietly, "John, can I go next? I have to tell Bobby something that will probably change the way he feels about me." She looked at Bobby, unable to make eye contact with him. "Bobby, I am not a good girl. I'm pregnant, and I don't even know who the father is. I would go to weekend college parties and wind up getting so drunk I sometimes had sex with guys I just met. I would blame God because of all the bad things that happened to me in my life. I felt alone after my dad died until the day I met Helen and Jane. They made me feel what I think is the kind of peace you mentioned, but it never got to the point that I wanted God in my life. I just thought you should know not to waste your time on a person like me, Bobby. You deserve better."

Helen spoke up. "People, could we please all hold hands? I want to talk to the Lord." They all joined hands together at the table. "Father, I know we are all here to serve Your purpose and time is a crucial factor. Lord Jesus, our first love, could You heal our little sister Mary and send the Holy Spirit to help her to understand?"

As if a soft wind breezed through, they all felt the peace that could not be described.

Mary felt empowered. She got down on her knees and begged, "Jesus, Lord, my first love, please forgive me for all the false blame and doubt. Please, Jesus, forgive me so I can forgive myself, and help me Lord, to know what is right from what is wrong. I feel Your love with all my heart. Thank You Jesus, tell Daddy I love him. Amen." Mary stood up and the room lit up with her smile. She looked at Helen and Jane. They were all smiling with tears of joy. Mary yelled out, "Praise Jesus!" and "Hallelujah!"

Helen and Jane couldn't help laughing, because just a day or two earlier, Mary had told them not to expect her to do that. Mary looked at Bobby, who was staring at her with loving eyes, she knew the love was for her; and she knew just how he felt, because she felt the same way about him.

Bobby said, "Mary, this is crazy, but I love you and want to be with you forever." She jumped into his arms and cried, "Praise Jesus! Amen to that, Bobby."

John said, "Fantastic. The Lord is with us. Who can stand against us?"

Ivory jumped in with an "Amen," and hugged him.

Once emotions settled down a bit, John said, "Bobby, I believe you have the gift of sensing danger. I have a gift of command; when I give a command in a certain voice, people are compelled to obey me."

Bobby said, "Now that you mention it, I remember how I felt when you gave us commands."

Ivory agreed. "Yes, everybody except Helen. She laughed at your voice." Ivory smiled at Helen.

Helen corrected her. "Ivory, I laughed because I saw the gift and knew I was in the place that the Lord wanted me to be."

"I know you weren't laughing at John," Ivory said. "You're too nice for that. But what *is* your power, Helen?"

Jane interrupted. "The Lord is with her always. That's her power, and it's huge!"

John asked Jane if she had a gift from the Lord. Jane looked a little embarrassed. "Well," John asked again. "What is it?"

Jane adjusted herself in her chair and shuffled her feet a bit. "I can look at someone and know what they are thinking."

"What am I thinking right now?" John tested her, while half-believing her.

"Are you sure you want me to say it?"

"Yes," he urged.

"You want to hug and kiss Ivory so bad, it actually hurts."

Ivory snorted. "Really, John. Try to control yourself."

Jane looked at Ivory; "You want the same thing just as much, or maybe a little more."

Ivory felt her cheeks flush. "Okay! Does anyone else have any gifts?"

"I'm sorry Ivory, sometimes I don't keep my mouth shut when I should."

"Oh, Jane, sweetheart, that's okay. This meeting is the most amazing thing I've ever been a part of...and I've been in some pretty amazing meetings during my career."

Helen exclaimed, "Ivory, tell them about your gift! It's amazing!"

Ivory looked at Helen, surprised, "Well, I'm like Doctor Doolittle. Animals obey me as if they love me so much that they have to do what I say to please me. I don't even have to speak. I can just think of what I want them to do; and they do it. Helen, I have never let anyone know. I felt like a freak, but now that I know it's a gift from the Lord, I don't feel like a freak anymore." She looked at John, hoping it wouldn't make him think less of her. John's eyes said it all. He thought she was an amazing woman.

Mary, almost sounding disappointed, said, "I have no super-powers. Am I still in the club?" This made everyone let out a laugh.

Helen said, "Mary, you have been chosen for something very special. Who knows what you will be able to do? You have just been born to live forever. You are no longer of the Earth, but are part of the body, and blood of Jesus Christ, the King of Kings."

John said, "Okay. Let's start by each one of you having these." He passed out encrypted cell phones. "Ivory set a changing algorithm code on these phones, and they all change at the exact same time with the same new codes; nobody should be able to track them. I'm sorry, but we have to destroy all other electronic devices."

"If you guys have pictures that you don't want to lose, I could download them onto a memory stick," Ivory reassured them.

"Great!" Helen said. Everyone handed their phones to Ivory.

"One more thing," John said. "I'm expecting company tonight or tomorrow, so please stay in these quarters, just for a day or two."

Jane said somberly, "An assassin."

"Yes, Jane, I will try and tell you more information. Sorry, but I'm used to keeping things to myself for security reasons. It might take me a while to get used to my new God squad."

Jane said, "That's a cool name! All right, we are now officially, the God Squad. What do you think, mom?"

"I love it, Jane."

Chapter Ten: A Dinner Guest

Raphe Corvino landed at Globocorps' private airport, on over one thousand acres of land in, upstate New York. A high-ranking, FBI Assistant-director, an American senator, and two secret-service agents met Raphe. They were there to pick up a 100 million dollar cash contribution-bribe, from Mr. Grey. Raphe recognized the FBI Boss. He had seen him in the news but couldn't remember his name. He had something to do with rigging the presidential election, but it seemed to backfire on him. Raphe didn't really follow politics. As far as he was concerned, they were all money-grabbing, backstabbing weasels. At least half of the head politicians in this country were on Mr. Grey and his elite Globocorp pals' payroll. The country was almost lost, but somehow a real American patriot had won the election against all odds, even with the existing corrupt government rigging it. Raphe laughed. He was secretly happy that the businessman won. Man, did it piss off Mr. Grey, who Raphe detested. The guy gave him the creeps. These corrupt politicians had no honor. He wished that the new president had them all shot for the treasonous garbage they were. After the corrupt FBI man loaded-up the donation, he drove him to a hangar, where he met up with the Globocorp crew. The Senator and the FBI man tried to shake Raphe's hand. Raphe just stared them down, he actually wouldn't mind killing these guys. He hated dishonorable people, there was no way he was going to shake their hands. Raphe was always ready, he had thought up a plan on the ride over, how he could kill these guys, without problems, but his boss-dad would be disappointed in him. Raphe was hoping they would make a move, so he could give these boys a well-deserved eternal rest! Their eyes told him different, they were afraid. The four of them walked to the black Cadillac SUV, and left.

The Globocorp team had orders to get him close enough to his target without being detected. Raphe's orders were to terminate any and all personnel on the grounds with extreme-prejudice (military vocabulary for 'kill everyone'). Then he was supposed to blow the place up so the only pieces left would be in a different state. He chuckled, Why such overkill?

Raphe entered the hangar and ordered the squad to follow him downstairs to an old bunker. Mr. Grey had it converted into an office for jobs like this. Raphe's, father, Antonio Corvino, was Mr. Grey's right-hand man. Raphe had been working for Globocorp since he was a boy. Raphe had done many assassinations for Globocorp. His father always told him that his targets were evil people. Raphe had just turned twenty-five years old, and he already had a reputation as one the best hit man in the world. However, lately he's been questioning some of the assignments.

He would never disrespect his dad by questioning his judgment. The main target was a woman doctor who, as far as Raphe's research had shown, was nothing but a good person. She seemed to be devoting her life to helping sick children and animals. From what Raphe found out about her, she was kind and generous. Dr. Ivory Black was a genius, and a stunningly exotic, beautiful woman. For the first time, Raphe wondered if he was doing dirty deeds for Mr. Grey. Raphe knew his father was a good man, but maybe Mr. Grey had been lying to his dad. Raphe put it out of his mind and concentrated on his other target. He looked forward to his secondary target; a man called Agent, or General, John White. This man, General White, was a challenge. He had already killed or captured six hit men; all of them sent to kill him, had pretty good reputations. Raphe was trained to never underestimate an opponent. He really didn't want to do the doctor, but orders were orders. When he was done with this, he was going to tell his dad that he needed some time to explore other forms of employment. He laughed at that idea, thinking of the look his dad would give him.

Raphe was born in America. His dad was born in Italy. Antonio Corvino, Raphe's dad, had moved to America with his parents when he was twelve years old. He became a citizen and joined the Navy and made the SEAL teams. He met Raphe's mom Maria Fiora at a party on the beach. Antonio thought he had met an angel from heaven, he told Maria that the first time he saw her. Maria thought he was the most handsome man she ever saw. She told him she was in love with him from the first time she looked into his eyes. She said she knew he was just as beautiful inside, as he was outside. They were married three months later. They couldn't stand to be away from each other.

Antonio had his missions to go on, and he knew Maria was safe near the base. It wasn't long before Raphe was born. The nurse put Raphe in Antonio's arms, and he was the first person that little Raphe ever saw. Raphe had opened his eyes for the first time, looking at his father's loving face. "It was like magic," Antonio told him. He used to tell Raphe that was one of the best moments of his life. Raphe remembered how beautiful his mom was and how she spoiled him, always hugging and cuddling with him.

When his dad came back home from one of his missions, he would train Raphe. He started training him in martial arts and how to handle weapons when he was only eight years old. He said someone has to be the man of the house and protect Momma while he was away.

Those were happy times. The only meal they didn't have together was lunch during the week because Raphe went to school.

The weekends were always a fun time. They were always together. One Saturday, they took Raphe to the beach they always visit. They surprised him and there was a carnival there. Raphe's mom went on the kiddie rides with him, but he was ten years old now and wanted to go on the bigger rides. Raphe didn't know it, but his mom had just found out she was pregnant and she didn't want to go on the crazy rides.

She asked Antonio to take him on the Ferris wheel. It was really high; she asked Raphe if he was too scared to go on it, and he said, "No. I want to Mom." His dad grabbed him, picked him up, and started carrying him. Raphe said, "Dad, put me down! I'm a big boy now."

Antonio said, "Sorry son, I forgot." They both got on the Ferris wheel. Maria was watching and waving until they went around, out of sight. It took a little while to load all the carriage seats with people. When they came around, they couldn't see Maria.

"Dad, I didn't see mom!" Raphe said. He had a bad feeling in his stomach.

Antonio said that she probably had to use the bathroom.

When they got to the very top again, Antonio started to scream. "Get us down! Get us down!" He saw four men, who he thought he recognized, and they were assaulting Maria. Antonio and Raphe could see from their high position, but people passing by couldn't, because they had her trapped in between some trees and bushes.

As soon as their seat on the Ferris wheel was fifteen feet or so from the ground, Antonio unlocked the safety bar, jumped off and started running toward the wooded area. Raphe jumped when it got a little lower and followed his dad. When Raphe got to where his dad was, Antonio was fighting one of the three men that were holding him back from saving Maria. A big, strong-looking man was raping her. His dad had broken one of the men's arms, and the other one's kneecap, and he was working on the third one when he heard Raphe scream "No! NO!"

Antonio looked. Maria had fought back hard, and the big man had snapped her neck. Whether by accident or not, Antonio went crazy. He pulled out a concealed combat knife he always carried, and killed the last guy who was fighting with him, almost decapitating him. The big man who was on Raphe's mom stood up. In utter rage, Antonio said, "Captain, you son of a bitch!"

Before the captain could say a word, Antonio sliced his throat. Before he died, Antonio grabbed his testicles and said, "Captain, you will no longer need these, you sick, sack of shit!" He then sliced them off and shoved them into the captain's mouth, as he gurgled his last breath.

Antonio handed the bloody knife to Raphe, and ordered, "If those two move, kill them!" Antonio checked his wife and covered her private area. He carried her out and yelled for help. He knew she was dead, but he was in shock. As far as he was concerned, the light of his life was just put out forever. When the police arrived, they questioned witnesses, and got a statement from Antonio, then let him go. They called the coroner for the two dead rapists, and an ambulance for the two who were injured. Antonio told the coroner he wouldn't allow him to put Maria in the same vehicle as the dead rapist! The coroner felt terrible for Antonio and little Raphe. He told Antonio that he would take Maria in his own personal vehicle, and treat her with the utmost honor and respect. Raphe felt numb and cold. He couldn't believe what just happened was real.

Three days later, Antonio was summoned to the military barracks, and was told the rapist that snapped his wife's neck was a SEAL team captain, which Antonio already knew. The captain's father was an ex-Navy admiral, now a senator. Antonio's commanding officer had dishonorable discharge papers waiting for him, even though there were no charges filed. His commanding officer said, "It's politics, Antonio," and it was bullshit, but he couldn't do anything to help him out. He also told Antonio that it might be a good idea to leave the country for a while because this asshole senator was trying to find a way to arrest him. The way things were in the world now. The piece of trash would most likely set him up somehow, to go to a military prison. "Antonio, what would happen to Raphe?" Antonio changed at that exact moment. His commander saw it in his eyes. "Antonio, don't do something crazy!"

Antonio snapped out of it and said, "Yes Sir, don't you worry, I'm out of here." He took Raphe and moved back to Italy. He got a job with a company called Globocorp. Antonio moved up fast in the company. He was highly intelligent and a lethal enemy. There was a place for people like him at Globocorp. Every day, Raphe was taught to be a killer. Raphe was instructed by some of the best martial arts professionals in the world. Antonio became a man possessed with revenge on the whole United States of America. He didn't spend a lot of time with Raphe anymore. When he did, Antonio would always tell him, "It is you and me, Raphe, against the world." Raphe missed the days when his dad was his buddy, and he really missed his mom's hugs and her happy, contagious smile. Raphe still had his dad, though, and he wanted to be with him, and make him proud.

This guy, General John White, his dad told him, was actually a friend of the family that forced us from America. Antonio told Raphe, "The reason we had to leave was because we didn't allow evil men to get away with raping and killing your mom." Oh, yeah! Raphe was going to like this assignment. Maybe he could get lucky and find a way not to do any other collateral damage; kill people that happened to be in the wrong place at the wrong time.

Raphe had studied General John White. He wasn't a typical military person. He was a General, made one by the new American president, but he was also an agent in the N.S.A. He liked to be called John by his friends. John never used all the power that the president gave him the entire time. He only used it when he was on a mission and it was necessary. John had trained to be a professional boxer but injured his back in a freak accident. So, he joined the SEAL teams after his back got better. His trainers called him for two years and begged him to come back.

John had moved on and found something more worthwhile, protecting his nation from enemies. He became a black belt in three different martial arts, but would always say none of them could punch worth a damn. The military tested everyone and found out John was an actual genius. He got a ticket to West Point. He broke records there, and was taught tactical maneuvers and battle strategies. John's skillset made him move up the ranks very quickly. He was given the most important missions and would not rely on anyone but himself to lead the SEAL team. This guy was one hell of a challenge.

Raphe asked his dad, "What did General White have to do with us fleeing the country, because you tried to save mom from the murderous rapists that killed her?"

"Raphe, you're going to have to trust me," Antonio told him. "Not every piece of top-secret information is available to you. Mr. Grey has made me take an oath of honor, and there are some things I can't even tell you, son, no matter how much I would like to." Raphe still trusted his father and understood an oath of honor. It's too bad he couldn't know the connection, because after reading the research on General White, he kind of admired him. His dad wouldn't lie to him, so General John White was a walking dead man.

Raphe and the team made their plans for insertion and pickup after the mission was accomplished. The technology that was available to Raphe was as good, or even sometimes far better, than the Americans had. A high-tech, electric-powered motorcycle would bring him about two hundred yards from the top-secret bunker that his targets were in. The motorcycle was designed to be invisible and could not be detected by radar. Raphe thought, kind of like the alien in that "Predator" movie.

He was also issued a suit of similar design. He made sure it worked before he used it on his mission. Raphe put it on and turned it on stealth. He became invisible, and then he practiced walking around the guards at the hanger. The trick was to not move abruptly. This technology relied on holographic images being projected onto the suit of the space that was there, as the person wearing the suit occupied it. This technology required a high tech next-generation super-fast computer. Even with all that technology, it still required practice. It was necessary to practice moving fluidly and with no abrupt movements, or else the result would be a wavy picture.

Raphe had done his homework on the suit. He was trained to become an expert with anything that your life depended upon. Raphe even sat at a table with three of the guards while they ate their lunch, and they never knew he was there. He was very impressed with the suit. He made sure the motorcycle and the suit were at full charge before he left for his mission targets.

Raphe was able to formulate a precise plan because they had actually bought blueprint plans of the bunker from some money-grubbing CIA, traitor to his own word, I can't even use her to fake it. Besides, it wouldn't work anyway. General White would probably kill her in front of me to show me how killing people is not a problem for him. He questioned her. "Jane, how do you know I'll keep my word? Most people don't these days."

"I know you are an honorable man Raphe, and I believe keeping your word is very important to you."

"All right," Raphe said. "I give you my word of honor, beautiful Jane."

"Okay," Jane said, blushing.

He thought, I'll let her loosen me up, but I'd better not eat or drink anything. It's probably got some kind of sodium pentothal or some other more potent chemical in it.

Jane pulled out a pin on his chair that allowed him to be able to have just enough movement in his arms to feed himself. He couldn't go anywhere. His chair was made of thick steel and was bolted to the floor. Jane went into a small refrigerator and asked Raphe if he liked salami or roast beef.

"Roast beef would be nice." He was actually starving, and he loved salami, so he asked for roast beef since it would be easier to resist.

Jane brought over the roast beef and a big bottle of water. "Raphe, there is nothing wrong with it. I would never be part of lying to you." He just stared at the sandwich. Jane grabbed the sandwich and took a bite out of each corner. Then she opened the water bottle and took a good, long drink. "Raphe, would you like me to sit here for a while to see if I start telling you my innermost secrets?"

"I would like you to sit here forever."

Jane stared into his eyes. "I feel the same way Raphe, but I have to leave now, so I can tell the others that you're really a good guy."

"But Jane, I came here to kill everyone," Raphe confessed.

"I know Raphe. The apostle Paul killed Christians, until God showed him the truth. Raphe, please eat. You have been out cold for thirty-two hours. You must be starving. I give you my word that the food and water is not anything but food and water. Do it for me." Raphe agreed. He tore into the sandwich and drank the water. Jane went to the refrigerator before she left and gave him a salami sandwich and another bottle of water. "I'll be back in a little while." She left and closed the door.

Jane went to the main living area in the underground cavern. John had found the cave as a kid hiking around the woods. He never told anyone about this place. When he went on vacation or had time off, he would work on it. John never knew why he had built this place and never told anyone about it. When he was young, he called it his bat cave. Actually, he still did. The cavern had excellent spring water running into a deep pool that never went dry. The stream was strong enough to run a water-paddled, electric power generator, which created enough power to light up the place and have hot water sinks and showers. John also had an escape tunnel that led four miles away underground, where it stopped in a munitions room stocked with all the latest weapons. He had even installed a ten-foot in diameter steel reinforced concrete pipe for over four miles. The pipe was an escape tunnel for a bullet train that could get John and twelve other people to the munitions room in a little less than four minutes.

There were two other tunnels; one led north and was an existing tunnel that he had reinforced. It was big enough for two people to walk side-by-side with a seven-foot high ceiling at its lowest point. The third tunnel faced east and was a main loading tunnel and entrance. It ran about a quarter of a mile. It was twelve feet high and twenty feet wide in a straight line. The doors were made of titanium coated steel and camouflaged to blend in perfectly from the outside. The bigger doors were only opened for loading and unloading supplies. There was a regular-sized door for people to enter and exit. It was cut right into one of the larger doors. This was the first time John felt it necessary to be totally off the grid for a while.

Jane had volunteered to watch Raphe, and she was ordered to stay far enough away that nothing could happen to her. She was supposed to come and get the General directly, as soon as the prisoner-Raphe showed any signs of consciousness. John heard a knock on his office door. He was going over plans with Ivory, about lining up a secure way to get her research team here unnoticed.

"Come in," John beckoned. The door opened and Jane came in.

"General," Jane hesitated, "I mean, John, he's awake, but before we go in, we need to have a meeting."

"Jane, there is no 'we' are going in! I'm going in alone to question him," John spoke sternly.

Jane knew what he was thinking. Raphe is probably going to have to be executed, after reading the top-secret file on him. John really didn't think there was a choice. Jane was adamant, "General I will not allow you to kill this man! I thought we agreed to pray about our decisions and that we are a team."

John was surprised by Jane's tone and replied, "There is a chain of command, and I'm at the top. You are right about one thing, Jane. We need to have a meeting, to go over how our team is going to operate, and organize it!" John, using his command voice, ordered Jane to get everyone ready in the briefing room, then dismissed her.

Ivory gave him an angry look, "John, you didn't have to use that voice with her."

"She was reading my thoughts as they came up," he said loudly.

"What? So you really are going to go in there, question this guy and then what? When you have tortured enough information out of him, you're going to blow his brains out?" She was looking at him like he was some kind of monster.

John was tired and he looked exasperated. "Ivory, I'm forty-one years old. I've been in the Armed Forces over twenty years. You were a captain in the Air Force. I've been in covert ops, mostly after West Point. Our new God Squad makes me nervous. I have trained and improved procedures all my adult life. I'm very good at it. I don't think an eighteen-year-old girl is qualified to give me orders." He saw Ivory ready to say something. "Please, Ivory let me finish." She did, but only because she saw he had a desperate look on his face. "Beautiful lady, don't get me wrong. I know this is meant to be. God's will is at work in bringing

Bobby spoke up. "General, I believe you are right, as much as I hate to say it."

Jane said, "I read his mind, John. He really believes he's doing good."

"Jane, honey, so did some of the worst killers in history. Look, guys, I'm not used to this. I'm trained to react a certain way to ensure the safety of my people. Show me a way out and I'll take it." John looked at Helen. "Helen, we need your opinion, please."

"You don't need my opinion. Everyone hold hands. I'm going to ask our Lord for His opinion, and I want you all to ask Him silently while I ask out loud please. Father, what should we do about this young man? He has come here to murder us all, and we forgive him." Helen remained still for a short time. "Thank you, Jesus," she said warmly with a smile.

"Whatever you say, Helen." John assured her, "I felt God's presence strongly again."

Jane said, "Well mom, what do we do?"

"We invite him to dinner," Helen declared. "The poor boy must be starving."

"Yes!" Jane squealed. Ivory and Mary were grinning because of the looks on both John's and Bobby's faces.

"Uh," John stammered. "Helen, can you repeat that? You want me to cut him loose and invite him to dinner?"

"No," Helen said, "Secure him as comfortably as you can. Tell him it's for our protection. Let him have enough room to stand and move around. John, the Lord has chosen this young man. He was molded in the fire his whole life for this moment. Raphe Corvino has been chosen, by Jesus Christ; our King of Kings, General. I believe he out-ranks you." Helen started laughing at the joke she just made.

Bobby looked at John curiously. "What's it going to be, General?"

"This is surreal," John lamented. "It's absolutely the last thing I would advise, but these are uncharted waters for me. Bobby, give me a hand to set up a chair for our dinner guest." John said sarcastically, "Ladies, maybe you could cook up some pasta and sauce with meatballs, and sausage for Raphe. He did just fly in from Italy!" And then he said, "Thank you Helen, you have saved me some pain."

"I haven't done a thing sweetheart. Your faith has saved you from pain."

Bobby and John got up and headed for their prisoner.

"Bobby, make sure you call me General when we're in front of him," John ordered. "He needs to know the magnitude of the situation."

"Yes Sir. I should tell you this guy works for the same people that paid one of our senators for information on the mission that got my men killed. He may have even run the operation."

"Bobby, listen to me. I need complete honesty from you. Are you going to be able to handle this? Because if not, I need to know now."

"Yes Sir. I will follow all your orders, but if I find out he was there or had anything to do with it, I don't know if I can forgive him and work with him, which seems like what's going to happen. Sir, you must have lost men. You know how it is."

"Yes, unfortunately I do Bobby. Here is how we play it for now. Do you trust me?"

"One hundred percent, Sir."

"Good. Let me do all the talking, and don't mention any missions or ask him any questions. Bobby, I promise we will find out if he was involved. Then you can decide what you're going to do, but remember this: You were chosen too."

"Sir you're starting to sound like Helen." They both chuckled.

Chapter Eleven: Cat and Mouse

Lucifer Santino, also known as Mr. Grey, or "His Lordship," as he liked to be called, found out that one of his four most trusted executive secretaries was selling secrets to his competition. Mr. Grey came up with a perfect plan to teach the other executive secretaries to be loyal, and test out their new Nano cell, biotech inventions on the guilty party.

His Lordship was excited to have a little fun. He ordered Doctor Spears to set it up. Lord Grey had a cute and friendly domesticated cat named 'Rosy', implanted with Nano cells. Then, he had Doctor Spears secretly expose the guilty executive secretary to enhanced pheromones. He had security bring all four of the ladies into the security office. They were told to wait there and that he would be in shortly.

The cat was left in the room with the ladies. It was purring and rubbing against the ladies' legs for attention. The cat particularly liked Sara Smiers, who happened to be the guilty party. Mr. Grey and Doctor Spears were watching from a monitor in a small laboratory a couple of rooms down the hall. The friendly kitty let Sarah pick it up and was purring, and massaging

Sara's lap. Sara had a cat at home, and she just loved the attention the cat was giving her.

He looked at Doctor Spears. "This had better work Doctor. I will not be made to look foolish without punishing those responsible for making me look that way!"

"My Lord, I am certain it will work," he grinned, sheepishly. "Thank you Lord Grey for allowing me to observe, it is an honor to work with you my Lord. This is very exciting."

The ladies were wondering what this was all about. They were talking among themselves and looked nervous, Sara was looking especially stressed. She tried to take her mind off her guilty conscience by softly stroking the pretty black and white bow-tie cat.

"Doctor, when I say find and punish the guilty party, 'Rosie!' turn the signal on full rage."

"Yes, my Lord," Doctor Spears cackled.

Mr. Grey bellowed with laughter. "Doctor Spears, I respect that you love your work, but don't let your lust for it make you over-enthusiastic. I have big plans for you if you can follow my orders to a T. If you cannot, then you will be of no use to me. Doctor, look at me!" Doctor Spears looked up sheepishly. Mr. Grey said, "Do you understand me?"

Doctor Spears said "Yes, my Lord."

"Let us begin, Doctor."

Lord Grey finally walked into the security room where the four executive secretaries had been nervously waiting for him. "Hello, ladies," he said suavely. "I am very sorry to have kept you waiting." He stared at each one of them in turn, separately, with an intensely critical demeanor. He could feel their fear; even the three innocent ladies were scared. Mr. Grey was six-feet, three-inches tall and had dark brown, almost black, piercing eyes. When he wanted to, he could scare most anyone with a look, and he knew it. "Ladies, it has come to my attention that one of you has been stealing from me." The ladies were frightened and started looking at one another. Mr. Grey walked over to Sara Smiers and took Rosie from her lap.

Sara said, "Excuse me, Mr. Grey, your cat has just torn a thread from my pant-suit, it's ruined."

"Miss Smiers, I am sorry, it will be replaced I assure you. Ladies, you will refer to me as Lord Grey from now on unless we are in public or relating with news media. Then it is Mr. Grey."

Sara had enough of this and stood up. She started to speak, but Lord Grey shouted, "Silence! I have brought you here to give the guilty party one last chance to confess her crime and to beg me for forgiveness. I will graciously forgive whoever is guilty, and allow them to keep their job, only if they confess within the next three minutes."

"Excuse me Lord Grey," said Francine, one of the innocent women. "But what happens to the three of us that are innocent if the guilty party doesn't confess?"

"Not to worry Francine, do you see this cat?" She nodded. "This animal is an amazing piece of new technology we have developed at Globocorp. This seemingly domestic cat already knows who is guilty and will attack, and kill the guilty party upon my command." Francine laughed nervously. Lord Grey also laughed. The other three ladies looked confused. They thought Lord Grey was making a joke, but it wasn't funny. At least Francine has a sense of humor, he mused...she's also not bad-looking. He looked at his watch and said in a loud clear voice, "Two minutes left, ladies!"

"I quit!" Sara screamed. She tried to open one of the two doors, but couldn't. She frantically tried the other door and that wouldn't open either.

"The lady doth protest too much, methinks," Mr. Grey said smugly, quoting Hamlet. "You have exactly thirty-nine seconds to confess and beg my forgiveness."

"Screw you, Grey! Let me out of here. I'm tired of your stupid game!"

He counted down, "three...two...one." Lord Grey placed Rosie on the desk. "Time's up! Find and punish the guilty party, Rosie!" Sara screamed as Rosie leapt onto her face and gouged out her eyes with her back feet as she clung to Sara's scalp. The other three ladies were screaming hysterically. Lord Grey assured them they would be fine as long as they remained loyal to him. Rosie was a blur of claws and teeth and proceeded to tear Sara to pieces. No matter how hard Sara fought, she had no chance. Rosie was so fast and strong, and went for all the vital kill spots. In a matter of four minutes Sara had bled out and was dead. Rosie kept going as if she would never stop. Finally, after ten minutes, Rosie stopped. Her brain was swollen, and her eyes had almost popped out of her head. Rosie was sunken halfway into Sara's abdomen when she expired. The other three women in the room were sobbing and holding on to each other, terrified. Francine let go of the other two women and started to vomit. They were all splattered with mucus membranes, blood, guts, and even small pieces of skin.

This is unexpected; it's better than sex! If I'm not careful, I won't be able to stop. Lord Grey felt like he was losing control, I must control myself! I have important plans and my world needs its leader. Lord Grey was having an internal struggle. He didn't want to let Doctor Spears see him out of control; or let him see how much he relished the murderous, gory act. He must exhibit a persona of control. He had to control his overwhelming desire to mutilate and kill the remaining ladies. After watching the murderous carnage caused by the killer cat that was under his control, he became enraged and homicidal. Lord Grey had to use every ounce of his willpower to contain his compulsion. It was a struggle, but he was able to control himself. The other three women in the room were sobbing and moaning. Mr. Grey composed himself and ordered them to be silent. They slowly whimpered and calmed down.

"Take note of this lesson, ladies, and tell no one. I will know if you do, and something far worse will be waiting for you. Look on the bright side! You were not Sara," he chuckled. "You will all receive a bonus and a raise for your loyalty to Globocorp. Ladies, you have my permission to go and get cleaned up. If you need it, you may see the company psychiatrist, free of charge," he chuckled again. The door opened, and the women scrambled for the exit, literally covered in blood and guts. They were led to a locker room where they could shower and scrub themselves clean. There was a change of clothes for each of them. They were told it was another gift from Lord Grey for their continued loyalty.

Lord Grey walked into the room where he had left Doctor Spears. "Doctor, you see, you *can* control yourself long enough to follow orders."

"Thank you my Lord, and may I say you were magnificent!"

"Yes, I was, and it was exhilarating. I can see why you enjoy your work so much Doctor. It can become addicting. Always remember: My orders first, our pleasures second. You and I will be doing this again soon. I want you to hold off on any major population control until I order it, or until Antonio relays my orders."

Doctor Spears grinned ear to ear. "It would be an honor to work directly with you Lord."

"Doctor it is vitally important that we gain the trust of Doctor Jennings, at least until we are able to apply this technology to human beings. Can you imagine the fun we could have with that?" Lord Grey burst out with a maniacal laugh.

Doctor Spears was so excited; he was having a hard time stopping his laughter. "Doctor, I haven't had a good laugh in a long time; it feels good," said Lord Grey. He patted Doctor Spears on the back with his blood stained hand. "Great work! Keep it up Doctor, and you will go far in Globocorp."

"Thank you my Lord," Doctor Spears said joyfully.

"Remain in Rome and prepare your team. Stay away from the compound. I don't want you to accidentally bump into Doctor Jennings," Lord Grey ordered.

Chapter Twelve: Dinner is Served

John and Bobby secured the chair to the floor in the dining room. They went to get Raphe for dinner; earlier they had locked him in a cell. They tranquilized him and put him in a straitjacket. He was then transported to the dining room on an appliance hand truck (usually used for refrigerators). John removed the straight jacket and they placed him in the steel chair bolted to the floor. His ankles were chained to steel shackles that had two feet of slack. His wrists were chained with shackles that had four feet of slack but were made out of strong, but lightweight straps. Raphe would be able to eat and have enough mobility to move around without being able to kill anyone. John gave Raphe an injection to wake him up, as Jane and Mary were bringing out dinner: spaghetti with meatballs and sausage.

John smirked. "Very funny ladies." They all chuckled. Helen walked in the room and Raphe thought she must be Jane's mom or sister because they had a close resemblance. If she wasn't Jane's mom, she was definitely a close relation.

Helen introduced herself to Raphe as Jane's mom. Raphe thought, amazing, she must have had her at a young age, because she was stunningly beautiful still, like Jane. Mary came in with a pitcher of iced tea.

"Raphe, this is Mary," Helen announced.

Raphe thought, what is going on another gorgeous lady? He smiled, "Pleasure to meet you."

Mary smiled warmly. "Likewise, Raphe." Her smile was bright and beautiful. She was almost as beautiful as Jane, Raphe thought. He had feelings for Jane the first second his eyes met hers. Raphe thought Jane was the most beautiful woman in the world, present company included.

Ivory walked in with a bowl of salad. He knew her from his research on his mission. Raphe was amazed at how beautiful she was in person. Helen introduced them.

Raphe said, "Pleased to meet you Ivory."

"It's a pleasure to meet you, Raphe."

Raphe was almost beside himself. How is it possible that all these women are so incredibly beautiful? He wondered. Then Jane came in with a couple bottles of wine, and he stared at her in awe. She stared back.

Helen noticed and smiled. "Raphe, this is my baby girl, Jane. I think you two have met already."

Jane put down the bottles of wine and said, "Hello again, Raphe."

"Hello Jane," he muttered, almost as if in a trance. They both continued staring into each other's eyes.

Mary said, "Hello, General," as John walked in. Raphe snapped out of it and gave John a dirty look. Then Bobby came in.

Helen said, "Raphe I think you have already met the General and Bobby?"

"Yes Helen, I have." He noticed that Bobby and Mary couldn't keep their eyes off each other. He also noticed that Ivory and General White seemed to be smitten with each other as well. Raphe thought, what a strange situation … it seems like some sort of a fantasyland. Jane laughed at his thoughts. He looked at her thinking, I wonder if she understood my facial expressions. Once Raphe looked at her, he never wanted to stop. Somehow he felt she didn't want him to stop either.

Helen sat down and asked if everyone would take a seat. John sat on Raphe's right and Bobby sat on his left, both out of reach of his restraints. Helen sat directly across the table from Raphe. Mary sat next to Bobby and Ivory sat next to John. Jane sat to the right of her mom, still staring at Raphe.

"Would you mind if I ask a question?" Raphe asked politely while he was looking at Helen. John had previously agreed to let Helen run the dinner meeting.

"Of course not Raphe. Ask away."

"Well, all you people know I was sent here to kill everyone and then blow up the place using twice as many explosives than was necessary, right?"

John said, "I knew about the killing, but the explosives – why use twice as much as necessary?"

"That part baffled me too. It was the first time I've ever received orders for an over-kill, if you'll pardon the pun. I failed my mission and was captured, but instead of a military interrogation, you're feeding me, and being hospitable. If this was the other way around, I would have not been this gracious. The way I see it; it would really be smart to execute me."

"I told you so Helen," John said, with a chuckle.

"Excuse me for a minute General. Instead of an interrogation then an execution, you throw me a dinner party with four of the most beautiful women I have ever seen, one of which I think I'm in love with," Raphe admitted.

"I love you too Raphe," Jane said.

"Shit," John said aloud, palming his face.

"General! I will have no cussing at this table," Helen retorted.

"Sorry ladies," he apologized.

Raphe looked around confused. "Am I drugged? Or am I in a nut house? None of this makes any sense!" Everyone laughed at him. "I don't get what's going on here! Is this some new kind of mind-control warfare?"

Helen chortled, "Yes, and watch out for Jane! She'll snip off your testicles and laugh while she does it."

"Mom!" Jane cried.

"Sorry," Helen laughed, "Sometimes I joke around before I think about what I'm saying." Everyone was still laughing, and even Raphe joined in. When the laughter died down Helen said, "I would like to say grace and eat this wonderful dinner before it gets cold. Please, let's all hold hands."

"Mom can I switch seats with Bobby?" Jane pleaded softly; Helen saw a tear in her eye as Jane whispered in her ear.

"The last time Raphe heard grace was when his mom said it the day she died."

"General, I think it would be fine."

"Helen," John sounded alarmed, "This is really getting a little crazy. Raphe could possibly kill her before I could stop him. I'll get my side arm just for a precaution."

"I don't think a gun at the table, especially pointed at someone, is a nice thing while we are saying grace."

"Okay Helen. I hope you know what you're doing," John scowled.

"Raphe, would you give me your word that you won't try to hurt my daughter if she holds your hand during grace?"

Still in disbelief, Raphe exclaimed, "Yes, I give you my word, Helen. I would never hurt her, and I would gladly sacrifice my life for hers if I had to." Helen and Jane shared a look. Helen smiled at Jane with a mother's love in her eyes. He was amazed at the love he could actually feel in Helen's eyes for her daughter.

Jane looked at Raphe. "My mom is so happy for me that I've found the love of my life."

Raphe choked up. "My mom was like that. This is the strangest thing that has ever happened to me. Jane, I can't imagine living my life without you in it. I didn't believe that things like this were possible."

"Hold hands," Helen reminded everyone. Even John and Raphe joined hands, albeit a little forced and harder than necessary. Helen started grace. "Father, thank You for all our blessings, and we are grateful to You for sending Raphe to us. This man has been through the fire and still holds onto his goodness and virtue. Lord, please show him the truth and remove the veil of lies that are blinding him. Father, send him the truth and the life. Please Father; send the Holy Spirit and our King Himself. I feel it's time for this man to make his choice to accept the gift of grace from Jesus. Your will be done Father, in Jesus' name we pray." Everyone felt the Lord's love and peace.

Raphe felt tears running down his face. He fell on his knees and cried, "I am sorry Jesus! Please forgive me." He wept with overwhelming peace and joy. He felt a love unimaginable in his heart. It seemed to him that his sins were worse than the sins committed against him, and it was easy to forgive everything that happened to him in his past, even what happened to his mom. He felt Jane's love and even John's. It seemed the entire room was filled with immeasurable love. He returned to standing, and Jane jumped into his arms.

"Thank You, Lord! Thank You, Lord!" Jane cried. "Oh Raphe! I have been praying for this moment since I first saw you. The Lord has answered my prayers. I am so proud of you Raphe."

"Jane I didn't do anything, except receive the greatest gift that I have ever received. I also love you so much - it is amazing." Raphe felt John unlock his chains. Raphe actually hugged him. Surprisingly to everyone, John hugged him back. "What's the deal?" Raphe asked.

John said, "Right now let's all sit down and eat something before it gets cold. And from here on out, just call me John." They all sat down and started eating.

Between bites Raphe asked, "What's to become of me John?"

"You're free to go or stay; whatever you want to do. Does everyone agree?" A unanimous YES came from everybody, even Bobby, who winked at John. Bobby didn't even care anymore if Raphe was involved in the mission that got his men killed. God's presence was so strong;

there was no doubt that Raphe was a good guy. "Raphe, after dinner, I'll show you what I have on Globocorp. Then you can join the team or not."

"Deal General. I mean, John. Uh, am I right in assuming that you know that your location was compromised, and we are now somewhere different?"

"Yes, you are Raphe. Thanks for caring."

Raphe glanced at Jane. "You know Sir, Globocorp has over half the politicians and the federal police agencies under their control.

"I know Raphe." John grinned.

"What I'm trying to say John, is that there isn't a base or a top-secret facility that they wouldn't find us at, and quickly!"

"Unreal," John said. "This blows my mind; you're trying to protect us?" He started laughing. Raphe wrinkled his eyebrows.

"I am sorry Raphe, but all this stuff that's going on is mind-boggling to me, also. Don't worry. We are off the grid and at a place that I made on my own. Only, I personally know the location. The government or anybody else has never known the location of this place. I found it when I was a kid and made it my bat cave. I have kept it a secret from almost every person I've ever known. The only other person that knows of its existence is my lifelong friend and loyal Captain, Joe Mills, but even Joe doesn't know the location. I made him wear a blindfold when we were entering the state. I needed it for the reasons we are using it now. I also put the deed to the land in someone else's name."

"Fantastic, that is amazing, and fortunate for us," Raphe said.

John said, "It never made sense until now. I know the Lord did it, through me. For over twenty years, whenever I had time, I would work on it and make sure it was secret. We are totally off the grid Son, except if we go outside and are spotted by a satellite. That's very unlikely, but we still won't take that chance, yet."

"That is a relief John," Raphe said.

After dinner, John asked Ivory if she could come to his office. He then told everyone he would like to have a meeting to formulate a plan to get Ivory's team of scientists here. John told them they needed a plan to get them here without the enemy noticing. John and Ivory walked into his office. He let her enter first and closed the door. He spun her around and said, "Now, where were we; before we were so rudely interrupted?" He kissed her, hugging her tightly and weaving their bodies together.

Ivory pulled away. "John, we have to stop. She had to catch her breath, she was feeling flush and her chest was heaving, she had never felt so passionate and wanton in her entire life. "John the world needs saving, and we have a limited amount of time to get a plan together, just to even begin to solve it." Ivory's voice was quiet, sultry and charged with sexual energy as she spoke... "John?" He pulled her back into an embrace and kissed her passionately for several minutes. Ivory said, 'The plan, John'...falling back into him. John caressed her upper arms and pushed her back. "This is unreal. I live a totally disciplined life. I can't act like a teenager in heat.'"

"Ivory maybe that's another gift you have, being an irresistible super vixen."

"John if I have it; you do too."

"Ivory," John said, "You're right. We have to put it on hold, or we will never be ready for the meeting. Please try and control yourself, woman."

"You started it," Ivory grunted.

"Ivory you know, you're the one who wouldn't stop." John quipped.

"John, you are the biggest jackass I know."

John started laughing. "Let's get to work. I'm sorry, ivory. If I didn't change the mood, I wouldn't have been able to stop."

She giggled. "To tell you the truth, me neither. All right John, this is what I need brought here if I'm going to have any chance at all of solving this Nano cell nightmare. I am going to need transport and communications. I'm going to need my super-computer. I'm going to need a vapor-proof-static-free laboratory setup somewhere in your bat cave. *Bat cave*. I should have known when we met that you were Batman," she laughed.

"I'm not Batman Ivory, he's an old man now."

Ivory stopped. "Are you telling me there really is a Batman?"

"No," John snickered, "That's just what I call the guy I bought the property from."

"That's adorable, but duty first." Ivory handed him a list.

"Is this pretty much all you need?"

Ivory thought for a moment, "So far, but we may need all kinds of other equipment when or if, we figure it out; but all of that will help us get started."

"Thank God we're still on schedule," said John. "Time to go meet the team."

When Ivory and John walked into the meeting room. There was fresh coffee and dessert. John looked at Bobby quizzically. Bobby shrugged, and then nodded toward Helen. "Helen this is very nice, but you don't have to bake whenever we have a meeting."

"I know John, but I was just so happy about dinner. I promise I won't do anything that takes up or wastes any time. I know time is our enemy. I thought, why not make some cookies to go with the coffee? You never know, we may not have much of a chance to sit down and relax, very soon," she said cheerily.

John looked at her in admiration. "Helen, you're right. We'll talk and have dessert, and coffee. After that, we gotta rock and roll!"

Ivory grabbed a cookie and took a bite. "My goodness, these are fantastic!"

Helen lit up. "Thanks! I love to bake!"

John tried one. "This is the best cookie I've ever had. Helen you could make a fortune selling these!"

"Thank you John, but I have much more than I'll ever need."

John looked at Helen as she was smiling and noticed what a beautiful woman she was. "You know Helen, I know you are not married. You are still young and beautiful. What's your story? If you don't want to tell me, it's fine."

"Thanks for the compliment John. I realize I haven't told you much about myself. Well… after I lost my husband, my one true love, I knew in my heart that nobody could match him in any way. You should have seen how happy we were. If he walked anywhere near where I was, even if I couldn't see or hear him, my body and soul would feel his presence. He also could feel my presence, the same way. We were one and whole, together. He was my life and my love, as I was to him. With him I was at my best. I thanked God every day for him, and I still do. I know God's plans aren't our plans. When he died... I knew God had made us perfect partners, and ten years with that man would be worth a million with any other man. After he died, I had a hole in my heart that I could not get rid of. Jane, our little blessing from God was just a toddler; and I knew I had to be strong for her. I prayed and prayed for God to heal my heart, and so our Father gave me a gift; I can feel the Lord's presence, always, and if God's presence is closer than usual, I feel it; just like I could feel my husband's presence when he was near. The Father healed my broken heart and filled it with the Holy Spirit, always, and Jesus our first and forever love. My husband's name was John, by the way." She smiled at John and he smiled back. "He is with God and they both are waiting patiently for me, because I still have a job to do here before I go home. Is that okay for now John? You know, I could go on for hours and I wouldn't mind. I love talking about myself," she giggled.

"Helen, you are one of the most amazing people I have ever met. You are our biggest blessing."

"Wrong again John. God is our biggest blessing. I am just His child, as we all are. I know it's hard on you sometimes, but you always listen and follow God's path, even when it disagrees with your training. I know that's tough, but your faith is stronger than your training. Use them both, but if you feel the Lord telling you to look right instead of left, listen! That last thing I just said wasn't even from me because I don't know what it means. Remember it, because the Lord just sent you a message. Someday it will be a very important choice in your life." Helen looked around the room. Everyone was looking at her in adoration. Sometimes Helen didn't realize how profound she could be. "What?" she asked.

"Mom, that's such a beautiful story, and the way you said it, it was like we could feel it. Am I right, guys?" Everyone agreed.

John felt like Helen could use some help. "Helen remind me not to ask you any personal questions unless we have a lot of time, like a whole day. Quite a story though." John winked at Helen. "People, snap out of it! Like Helen said, we have a lot to do; and very little time to do it."

"Thank you John. Now, I am going to say a prayer and go to bed. Lord help my new family to make the best plans, and may they all follow your will in Jesus' name. Amen. Good night team and don't stay up too late." Helen giggled. Jane and Mary stood up, and hugged her goodnight.

Chapter Thirteen: The Plans of Men

John passed out papers to everyone. He said, "Here is the layout of this entire compound, as well as every way in and out. I've formulated an insurgency plan for Ivory's tech team. It's pretty basic and shouldn't be a problem." Everyone studied it. When they were done John said, "On a different topic, I would like to start planning a raid on Mr. Grey's compound. We have little or no intelligence on the compound or the outer buildings."

Raphe chimed in. "I can help you with quite a bit of that."

"I was hoping you would say that, son."

"Grey's place is an extremely high-tech fortress. The well-armed guards all have similar stealth suits that I had on when you caught me. There are alarms that if triggered, will bring in two hundred armed men," Raphe explained.

John announced. "Tomorrow, I'm going to talk to the president and fill him in. I'm not even sure that we will implement a plan to raid Mr. Grey's compound. I just have a feeling that it would be a good idea to have a plan, in case we have to."

Ivory asked, "Excuse me, John, but why didn't you show me this in the office earlier?"

"If you remember," John said, "We were pressed for time. I needed a list from you and didn't know how long it would take."

Ivory smiled, a little embarrassed. "Yes, right. Sorry John." She pinched his bottom.

He jumped a little and hoped nobody saw. "It's okay Ivory," he mumbled, a little irritated.

Ivory said, "I'm going to start a detailed print and an engineering design, on the best way to install that vapor-proof lab in here. I saw a great spot. I'm going on the other side of your bat cave."

Mary perked up. "Can I come? I went to school for design. Maybe I can help!"

"Sure," Ivory said. "Come on."

Jane asked, "Could you guys use some help measuring and moving stuff around?"

Mary was excited. "Come with us Jane! We'll leave these tough guys to figure our new guests' travel arrangements."

"Yes," said Ivory. "We would only be a distraction. The three of us would be too much for these bad ass men to handle, they wouldn't get anything done."

John was getting slightly annoyed. "Are you done, Ivory?"

She could sense his irritation. "Not quite!" Ivory walked toward John staring in his eyes, she caressed his face softly and sensuously kissed him. While she was kissing him she put both her hands on his chest and pushed away, like something was holding them together. Ivory looked at John with puppy dog eyes, and whispered, "Sorry, I can't help it." She straightened up and said; "Now I'm done," as she sauntered away with Jane and Mary.

When the ladies left, Bobby and Raphe started laughing about the look on John's face. He seemed confused and embarrassed. Bobby had not seen him like this before and said, "General, Raphe and I have talked about just what you're going through."

Raphe agreed. "I know I just arrived here, but Jane is the only thing I can think about! How do you guys get anything done?"

Bobby said, "We're going through the same thing. It's like we can't control ourselves and neither can the girls."

Raphe added. "Think about this, John - four absolutely gorgeous women are accidentally inserted into a situation. The three of us fall in love, I mean, like the love Helen described. Do you guys feel that's strange also, like not a possibility... but it's happening anyway?"

"Yes! And it's messing with my brain. I'm indecisive and distracted all the time. Sometimes, I almost don't have the willpower to stop thinking about Ivory, even though the world is in big trouble. I have to do something about it."

Bobby told him, "Raphe and I have talked about it, and we have come up with a plan that could possibly work."

"Yeah? What is it?" John was interested.

"Well," Bobby said, "We meet with the girls and ask them if it's okay with them, that during our duty hours, you use your command voice to make us concentrate on what we are doing."

"That's your plan? I am supposed to walk around and make sure everyone remains non-romantic, like some kind of love guru babysitter?"

"Sorry Sir, but that's all we could think of."

"No!" said John, "Don't be sorry. This is a problem, and you guys saw it. Even though you don't want to sacrifice time away from the girls, you realize you have to. Thank you for the initiative guys but it's a bad plan. First of all, I don't even know if that would work because I have to be in command of myself. If Ivory is around, I'm not. Here is what we do. Have a meeting, all of us, and ask Helen." John couldn't believe the absurdity of their problem. He chuckled.

"John," Raphe said, shuffling in his seat. "I'm not sure Helen would approve of me. I'm really not good enough for her daughter."

"I'll put in a good word for you son."

"Thanks John."

John said in his command voice, "Now, let's get our insertion plans done." Bobby and Raphe both said, "Yes Sir," and started working on it.

John smirked, "At least my command voice still works. At that moment, they all heard someone screaming in agony.

"NO, NO!"

John smashed his hand on the wooden table. A drawer popped out. He threw two nine-millimeter handguns to the guys and grabbed the judge for himself. As they ran toward the screams, they realized it was Helen. John got there first. The door was unlocked. He motioned for Bobby and Raphe to watch his back. He opened the door and Helen was having some kind of a seizure.

He yelled out, "Clear! Someone get Jane in here."

The girls had heard the screaming and Jane knew it was her mom. She came flying through the door almost at the same time John had told them to get her.

She shouted, "Mom! Mom!" It didn't work. She got on top of her mom and hugged her, crying "Please God, wake her up!" Helen woke and saw Jane; she started sobbing and shaking. Jane had never seen her mom act like this. "Mom, are you okay?"

"Yes, but those poor children. My Jane," Helen hugged her. "We don't know how lucky we are." Everyone crowded in and asked what happened. Helen started to tell them, but stopped and said, "Jane, don't touch it," then she faded off into a deep sleep. Helen's right arm started to light up with a surreal, glowing light. The light felt like it was alive. Helen's forearm turned bright white.

"Mom?" Jane yelled. Helen didn't respond. "Her arm is burning hot!" She reached out and touched it despite her mom's warning. She pulled her hand back quickly and passed out. Raphe grabbed Jane. She was breathing and seemed to be okay, just sleeping.

They were all staring at Helen's arm, and words started to form on it. "THE GREY MAN OUT OF ROME, YOU CHILDREN SHALL BATTLE. I WILL BE WITH YOU. DO NOT BE AFRAID. YOU HAVE BEEN CHOSEN FOR THIS. THE GREY MAN SHALL NOT BE KILLED. I SHALL JUDGE HIM, SO SAYS THE LORD YOUR GOD."

Raphe's eyes opened wide and he almost forgot he was holding Jane. It took him a few minutes to get over what he had just witnessed. Raphe regained his composure and spoke in a quiet, yet serious tone. "I have met the Grey man, and have been in his castle. He is the CEO of Globocorp. My dad is the top security man, and is in contact with him almost every day, in person." Raphe was stricken with sadness and wrestled with his own thoughts. How could his hero, his whole world, do so much evil? What happened to his father that he knew deep in his heart, loved him? A realization popped in his head. I will be fighting my father. What if I have to kill him? What if he has to kill me? Would he?

John looked at Raphe and so did the rest of them. He knew what Raphe was thinking. It was the same thing he would have thought. All he could say was, "Raphe, we will do our best to try and help your dad."

"John, you don't know him like I do. He won't be captured alive. He is too smart for that. You actually remind me of him. He's that good."

John said, "I've been on over forty missions. You probably already know this, but anything can happen. One thing I know, if God is with us, nothing can stand against us. That's a fact Raphe, and we all know God is with us! When Helen's up for it, we will pray for your dad."

Raphe gave him a grateful look. "Thanks John, you're right. After what I've seen here, anything is possible."

Helen was awake and her arm was no longer glowing. "All things are possible through God, Raphe," she said weakly. Everyone was looking at Raphe and hadn't noticed she was awake. "I give you my blessing Raphe, you are good enough for my Jane. What God has put together, let no man or woman tear apart!" Helen giggled. "I'm so happy that she will know my happiness with her father."

Raphe and John looked at each other in wonder. "Thank you Helen," Raphe said, relieved. "I really don't think I would have ever been be happy again, without her."

"You're welcome son. Now come down here and give mom a big hug." Raphe did, and it felt like he was hugging his own mom again. Raphe didn't want to let go.

Jane started to move. Then suddenly she jumped up and cried, "My finger is burning so badly!"

"Oh, honey," Helen, said. "Let me see." Raphe jumped up and went to comfort her. Mary and Ivory went to look at it also.

Fortunately, Ivory was not only a research doctor but also a medical doctor. She said, "Jane, let me have a look at it." She looked at John, and he knew it had to come off before gangrene set in. It was a fourth-degree burn, down to the bone. "Jane, I'm sorry to say this but your finger has to come off, or it will continue to infect your entire hand."

"No!" Jane cried in pain and sorrow. Watching this broke Mary's heart. Jane was like a sister and was the best friend she ever had.

"Jane let me see it." Mary looked at it so closely that her tears fell into the wound.

"That feels better. The pain is going away some," Jane said, relieved a bit.

"Father please, heal my sister, in Jesus' name." Jane's finger started getting lighter, and seconds later it looked healed. Jane wiggled her finger and gave Mary a hug.

Helen said, "Now we know your gift Mary. Thank you for stepping out in faith."

Mary drying her tears, said, "You're welcome Helen, and thank You Jesus for my gift."

Jane astonished, yelled out, "Mom, look!" There was a sparkling glow the size of a pinhead at the tip of her finger where she had touched Helen's arm. "What do you think it is?"

Helen said, "I think it's a lingering trace of God's glory."

"Do you think it will always be there?"

"No Jane, God's glory is not ours to keep. All the glory goes back to the Father. It might be there for a while, but I believe eventually it will fade and go back to God."

"Mom how come your arm is back to normal?"

"Because it was God's will that my arm be filled with His glory. It was not His will that anyone touch it."

Jane looked ashamed. "Sorry Mom."

"Honey, it might have been His will that you touched it, because you were healed, and our Mary discovered her gift. Who knows the mind of God? It may be that the glory in your finger will be something you need in the future. His plans are not our plans. I don't have all the answers Jane. It's like how a baby plans to stick a metal object into an electrical outlet. You stop the baby and say no. The baby gets angry because she didn't get to do what she wanted. You have ruined her plan and she doesn't understand you just saved her from pain or even death. The baby cries and throws a tantrum. She cannot possibly understand why you did that. To the baby, you're just a mean mommy. That's how we are to God; we're like that baby. There is no possible way we can make plans or want things that will always fit God's plan. Every single thing that God does is for our good and the good of all His children. Not one bad thing comes from God. Even though people think, 'Why didn't God do something about this or that?' God is like that mother with that baby. We cannot comprehend His plans, but just know 100% percent, all good comes from God. Sickness and death come from sins of the flesh, always wanting more. It's the human condition! The evil we are fighting now, I'm guessing, comes from Satan himself. Have faith that God knows what He's doing, and remember the world will hate us, but we are not of this world. Every one of us here are already in God's world. This world is just a training ground, a place to allow you to use your free will to choose if you want to be with God or not. All of us here chose Jesus; we are no longer of this world. We are with God doing His will until He takes us home. Like it says in Psalm 23, "The Lord is my shepherd; I shall not want."

"The only way to be satisfied with your life and stop constantly wanting; the only way to be at peace and live a life of love, and happiness is to ask Jesus, the Prince of Peace, into your life. That's the only thing people need. It's the only way to be truly satisfied and at peace. Let me say a quick prayer and then I will go to sleep. I feel drained. Father thank you for all these amazing blessings. Please let us get the rest we need for tomorrow, in Jesus' name, amen."

The next day at breakfast, everyone said that was the best night sleep they had since they had gotten there. During breakfast John explained to Helen the unique problem they were having. He said, "I have never in my life been out of control. When Ivory starts her lewd advances toward me, I just can't resist."

Ivory looked mad. "Really? Is that a professional way to put it?"

"Sorry Ivory, but you know nothing is ever my fault. I'm the general." Everyone laughed. Helen kept laughing hysterically. After some time, John said, "Helen?"

Helen put her finger up and kept laughing. Finally, she said, "That's one heck of a problem you guys got there." Then she laughed again while everyone stared.

"Mom, we're serious," Jane scoffed.

"Sorry," said Helen, "But I guess I needed a good whole-belly laugh. You all are certain that God has put you together like He did for my John and me? Are you willing to commit to this relationship for life and have God's blessing?"

John and Ivory looked at each other and said, "Yes."

Helen said, "Hold the hand of the one who our Father has gifted to you. Hold the hand of your blessing and your true love, your gift from our Savior. Father, you have brought these couples together. You have made them for each other since before time began. They are all true forever loves and we thank you, and acknowledge that very rare and miraculous gift. Please help them to treat each other like they would want to be treated. Keep your Holy Spirit in their hearts for each other every second of every hour of every day."

"Do you, John, take Ivory to be your wife?"

John said, "I do."

"Ivory, do you take John to be your husband?"

Ivory said, "I do."

"Bobby, do you take Mary to be your wife, and to be a good father to her child?"

Bobby said, "I do."

"Mary, do you take Bobby to be your husband?"

Mary said, "I do."

Helen smiled. "I bet your dad is smiling right now."

Mary's face glowed. "Love you, Dad," she said proudly.

"Do you, Raphe, take my Jane to be your wife?"

Raphe said, "I do."

"Do you, Jane, take Raphe to be your husband?"

Jane said, "I do."

"Wow," Helen said. "I can feel your dad's love. Father, bless these unions in Jesus' mighty name. Amen."

John asked, "Are we married now?"

"Yes!" said Helen, "and it's legal, I'm licensed. You all may kiss your brides and start your two-and-a-half-day honeymoon. There is really not much to do until the staff and equipment get here. Go consummate your marriages. You were like two perfectly matched magnets, so close but not touching. Now you are one. Problem solved. I'll be in the hot spring and I am writing a book so I could use some alone time. I'm sure you also will be busy." She laughed.

Chapter Fourteen: Antonio's Training

Antonio was pacing in his office, waiting for a call from Mr. Grey. He was worried. Raphe was missing, and he was afraid he was dead. The phone rang, and it was Vie, Mr. Grey's personal secretary. She said, "His Lordship will see you now."

Antonio hurried into Mr. Grey's office. He knew there wasn't much time to save Raphe – if he was still alive. Raphe was expected back two days prior, and had missed his evacuation contact. Antonio felt Raphe was still alive, even though reports had come in saying he was most likely killed. The report stated he was blown up in an American jet he had stolen in an attempt to evade capture.

Mr. Grey was standing solemnly. He looked at Antonio like he pitied him. Mister Grey said, "Antonio, I am also worried about Raphe." Antonio asked Lord Grey if he could send a team, with himself leading it, to locate Raphe, dead or alive. Lord Grey said, "Antonio, either the boy has passed, or he will find a way to get in contact with us. I know how you must feel, but don't believe the worst. Raphe is one of the best-trained men in the world. Going after him may even endanger his position. My best man going out there possibly making it worse is not a good idea. If we haven't heard from him in five days, I'll reconsider."

"Lord," Antonio sighed, "He's my only son, I can't lose him."

"My friend, I know how you feel but Raphe has been out of touch before. Sometimes things go this way. Give him some time. He will come through."

"Yes Lord, but I'm feeling nervous because the last six assassins we sent after General White have been killed."

"I know Antonio, but they were not Raphe Corvino. Raphe is one of the best in the world, if not the best."

"I know Lord, but I have more experience and I trained him. I believe that, possibly, the greedy two-faced American politicians that work for us compromised him. I know I can take out this General White."

"I do too, but you are far too busy running the entire security for Globocorp to go gallivanting around the globe looking for someone who is probably just hiding out until he can get back."

"I've got a bad feeling Lord, please!"

"I'm sorry Antonio, but I believe in Raphe and we must give him more time. That is my final word on it." Antonio knew he would get nowhere. Maybe Mr. Grey was right.

"Come with me Antonio," Lord Grey beckoned, "And we will have a nice dinner and then some entertainment." He thought Antonio really hasn't been himself since Raphe has gone missing. Raphe is probably dead. Last night after dinner, Antonio just wasn't into the orgy with his usual gusto. He knew he was lucky to have such a hate-filled man working for him.

The hate Antonio directed toward the Americans was so powerful you could actually feel it projecting from him. Antonio's high intelligence and loyalty made him a perfect asset for Mr. Grey's plans, not to mention his expert tactical skills. Antonio left to get dressed for dinner. Mr. Grey laughed a sinister laugh. He just thought of a way to get Antonio even more devoted to his hatred toward America.

Mr. Grey called out to Vie. "Yes, Lord," she answered seductively.

"I want you to set up a meeting with Colonel Barry Jackson and Doctor Spears, for 2:00 p.m. tomorrow afternoon. Let them know it's a top-secret, private meeting in my private office!"

"Yes Lord, will there be anything else?"

"Actually Vie, I do believe I'll need to release some tension after the meeting."

"I will set something up...or did you have anything specific in mind?"

"No, surprise me Vie." He snickered.

"Yes Lord," she purred and cackled for him.

What a great employee Vie was. She loved her work and seemed to anticipate his needs. It was turning into a great day.

The next day Mr. Grey was in his top-secret office at 1:00 p.m. He had arrived early to make sure everything was planned to perfection. He was thinking about the ingenious idea he had, to plant a seed in Antonio's mind that General John White was somehow connected to his wife's rape and murder. That somehow he was the one responsible for him being punished for trying to save his wife. Antonio had killed a senator's son, who was also a Navy SEAL Captain. This same man had raped and killed Antonio's wife, Maria. Three of his friends were waiting in line to rape Maria, when Antonio arrived to save her. They tried to stop him from helping his wife. He had wounded and beaten two of the men and killed one, trying to get to her. The SEAL Captain snapped Maria's neck before Antonio could get to her and save her. Antonio killed him also. The two injured men were set free with no charges brought up.

Lord Grey laughed, "They would have been better off in prison." He had ordered Antonio to abduct them and bring them back to his private torture chamber. Lord Grey had instructed Antonio in the fine arts of torture. Antonio took to it like a duck to water. He was not sure if Antonio would have gotten into joys of torture, if it hadn't been for those two men. He was starting to feel that Antonio was slipping away. He couldn't feel the hatred that he used to feel emanating from Antonio. Lord Grey would have to feed his hate. Antonio was an asset Lord Grey would not lose. He was the smartest, most reliable man in Globocorp, beside himself of course. Lord Grey and Antonio had become close. He had taught Antonio the fine arts and pleasures of inflicting ultimate pain on useless common humans. "Good times," he sneered lustfully. Antonio just needed a hate-filled mega-booster shot and then what fun they would have together.

Both Colonel Barry Jackson and Doctor Spears were heading down the elevator, right on time. Mr. Grey waited for them to knock and then gave them permission to enter. He greeted them both professionally. "Hello Colonel. Hello Doctor. Please take a seat. We have a lot to do in a short time."

"Yes Sir," said the colonel.

"Yes my Lord," said Doctor Spears.

Mr. Grey said, "Barry please call me Lord, Lordship, or Lord Grey, unless we are in public. Then it's Mr. Grey."

"Yes Lord. I have acquired the assets that you have requested. They are in room 224 if you want to inspect them."

He brought up room 224 on his security screen. He saw an attractive young mother with two sons. The two boys were playing together, and she was reading a book. She had been told that her husband was receiving a medal and a commendation for his part in a top-secret mission, and had asked if his family could be present. They were flown in a private jet straight to the castle. Their room was upper class. They had been implanted with tracking devices on the plane ride over and had no idea. They thought they had just fallen asleep, but were actually gassed and injected with a tracking device so small they didn't even notice.

"Nice work Colonel."

"Thank you Lord Grey."

Lord Grey said, "Colonel Jackson, I want them kept in that wing until tomorrow. My president of security and I will be going on a five-day trip to my private island to investigate some illogical math problems that one of my vice presidents is having. I want you Colonel, to have your most trustworthy man allow them access to our theme park. Tell them it will be at least five days until Daddy gets here. Tell them to enjoy their vacation. Inform them that a suite is being prepared for them and will be ready at 10:00 a.m. tomorrow morning." Lord

Grey didn't want to take a chance that Antonio might run into them, even though he probably wouldn't recognize them. They were leaving at 9:00 a.m. and would be in the air before 10:00 a.m.

"Doctor Spears, I will have the coordinates within the next forty-eight hours. Once you get those coordinates, located somewhere in the USA, how long will it take you to implement our latest Nano cell technology?"

"How large of an area, Lord?"

"No more than two square miles."

Doctor Spears thought for a few minutes and did some calculations on a note pad, then went over it again and added a day just in case he was off. He knew failure was not an option with Mr. Grey. "Four days, Lord."

"Doctor Spears you will notify Colonel Barry Jackson exactly when your mission will be done. Barry you will have the place totally destroyed. No more Nano cell evidence left on the scenes, but wait until I give the okay! Are we clear on this Dr. Spears, Colonel Jackson?"

"Yes my Lord." They replied.

"Gentlemen, this mission is one of the most important missions to me personally and to Globocorp worldwide. Failure will not be an option that you will enjoy." Mr. Grey gave them a look of pure evil! It even scared the colonel.

"We will not fail you, Lord," they said simultaneously, almost trance-like.

"Good answer, men. Success will have great rewards. You will be hearing from me soon. Dismissed."

Mr. Grey was in his office waiting for Antonio to arrive. Vie called, "The only important meeting you will be missing is your 3:00 p.m. with Doctor Jennings."

"Vie, give Doctor Jennings my apologies: Tell him I've decided to let him get used to socializing. Tell him I'll contact him in five days and set up a meeting. Let him know I have decided that he deserves some time to enjoy life's pleasures."

"Yes my Lord. You're good to go."

Lord Grey was starting to get excited about his trip. "I see Antonio coming toward me on the screen, send him right in, Vie."

"Yes my Lord." Vie replied.

Antonio walked into Mr. Grey's outer office. Before he could even speak, Vie said, "Go right in Sir. He's expecting you."

"Thanks Vie," Antonio said nervously. He opened the office door and saw Lord Grey pacing back and forth looking agitated about something. He said, "Lord, is everything all right?"

"No Antonio, it is not. Don't worry it's not about Raphe." He saw a relieved look on Antonio's face. "I am going to need you and five of your men to escort me to my private island. I have good reason to believe one of my most trusted and oldest employees is embezzling from me. He is too high up in rank I am personally going to have to address this problem. I will make quite an example out of him. My people have to learn what happens when they fuck with me! I will instill so much fear, that if anyone who works for me even thinks of betrayal, they will shit themselves from sheer terror!" Lord Grey paused for a moment to control his rage. "Excuse my outburst Antonio, but on top of trying to save the world, I am forced to waste my time with petty common filth. Antonio! I have just had an epiphany.

You've heard the saying 'when life hands you lemons, make lemonade'?"

"Yes, I have Lord."

"Well that is precisely what we are going to do. Road trip!" Lord Grey shouted and burst out laughing. "Antonio this trip may turn out to be something we both needed, a chance to relieve some stress and tension. Here is what I've got, and I know it's a very short time to plan a security detail, but it has to be done." He handed Antonio an itinerary. "I'm asking you to do this for me as a favor. When we get back, I'll return the favor my friend. When we get back and if there is still no news about Raphe, you can handle it as you see fit. I still have to see your plan and clear it. This is an emotional one for you, and I don't want to start a war, yet." He smiled at Antonio.

He respected Antonio mostly because he was fearless. Antonio wasn't even afraid of him, which was refreshing to Lord Grey. It was nice to have a loyal employee that worked for him because they genuinely liked him and didn't fear him.

Antonio looked at Lord Grey nervously. "Lord, if we're going to do this in any kind of safe way, I have to leave right now. I will be up all night making sure I set this up properly. Your safety is my responsibility. Nothing can happen to you on my watch. I would never forgive myself, and the world would lose everything. Are you sure you have to go so soon Lord? Is there no other way?"

Mr. Grey looked at him with adoration. "Unfortunately, there is no other way my friend. I am sorry that you will be up all night."

"That does not bother me Lord. What bothers me is making sure you're safe without time to check all the variables. I advise against this. Please give me one more day."

Lord Grey, admonished. "I'm sorry my friend. They will not expect us, and we will have the element of surprise on our side. Antonio don't worry so much. I have many loyal friends and worshippers in key places. You're not the only one who knows about security. It does give me great pleasure to see how much you care for me. I am truly impressed by your loyalty, and your intelligence with my plans to help the world."

"Thank you Lord. I should be running right now. I need to get these preparations going as soon as possible."

Lord Grey dismissed him, "Thank you Antonio. Go right ahead. If you have any questions, don't hesitate to call Vie. She has every detail I know in her office, and she was told you might need her. She is on call."

Chapter Fifteen: Company Calls

John was finally able to concentrate on a good plan without misdirection. Thank God he was finally able to think about something besides Ivory's outgoing personality, her unbelievable intelligence, her sexy green eyes, and her voluptuous breasts, not to mention her perfect ass. John was thinking about her now, but was also able to think about his job. Before, all he could think about was Ivory. John knew it was imperative to try and save the world. He thought - it's either the world or Ivory's ass. He chose Ivory's ass every time; he laughed, until now. Now he could concentrate on saving the world. He could be with Ivory whenever they could spare time; sometimes they would be working together. He was back with extra talent on his team! The best of both worlds... now to come up with a plan to keep them both!

John was making his fourth study of all his plans and itinerary. He was putting his mind in the place of his enemy's mind. What would he do if they did this? How would he counter this move? How would he counter multiple moves? It was like a life and death chessboard. He had already finished his research team's arrival plan and everyone's escape plan. In case the enemy discovered them, he had three tunnels to choose from: one going north, one going west, and one going east. The tunnel going west was the escape tunnel for his team. There was a bullet train inside a steel reinforced, concrete conduit that went for four miles to a safe underground bunker. There was room for twelve on the bullet train, plus a good-sized storage compartment.

The eastern tunnel was his only real choice to bring the research team in. It was a quarter of a mile long, and entered a massive underground cavern that the research team could use to set up their equipment. There were eight researchers coming. Two of them were at the top of their particular scientific fields. They would be arriving in an enclosed troop transport vehicle, designed for any terrain. Everything was camouflaged, but that didn't mean they would be completely safe. It was as good a plan as he could come up with. The transport airplane was to drop them near the eastern tunnel. Then they would drive right up to the tunnel door under a camouflaged canopy. The research team would bring in their equipment and go to work. He had coordinated this plan with Ivory. Just then, there was a knock at the door.

"Come in," John ordered.

Ivory walked in and gave him a sexy look. She came around to the back of his desk, wrapped her arms around his neck, and said seductively, "Hey stud, you busy?" Then she held his face and gave him a long, passionate kiss. She stopped and stared into his eyes. I could get lost in these forever, she thought.

"Well, Ivory, I am kind of busy right now." Her facial expression went from sensuous to visibly upset. John grabbed her, picked her up, and held her up against the wall, lifting up her skirt.

"I can't believe I fall for your tricks every time."

"No underwear, Ivory?" All she could do was moan.

Thirty minutes later, while they were getting themselves together. John's phone beeped. "E.T.A. 1 hour." John told Ivory her team was expected in one hour.

"We should head down there soon," she said in a very professional voice.

"Yes. Now would be a good time before you start to get all worked up again and make us late."

Ivory laughed. "I love you."

"I love you too."

Ivory could sense that there was something bothering him. "John, what's eating you?"

"I'm scared Ivory. For the first time since maybe ever, I'm scared, and it's a bad feeling. I can't operate efficiently if I am afraid to die."

"Haven't you always been afraid to die John?"

"No Ivory, not that I can remember. I'm so happy most of the time, I mean a happiness that I didn't know was possible."

She stroked his face "Me too, I never thought this kind of happiness existed on Earth. The love I feel for you is so strong. I feel like if you were gone, I would just shatter to pieces. John remember, if something happens and we are doing God's will, we will be rewarded a hundred, or even a thousand-fold. I can't remember the number the Bible tells us."

John said, "I think more than one of you would be more than I could handle." They both laughed. "God is with us. Who can stand against us? Let's move, my beautiful vixen."

When John and Ivory reached the dining room, everyone was there waiting for them.

Raphe asked, "General we would like your permission to help our new arrivals and make sure they are safe." Bobby walked up to John and handed him his holster with two 9mm 16-round pistols and four extra, loaded 9mm clips.

Ivory asked, "Hey! Where is mine?"

Bobby said, "Sorry Ivory, we didn't know you could shoot."

John offered, "Here honey, take one of mine."

Ivory refused, "No thanks lover. I like mine. Give me three minutes. My gun belt and weapons are in my room."

John looked at everyone and shrugged. "She's a better shot than I am. She was a captain in the Air Force and got hooked on target shooting. She never missed a day until all this madness started. She told me it calms her." He chuckled.

Mary noticed Ivory first, "Here she comes, locked and loaded!" They all got a laugh out of that. The mood was filled with excitement. They had not seen any other people or even been outside in over a week.

"People remember, it's General White in public, and you might as well start saying it now, so you get used to it again. These people are expecting a top-secret military operation, not a country picnic." John asked Raphe to open the titanium steel doors and let some sunshine in. When he did, they all heard a rattling sound and saw that there was a 4 or 5-foot timber rattlesnake coiled near the door. The snake was probably finding a cool area out of the sun, but it was now coiled and ready to strike. Raphe stood perfectly still. Before the snake could strike a shot rang out. The snake was dead. Everyone saw that Ivory had drawn her weapon and fired from twenty feet away. Jane ran to Raphe and hugged him.

Raphe said, "Great shooting Doc! Wow, I'm impressed!"

John said, "I told you guys she was good, but even I didn't know she was that good."

"Thanks," Ivory said modestly as she holstered her pistol.

"That was loud!" Mary said. "I think your new nickname should be Doc Holladay."

John looked at Ivory with amazement. She just winked at him and smiled. "Ivory, is there anything you're not an expert at?"

"You General, but I'm working on it." The group shared a laugh.

"Men grab a good stick, or one of the yard tools around here. Let's go out under the canopy and make sure there are no more surprises," John ordered. "I'm sure Wyatt Earp here can cover us " While they were almost done checking out the area for snakes, they heard the troop carrier coming.

Helen shrieked with enthusiasm. "Company is coming! Isn't it exciting?"

The transport vehicle drove in right under the canopy. The driver Corporal Tanner had enough room to maneuver, and back up in the tunnel so the equipment would be easier to unload. The passenger Sergeant Wilkes got out and saluted General White.

He handed him a sealed message. John opened it and read, (J. B.. 4. D. O)

"Thank you Sergeant, at ease. Please help the research team unload their gear. My lieutenants will show you the way." Raphe and Bobby both looked at him and nodded. "Doctor Black would you come over here for a moment? I'd like you to meet someone."

"Certainly General." She couldn't help but giggle at the formality they were using. John got a smile out of it too. In the right rear of the truck there was a beautiful German shepherd dog sitting in a large crate. His collar read, 'Opt.' He had a perfect coloring of golden brown, white and black, ideally mixed in the right places. "Wow! What a beautiful dog!" Ivory opened up the crate and Opt jumped down from the truck and sat in front of her.

John was blown away. Opt never left the crate without a command. Plus, he was amazed that Opt didn't come directly to him. Ivory smiled at Opt and he rolled on his back so she could pet his belly. John was shocked. Opt was trained to growl, to warn people to stay away from him. If the growl wasn't enough, he was trained to snap and show his teeth. Ivory was squatting on the ground rubbing his belly, and he was licking her face. What a beautiful sight it was to see, his best and most loyal friend, in love with the most intelligent and talented woman in the world. After taking it in John said, "Excuse me Opt, but she is my wife, and I'm happy you two hit it off, but we are burning daylight here." Opt seemed like he just noticed John was even there. He jumped up and ran to him, sat in front of him bursting with excited energy. Before meeting Ivory John was the only one that Opt trusted enough to put himself in submissive positions for.

John took some time greeting and playing with Opt, since it had been so long since they'd seen each other.

Ivory said, "General I thought we were burning daylight."

"Well then get over here!" John ordered and she came running into his arms. He caught her and they kissed, as Opt ran around them like an energetic puppy. Opt came near them, sat down, and whined a little.

"What Opt?" John demanded.

Ivory said, "He wants to leave to use the potty."

"The potty?" Opt took off, and John looked worried.

Ivory whispered, "Don't worry lover. I told him it was okay." Before she could tell him to kiss her, John was already doing it. She wondered, maybe he could read my mind? Suddenly, they heard Opt growl.

"I'm sorry to interrupt, but we're going to need you to show us how to hook up that computer of yours Doctor Black. My name is Susan. I'm a laboratory technician. I have been assigned as your personal assistant." John and Ivory both looked embarrassed, like they had been caught behind the barn. Ivory went to shake hands with Susan. Opt growled. She looked at him and he lay down before John could even give the command.

Ivory said, "Hi Susan. This is General John White."

"Hello Sir." Susan smiled.

"Hello Susan," John said feeling embarrassed. "I'm sorry you had to see that unprofessional display of emotion. We're newlyweds and she just can't seem to keep her hands off me." Ivory punched him in the arm. "See what I mean Susan." They had a laugh.

"Yes Susan, this is General John White, my husband." Then she looked at John and realized that was the first time she had introduced him as her husband. He also realized it, and felt great. They shared a loving look.

Susan giggled. "You guys got it bad." Opt yelped out a friendly bark like he thought so too.

John thought, what the hell? Am I in a friggin' Lassie movie? This whole mission has been surreal. My wife and I, he smiled, "Time for me to get to work. Ladies, I'll let you get to it. It has been nice meeting you Susan."

"Thank you, General. It's been a pleasure," Susan replied.

As they were heading toward their makeshift laboratory, Ivory told Susan to please call her by her first name. She was growing tired of the formalities already.

Susan said, "Okay Ivory, but I have to tell you, I'm a big fan."

"Thanks Susan, but I'm just a regular girl that has been lucky enough to be able to do what I love."

Susan joked. "You mean like the general?" Ivory busted out laughing. Susan said, "He is a manly man. Smoking hot. But, don't worry. I'm into the ladies. Beauty is beauty, though."

Changing the subject Ivory said, "Susan, this mission we're on have you been briefed?"

"Not really," Susan replied. "Just that it could be dangerous."

John was excited about the message he had received. It read, "John, be there in four days, over." That meant that Joe was coming soon to help. Joe had been the General's right-hand man for a large part of his life.

They had started out together in the SEAL teams. Joe had fallen in love, married, and had two boys. One he named John. The other one was Joe Junior. Joe's wife, Kathy, was a sweetheart. John had told Joe to stay in the States, and if he needed him he would let him know. That was right after they were married ten years ago. John had spent time with Joe and his family when he could. He loved to visit on Christmas and spoil the boys and Kathy with extravagant gifts. They were the only real family John had. He thought they couldn't be closer even if they were blood relatives. He had a bad feeling about letting Joe in on this mission. It was very dangerous for him, and his family. Joe had insisted that he come, and that he needed to talk to him in person. Joe didn't know the location of the bunker. He would be parachuted in. The coordinates would be given to the pilot by an encoded encryption that only the pilot's communication device could decipher. John always followed security protocol. No exceptions, even for himself.

John's base communicator beeped; it was Ivory. "General, we will be set up and working in two hours."

"That's fantastic news Doctor Black. Keep me posted."

"General how about a private meeting in your office, at say 5:00 p.m.?"

"That sounds great Doctor keep up the good work."

Bobby walked into his bedroom and noticed Mary was getting ready to take a shower. He saw her wink at him. Then he saw that she had his clothes laid out with a fresh towel. He thought Mary is the sexiest most beautiful girl in the world. Bobby stood there just staring at her.

Mary said, "Excuse me Sir, but I think we should shower together soon before my husband gets back from work." Then she let her towel drop to the floor, exposing her naked body. She turned around, and bent over to slowly pick up her towel. Bobby had her in his arms and in bed before she could flutter her pretty little eyelashes.

As they were making love Bobby said, "You know ma'am, It would be very dangerous for any man if your husband were to catch us right now."

Mary said, "My handsome husband please don't stop, ever," and she moaned his name. While they were in the shower Mary asked Bobby if he could teach her to shoot like Ivory.

Bobby replied, "I don't think I could teach *myself* to shoot like Ivory." They both laughed. "I *could* teach you to shoot, though."

Mary said, "really Bobby? Would you? It looks like fun. I do believe I'm the luckiest girl in the world to have you."

"Mary I cannot believe you are my wife. It's like I don't deserve to be so happy. Let's get back to the room. I want to show you some gun safety."

"Yeah, right." She giggled.

John had just finished going over Corporal Tanner and Sergeant Wilkes' service records. They checked out okay. He explained their duties to them. He looked up and said, "Men, what I'm about to tell you and show you is classified. This mission is of vital importance to our country and the world." He then showed them a blueprint of the entire compound. He told them, "If you hear an order to evacuate go to the north tunnel. If everyone that you've brought here with you is accounted for, leave immediately. If they are not all there, contact them on your base communicator. If you have to wait contact me, I will tell you if it's safe to wait, or to leave immediately! Then, you will lead them through the tunnel. The tunnel goes down to about 100 feet gradually for one mile, then starts going up slowly for about four miles. It comes out two miles east of a town called Kingsford. Head there in a straight line west. Keep hidden until you get close. Your civilian scientists have already been told to change into normal citizen clothes. You men will change clothes, bury your rifles, and keep only your side arms, concealed. Take your crew into town and go to the Green Comet Diner. It's open twenty-four hours a day, seven days a week. You will be picked up there within three hours or less. Any questions?"

"General, does this have anything to do with those two crazy animal attacks?"

John gave them a stern look. He said, "Normally I would say sorry that's on a need-to- know basis only. Men I'm thinking this is now a you-need-to-know situation, because then you will definitely remember to close and seal the steel door entrance to the tunnel. But yes, it does! These animal attacks are not a natural occurrence. The animals are being mind-controlled by some of the richest and most powerful people on the planet. Some of these people are in our own government. You are not only fighting a sick and twisted murderous group of powerful foreigners, but you will be facing enemies within our own country. Some are money-grubbing traitors, and some have been planted. Truthfully, we are out-gunned and the only thing that will win the day is our loyalty to the people of the United States of America. Both of you accepted this mission knowing it was dangerous. Both of you are decorated patriots and love your country! Win this mission or lose our country to socialist-communist globalization. I answer only to the president, and if I call he will drop everything, and immediately talk to me. That's how important this is. You two Green Berets have been chosen for one of the most important and historic missions, possibly in the entire history of our country." He looked at them seriously. "Can your country count on you to succeed?" He asked them in his commanding voice.

Both men yelled, "Yes-Sir!"

"God bless America, and your mission. Dismissed."

The two men left at about 4:40 p.m. He was expecting Ivory at 5:00 p.m. He kept thinking about the message he had gotten earlier from Joe. What kept coming to mind was why Joe had to see him in person. Joe said it was important. Something was up. He knew he could trust Joe to die for his country, and for him. Could someone have gotten to him somehow? Joe didn't know about the details of their operation or what the cost of failure would be. He wanted to see what Ivory had to say. She was due in two minutes.

Chapter Sixteen: Complications

There was a knock at the door. "Enter," he beckoned. He looked up when Ivory entered. She noticed something was wrong as soon as she saw him.

"I'm glad you're here Ivory."

"What's wrong John?"

"Ivory I'm starting to think we have been compromised. I received a message from Joe as we were organizing your research team's arrival. I talked to him about a week ago. He said he had to speak to me in person, and that it was important. At the time, I was like a teenager in heat and didn't think anything of it. I actually thought it would be great to see him. Now that we are married and things are not totally out of control. I have been thinking Joe would never do something like that. It goes against security protocol."

"Does Joe know what the mission is about?" Ivory inquired.

"No he doesn't, and he knows better than to ask," John answered, sounding worried. "When your team arrived, Sergeant Wilkes gave me a handwritten message." He showed it to her. (J. B.. 4. D. O) "It is Joe's handwriting and it means, 'be there in four days'. It's a kind of simple code we made up in case we got separated on our missions and had to send a message. We are the only ones who would know it. In all the time I've been on missions with him or anywhere important, we have never used it. The code was made when we were on a recon mission that was a wash. The place that we were ordered to observe was not the place where the bad stuff was happening. I was young and we were bored so we made up a code, and wound up using it as a secret language, at parties or to joke with his wife and kids... stuff like that. This was the first time the code was ever used on an official mission. Ivory do you remember when we met, and I joked around with you about how your name was a little bit like the, 'Who's on First Abbott and Costello' comedy act?"

"Yes."

John said, "When you asked me what race I was, I said human. That's because I don't know what race I am. I was an orphan and so is Joe. We met at our second foster home. We became like real brothers. We both joined the service at eighteen years old and we both made the SEAL team. I spent one quarter of my life crawling through swamps and running through jungles with Joe. He has saved my life many times and I've done the same for him. We have seen and fought horrible things for God and country together. I don't believe two men could be closer or more loyal to one another. I'm feeling emotional, at a dead end, and because it's Joe, I'm having a hard time floating like a butterfly and stinging like a bee. I was hoping you could help me look at it from a different perspective. That's what I do. I look at a mission from every perspective – from mine, and from my enemy's. I look at it like a game of chess. If

I move here, how could they get me? If they move here, how could I attack or change plans?"

While John was telling Ivory his story, he was pacing and looking down concentrating. When he looked up at her she was crying. When she saw his eyes looking her way she ran to him and hugged him. "You poor man! I'm so sorry for being such a jerk, and for being condescending when we first met."

"Ivory honey you have been the best thing that has ever happened to me since the first day I met you, and every day it gets even better. My life was what I chose it to be. God put me where I would have the best chance to come to Him. Don't feel bad for me. I'm working for God, and so are you. Okay sweetheart?" John couldn't believe it, Ivory even cried beautifully. "I only have one complaint."

"What is it John?"

"It's about our love-making. I have a few pointers I can give you."

"Oh really?" Ivory said in a slightly annoyed tone. "What are they honey?" She was sarcastic.

"I think we should do it twenty-four hours a day, seven days a week."

She laughed and wiped her tears. "I knocked on your door ready to jump your bones. In the last," she checked her watch, "Eight minutes. You have had me: crying, laughing, now I am worried! Let's look at this from my perspective."

"I'm listening."

"I believe you are right that something is wrong. I don't think Joe would want to come here personally if something wasn't horribly wrong. I also don't think he would have sent you that message in that code you guys have if he wasn't trying to give you some kind of heads up. Joe is now involved! This Mr. Atlas Grey has half our country's government infiltrated. Could he possibly have found out how close you are to Joe and his family? And if he did, how could he use it against you, and us?"

John's face turned scary mean. He reached in his pocket and pulled out an unfamiliar-looking phone. Sort of like an old flip cell phone. All he did was open it and put it to his ear. He was doing a breathing exercise to calm down, she guessed.

John said, "Mr. President, I need a location on Captain Joseph Mills' wife and children, 'Priority one!'" He closed the phone. "Ivory that's got to be it. That walking bag of evil has Joe's family. Shit! My little buddies and Kathy! Please, God, don't let them be tortured. If it's in your plan for them to come to you, please let them go mercifully. I ask this Father, as a personal favor in Jesus' name."

A sound came from his pocket. He opened the phone to listen, and said, "Thank you, Sir." John turned to his wife. "They have them Ivory. Just outside of Rome. I need twenty minutes Honey. I'm going down to the gym to kill the heavy bag. Ivory, please call a meeting with our team only in one hour, in my office. I'm sorry Baby, but I have to vent, or I won't think straight. Love you."

Ivory said, "Love you too." She was trying to be strong for him, and not cry.

John was walking into the gym with his hand-wraps and punching bag gloves. He noticed there were three people working out, two women and a man. He remembered them from the lab tech team. He asked them politely to leave because he needed the gym for half an hour.

Susan happened to be one of them. She said, "Yes Sir," and picked up her towel and started to leave. The other lady pretended she didn't hear him.

The guy said, "Buddy you will just have to wait until I'm done!"

John looked at him and used his command voice. "Leave now, or you will have to be carried out!"

They both stopped what they were doing and said, "Yes Sir," and left as quickly as possible. John then locked the door and started to punch the bag. From all his training, he knew to start slowly until he was loosened up. Then he poured it on as fast and as hard as he could until it felt like his heart would jump out of his chest, and he couldn't catch his breath. He then circled the bag, throwing jabs, until he was ready for round two. He did it again as fast and hard as he could. Finally, he stopped when he couldn't hold his arms up, and his punches had no force. He fell down on his knees and begged God. "Please don't let them hurt my babies, my sweet little nephews, or their mom, Lord."

He felt drained and hugged the bottom of the heavy bag for support. Then John clearly heard, "Do not be afraid, Son." It sounded like Joe's voice. He quickly looked around and yelled for him, but no one was there. He checked the wall clock. There was no time to take a shower. John had to leave for the meeting with his team. He stripped off his sweaty shirt and threw on a clean one, washed his face, and drank some water. He left his things and hurried to the meeting with a towel drying his face and arms on the way.

When he got to the door he could hear his team talking and decided it was a good idea for him to and calm down. He started to take deep breaths. He thought about Ivory and all his new friends. He had to stop – that was making it worse. John pushed opened the door, and everyone was present. Helen was actually sitting behind his desk in his chair.

"Come here General," Helen insisted. "I need you to hear something." John really didn't like looking out of control or weak, but he couldn't refuse this beautiful lady. It was like he was being pulled toward her. When he got close, Helen hugged him above the shoulders and whispered in his ear. "Hey, John, it's not over until it's over. We keep on trying even when we're dying. Do not be afraid. Son, if God brings you to it, He'll get you through it."

John froze. That's exactly what Joe used to say to him when it looked like his men were going to die, and John would feel responsible. Helen reached over to hug his chest and said, "This is God's mission John. You're not responsible. God chose you for this just like He chose your team. You work for Him, John. He needs you to have faith. You are not alone. He is always with you. You are His team's leader, and He loves you, and wants you to do the best you can, because leading the fight against evil is one of the gifts God has given you. Trust that He knows what is best and use your gifts to the best of your ability."

Helen and John started swaying. She had to let him go or else she would have fallen on top of him. "Wow, what a rush!" She felt dizzy, so she sat down in John's chair. Ivory ran over to John and checked his vitals. Helen reassured Ivory that John was okay.

Helen then said, "Ivory, honey, he's more than okay. The Lord has just given him a whopper of a blessing. Wow! If he got more than I did, I expect he will rest for a while. If you all don't mind, I'm going to rest my head." She put her head down and the rest of the team waited for them to wake up.

When John started to move and moan a little, Ivory reached over to hug him. He stood up a little shaky. With tears in her eyes she yelled to the others, "All of you come here and feel this! I can't explain it." When each one of them touched John, they felt a love so pure and potent, they could not stop their joyful tears. Helen woke up smiling with a joyful cry.

"Mom, what's going on?" Jane asked.

"Jane, Jesus just let me hug your dad and he said he was so proud of you. He said we soon would be together for eternity. I'm sorry honey, but I didn't want to leave him. I felt as if I had just showered, but then had to jump back into a pile of mud." Jane was so happy for her mom. She knew how much her mother wanted to be with him again.

Jane said, "I love you Dad. Thanks for being proud of me."

Helen looked around the room and noticed everyone was touching John and shedding happy tears. Helen slapped his shoulder and said, "Somebody's batteries just got charged big time!"

John looked at her, picked her up, and threw her up in the air and caught her, like she was a child. He said, "Thank you Helen, again, for stepping out in faith and putting it all out there. I'm back, and no more worry. If God is with us, who can stand against us?"

They all looked at him as he stood there. Their General looked like an ancient warrior, mighty and victorious in all his battles. For a second, they saw his eyes glow, as if there was an enormous power inside him that his mortal body was barely able to contain. He said, "I know we have to plan, but right now I have to apologize to a few people, and we should enjoy a meal together and thank the Lord God. Then we'll come back and plan our victory. Sound good?"

They all agreed. John asked Ivory if she would come with him because the person he was rude to was Susan, and two of her lab techs. The others would get started on dinner. When Ivory and John were alone, she wanted to know what happened. "What did you do?"

"I was losing it, thinking about my family being tortured by Mr. Grey. I had to hit something or I thought I would have a meltdown. When I got to the gym, there were two women and one man working out. I asked them to please leave for a half hour. Susan said she would and left right away. The other girl acted like she didn't hear me. The guy called me buddy, and told me to wait my turn."

"John, you didn't hurt him, did you?"

"No, sweet cheeks," and he slapped her butt. "I used my command voice, and told them to leave then or they would have to be carried out."

"Thank you Lord," Ivory said. He looked at her with a raised eyebrow. She said, "The look on your face scared me John. I know you would never hurt me, darling. I was worried that you were so hurt inside, that if anyone gave you any crap, you could possibly kill that person accidentally. I group-called the team and set an emergency meeting. We all prayed, and Helen said it was going to be all right. Then you walked in, and…Wow."

"Ivory I have never hit anyone who wasn't trying to hit me, except the enemies our government sent me to battle. I have the command thing. I use it before it gets that far."

"Oh yeah. Ivory smiled. "I forgot about that. You better never use it on me!"

"Not even at night in bed would I use it on you." John said innocently.

"Well, that might be kind of fun, actually," Ivory giggled.

The techs were all having dinner in the laboratory dining area they had set up. Ivory walked up to Susan and said, "General White wants to apologize to you and the two others about what happened in the gym earlier. He had gotten some extremely bad news and needed to hit the punching bag. I guess he didn't want anyone to see any weakness in their leader."

Susan said, "As soon as I saw him I knew something bad had happened. Man, when he is angry, he is scary!"

"I know, it was the first time I have seen him like that. When he left his office after the news came, he looked like he could kill someone, if they gave him any reason at all."

"What did you do Ivory?"

"I called our team and we had an emergency meeting, and prayed."

Susan laughed. "How could a genius scientist like you believe in a God who hates?"

"Susan, God doesn't hate." Ivory countered. "He is pure love. People and fallen angels hate."

"Doctor Black, I can't get into heaven," Susan said begrudgingly.

"Why not?"

"I'm a lesbian, Doctor!"

"So? What does that have to do with it?"

"We're not allowed in, according to your bible."

"Susan for a highly intelligent woman, you sure are ignorant sometimes. Have you ever even read the bible?"

Susan said matter-of-factly, "Yes. The part that says being gay is an abomination."

"Oh, Susan. The Old Testament people had the law, the Ten Commandments, plus a huge list of specific sins. As far as I know, all the people who were born and died on earth, that have accepted Christ are now in heaven, and they were all sinners. The only one born, lived, and died without any sin was Jesus Christ. Susan, can't you see we are all sinners? A sin is a sin, even if you have one thought about doing something wrong in your entire life, something that would cause innocent people to feel mental or physical pain. Without accepting Jesus, you're not going to heaven. I will bring a bible with me tomorrow. We don't have a lot of time, but I will show you how you're wrong. We have free will. Jesus Christ suffered every single person's emotional and physical pain that their sins caused them, and others. He did that for everyone that ever lived and for everyone that will ever live. There is not one person on this earth that can't choose Jesus. There is not one person on this earth who is not a sinner. A man once asked Jesus how to get into heaven, and Jesus replied to love your neighbor as you would yourself, and love the Lord God with all your heart, soul, spirit, and mind. Susan, do you and your girlfriend go around hurting people? Or do you treat people with compassion and kindness?"

"Well, we try to be kind, of course!"

"That's all any of us can do, try hard to be good to other people. My husband didn't succeed at the gym today. If you knew the news he received, you would think he didn't do too badly. Susan it seems the only thing stopping you from heaven is you not choosing Jesus." Ivory paused a second. "And by the way, if you call me Doctor in that tone again, I am going to get very angry. I respect you, and you respect me. That's my trigger, disrespect. I can't handle it. It's something I'm working on."

"I'm sorry Ivory." Susan said.

Just then they both noticed John waving them over. "Doctor Black, I have apologized and explained our situation to our tech team. I have a plan. I want these people out of here before Joe gets here. This means you have about three days to figure out a way to stop this Nano cell tech."

Ivory was agitated. "Excuse me General, but that would have to be a miracle."

"Doctor Black," John chided. "I thought you believed in miracles! I know it sounds impossible, but just do your best with the time you have here. If there is anyone in the world who can make this happen, it's you. I have witnessed your genius first-hand. After meetings with his cabinet, the President picked you himself! One of your many charms is you don't even realize how unbelievably talented you are."

Susan raised her hand. "I agree!"

John said, "I have faith in you and your team. And Susan, I'm very sorry about my rudeness in the gym. I hope you can forgive me."

Susan smiled at John. "Already forgotten Sir."

He smiled. "Thank you. Okay people," John addressed them all. You guys will be almost in another town in civilian clothes before the enemy even locates this place. Your ride might be there already, or you may have to wait an hour or two. These two Green Berets will lead you to your destination. Tomorrow, we will have one test drill. We need to know how much time it will take for everyone to get to the tunnel entrance. If anyone in town asks what you are all doing there, just say you were hiking the trails. I want to thank you all for your hard work and patriotism. Now, if you will excuse us, we need to eat our dinner, and then we will make our plans. I'm starving. Good night and God bless you all."

"John, there is something different about you," Ivory said as they headed for the dining room.

"Ivory I am not afraid anymore. I'm not in charge. I'm not responsible if any people die or get badly wounded. I'm leading the team, but it's not my team, it's God's team, and God is with us. I feel like a great weight has been lifted off my shoulders."

"'It's more than that John. It's like you project an arresting confidence. When you gave me that pep talk, I felt like I could accomplish anything! And when you talked to the team, I looked around at them. They were all in awe of you. Susan couldn't keep her eyes off you."

That made John laugh. "Ivory she probably has never seen such a ruggedly, handsome man before. You can't blame her for that!"

His smile made Ivory giggle. "She likes the ladies, General."

"Oh," John replied. "Well, I feel great! I do feel different Ivory, my beautiful genius, I feel a peace I've never felt before." He slapped her butt and started tickling her. Ivory tried to get away, but he caught her and kissed her against the wall of the tunnel. Ivory felt it also, a peaceful feeling, like she could let go and put it all out there, totally uninhibited, without fear of anything. She also felt John kissing her with every molecule of her body and mind. The love and excitement were almost unbearable. She stopped, and John saw a tear on her face.

He was concerned. "Did I hurt you?"

Her eyes spoke volumes. She loved him. "Quite the opposite. I felt the peace you were telling me about. Amazing, that kiss, I've never felt such love."

John said, "Same here." They were both breathing heavy. "As much as I want to throw you over my shoulder and ravish you in our bedroom, people are waiting for us, and it is important. I don't mean dinner. I mean thanking God and coming up with a plan we can live with, literally."

"You're right, you big tease," Ivory, told him. "But you owe me tonight."

"Believe me," John said, as he scanned her body. "You will be over-paid tonight."

Ivory took a deep breath and said, "We'd better stop and get our heads back in the fighting game."

John laughed. "You see, lady? How smart you are? That was my line! And it was you who analyzed that Joe was in trouble, and we were about to be discovered by the enemy."

John and Ivory walked into the dining room. Jane was the first one to greet them. "Perfect timing! You must be hungry."

"I am very hungry," John said. Ivory and John sat down with the team.

"Do you guys feel peaceful and calm? If so, isn't it strange considering what is going on?" Mary asked.

Raphe said, "Yes. I can honestly say I've never felt so calm and happy."

Everyone was in agreement. John looked at Helen and gave her a warm smile. He silently thanked the Lord for Helen.

Jane smiled. "Aw, that was sweet John."

"Jane that's bad manners," Helen warned.

"I'm sorry John," Jane said, "But I was looking at you, and you seem so...different."

Bobby and Mary agreed simultaneously. "Yes, you do!"

Raphe said, "I've noticed it too, General."

"People!" Helen announced. They all looked at her. "We are family now. I love you all and I want you to try your hardest to follow God's path that He has laid out for us. Our Father has blessed John with the Holy Spirit through our savior Jesus Christ, who loved us so much He suffered, and died for us. The doors of heaven were closed, and mankind closed them with sin. Mankind chose to refuse paradise. It wasn't enough. With mankind, it is never enough. Our Father sent His only son to open those doors for those of us who would choose to come back. We are eternally grateful for your love Father. Helen looked at John, "When you were blessed and sleeping in the Spirit, did you have a vision?"

John did, and it was so beautiful. He just remembered every detail. His eyes looked like they were seeing something else. He felt like he was almost hallucinating – like he was in a different place; but he knew he was still with his team in the dining room. John remained perfectly still. "I saw the most beautiful beach that went on forever and ever. The sand was slightly glowing. Curious, I bent over and picked up one grain of the sand. I looked at it between the tips of my fingers and felt the power of everything good. Grace, mercy and hope, but love was the most powerful. I felt every good thing that God wanted for us. I felt it in that one grain of sand. It was so powerful. Somehow, I knew it could explode and start a new universe. I thought this is only one grain of sand, among so many more. They could never be counted. My mind could not really comprehend it. The grain of sand I was holding started to get so bright I could only see light, but it was a living, feeling, powerful light. The light then entered my body and soul. I felt a love so strong and beautiful that I could barely move. I had to lie down, as I lay there filled with unbearable joy. I saw a man come toward me; as he squatted over me, He spoke.

"He said, 'Hello John,' and smiled. It was Jesus. He said, 'I'm sorry you had to suffer so much on earth. You chose to help your brothers and sisters. I will be with you John, always.' Then he picked me up and hugged me. He looked at me and wiped the tears from my eyes. I asked, 'Is all this love from that one grain

of sand, the power to create a whole universe for me?'
He smiled and said, 'Yes John, and every single grain
of sand on this beach is also for you, and for all my
children.' Then He transformed into the King of such
immense power and glory that I had to cover my eyes
from his gaze. Somehow I knew. My mortal body would
not survive looking upon His face. A glorious power
and love so fierce that one quick glance would oblit-
erate a mortal man. I then heard a voice so beautiful, eternal and living, that I automatically fell to my
knees and shook from the power of it.'"

"My King said, 'John, lead my team-my children as
you are my child. Lead them on the path I have placed
before you. Have faith that your Father has laid this at
your feet since before time began. You have been created for this task and many others. Have faith John,
whatever happens is God's plan, and what is best for
His beloved children. John, your team has been chosen
as you also have been. Go forth with the blessing of the
King of Kings.'"

As John stood there, he shed his tears through every word he spoke. He was back, visibly shaken and
tired, but full of joy. He looked at Helen, and she also
had been shedding tears with him.

"Whew John," Helen began. "You have been anoint-
ed and blessed by Jesus, The King of Kings Himself.
Never in all my life have I seen such a sight. Thank you
Lord, for showing me."

"You were there with me Helen?"

"No, I was just shown a vision, but you were actually there in spirit! John you actually hugged Jesus and
He wiped your tears away."

John felt unsteady again.

"Guys let's eat," Ivory said. "The food has got to be cold by now, but I think my man here needs something quick and some water." They all dug in. The food was still hot and better than the most fantastic meal they ever had.

Helen said, "Blessing after blessing, and its not even Christmas!" Everyone was in such a good mood. They couldn't help but laugh.

After dinner, John turned to Ivory and said, "I feel like I could pick up a car right now."

Ivory laughed. "Me too!"

John saw that everyone was finishing up. "Guys, how are you all feeling?"

Raphe said, "I feel like I could run a marathon." They all experienced a full-body boost in energy.

"All right," John said. "What do you say we all clean off the table and get to work on our plans?"

Mary was confused. "I don't get it; did someone put amphetamines in the food?"

Helen chuckled. "No, Mary. The Lord has filled us with another blessing. Keep them coming, baby!" Helen yelled as she was dancing around, while cleaning up.

Mary cracked up. I love that lady, she thought.

Jane smiled. "Me too Mary." Mary gave her a playful, naughty look. "I was looking at you! I couldn't help it," Jane said softly.

Mary grabbed her in a hug and said, "Thank you for being my best friend and sister. You helped me more than you know."

Jane squeezed Mary a little harder and said, "I love you too, Sister."

John told them his plan. It was simple. "When Joe gets here, we kill any kind of tracking device he has on or inside him. Then we get on the bullet train and go to my emergency kick-ass command center complete with a stealth jet, and lots of fun 'toys'. That's my plan. I have thought about this for hours, and I can't come up with anything better. What do you think?"

Raphe said, "It really sounds like our best choice." Bobby and Ivory agreed. John looked to Helen for confirmation.

"Unless the Lord has something to say through me, you're the boss. I don't know much about this kind of stuff."

Jane said, "Sounds good to me!"

Mary concurred as well. "But what about Joe's family?"

"Great question, Mary," John said. "We are working on that and should have that plan ready, which is quite complex, sometime tomorrow after dinner. We are trying to keep it as simple as possible, but it's not been an easy task. Sometimes it can take weeks of planning for a five hour mission!"

"Would you mind if I helped you guys? Mary asked. I promise I will behave," She glanced at Bobby. "How about you Jane?"

"No thanks. I have a feeling I'm supposed to go with Ivory. Would that be all right?"

Ivory smiled. "Better than all right Jane."

The next morning after breakfast, Ivory and Jane walked to the lab. Ivory told her that she didn't sleep much the night before.

"Last night was the best night of my life," sighed Jane.

"Me too!" Ivory smiled. "Last night was the closest I've ever been to heaven. I haven't slept at all and I can't understand why I'm not exhausted."

Jane said "Same here. I'm not tired one bit!"

"Jane, why did you want to come to work with me? Are you interested in science?"

"I like science Ivory, but the truth is that I get feelings; strong feelings that pop up in my head. I had that feeling last night when I asked you if I could come with you."

"What happens when you follow these feelings?"

"Sometimes, something small that my gift was needed for or sometimes, something mind-blowing. Whatever happens is always good."

Ivory gave Jane a hopeful look, "I could really use some mind-blowing today."

"I never know what is going to happen, but I hope it's a big help."

Ivory thought, Just being with you, kid, is a big help.

"I feel the same way Ivory."

They both walked into the morning meeting with the tech team. Everyone was there already waiting. Ivory always showed up a few minutes late because she hated waiting.

"Good morning everyone. We have a guest today. This is Jane."

"Hello," they all said.

Susan greeted her and shook Jane's hand. Jane heard her think, "What a hot body, and such a beautiful face!"

"Hi Susan. You're Ivory's personal assistant, right?"

"Yes, I was just about to say that."

"It's a pleasure to meet you Susan."

"Nice to meet you too Jane."

"Let's get to it," Ivory ordered. "Has anyone come up with anything new?"

Nobody spoke.

"Does anyone have any ideas, or even theories?"

Jane felt the feeling to look at a shy, nerdy-looking guy. He was thinking about frequencies. He thought, I have a theory, but it's probably wrong.

Jane interrupted the moment. "Excuse me, Doctor Black, may I ask someone a question?"

"Go right ahead Jane." Jane looked at this man's nametag. It read 'Anton'.

"Anton, I find frequencies fascinating." Jane gave him her best smile. "If you were to make a wild guess, what would it be?"

"W-, w-, well, it's not very scientific to guess Jane," Anton stuttered.

Ivory said, "Anton, we have one one-hundredth of the time we need to even come close to solving this. If you told me your guess would be that a sinister alien chicken from Mars was responsible, you would be the bravest person in this room."

Jane begged him, "Anton, please say it for me. I'm just a student, and to hear a guess from you would be very helpful for my studies."

"All right Jane, since you're a student and want to hear something about frequencies, I'll guess. When you get back to school, remember, this is not the right way to proceed scientifically. A wild guess would be that there is not one, but *two* different Nano cells that enter the brain. One would be the receiver and pick up a certain, maybe, subsonic-coded frequency, then relay it to the control Nano cell. However, that guess still wouldn't explain the total savagery of the mammal we have studied. We are still missing an important ingredient."

Anton's theory changed Ivory's perspective. Seeing it from his point of view, she said, "That's it!" Ivory looked at him in shock. She ran over to Anton, grabbed his face and said, "Anton, you're a genius!" She kissed his forehead. "I want you to analyze some of the Nano cells. Feed them subsonic frequencies. See if you can crack the code. Who is the biologist in the room?"

A woman raised her hand and said, "I am."

Ivory read her nametag. "Tina, I want you to check every shred of evidence for any traces of pheromones."

Tina, after thinking for a minute, said, "Oh my God."

Ivory asked, "Does anyone have experience with animal biological frequencies or anything close to that?"

A man in his forties raised his hand. He said, "I've had quite a bit, but it's been a few years Doctor Black."

Ivory read his nametag. "I feel you, Frank; it will come back to you. Maybe not right away, but with you and Anton bouncing ideas off each other, you never know what can happen. Look, we are a team. The country is at stake. We are trying to save possibly the entire world. All I'm asking is for all of you to work together and to do your best. I'm not asking you for a miracle, but I am hoping you come up with one. One more thing; is there someone here who can build magnetic pulse emitters with a range of two hundred thousand square feet, and some with a range of a one thousand square feet?"

Susan thought, I suppose she is going to tell me it's a gift from God.

Jane declared. "It is a gift from God, Susan, and I'll prove it. Tina is your girlfriend, when you and I met you thought I had a hot body and a beautiful face."

Susan's mouth hung open and she stared at Jane. "How are you doing this? What's the trick?"

"No trick. Think of something that is so bizarre that there is no way I would know it."

"Okay," Susan said, "I'll play along. Are you ready?"

Jane said, "You're thinking this is bullshit. The man on the moon is a fag. I usually try not to cuss, but you're worth it."

"Why am I worth it to you Jane?"

"I think you're cool, but you're worth it to God," Jane told her. "Not me."

"Yeah, a God that calls gay people abominations."

Ivory started to say something, but Jane interrupted. "I got this, Ivory."

Jane glared at Susan. "I don't know how you came to that assumption, but it's a lie. God doesn't ever call people names or hate. God is pure good. No evil exists in Him, and no evil can exist in front of God the Father."

"Are you are telling me I would turn to dust because I'm gay, and you're okay with that?" Susan huffed.

"No, Susan. That's not what I'm saying. I'm saying every single person on this planet would turn to dust in God the Father's presence. We are all sinners. Only by accepting the Son of God's sacrifice can you stand before God the Father, and that's only after you die here first and your body is made eternal. Susan, what if I told you

I had proof right now on my person that God exists? Would you want to see it?"

"Absolutely! Who wouldn't want to?" Jane showed Susan the small round circle of glory that God had left on her finger after Mary healed her. "That's your proof? It could be an LED light embedded in your finger."

"Touch it," Jane dared her. "It won't hurt you."

"I am *not* touching that. Please, can we stop this so I can get some work done?"

Jane said, "Ivory, can you come over here and touch this in front of Susan? That way she knows it's safe."

Ivory came over and touched it twice. "Jane, if Susan is scared to see if that really is proof that God exists you can't force her to touch it."

"You're right, Ivory. I guess I'll go back to see what mom's up to."

Jane knew Susan wanted to touch it, but was distrusting and thought it was some kind of a gag. "Last chance Susan. Do you think Doctor Black would allow me to purposely hurt one of her team members? Her family? Where is your scientific curiosity? Oh well. See you guys later."

Susan thought for a second. "Stop! I'll touch it, even if it's only to prove you're pranking me." Jane walked over and held out her finger. Susan reached out and as soon as she touched it she fell into a dream sleep.

"Whew, Ivory, she was a tough nut to crack." Ivory and Jane chuckled. "I still have the light in my finger. I thought it would leave when I used it." Jane was surprised.

"You would give it up for just anyone?" Ivory asked.

"No never! I only use it when and where God wants it used. Mom told me it's not mine to keep. All glory goes back to the Father."

John and three of his team members were working on a plan to travel to Rome as soon as Joe arrived at John's compound. He had good intelligence that Mr. Grey and his head of security would be on one of his private islands for five days. He was also able to get a blueprint of Mr. Grey's castle and the entire compound. John knew it was not complete, and that there would be places not on the blueprint; places they most likely needed to get to if they were going to save Joe's family.

He had Raphe going over the print to see if he could remember anything about the castle that was not on their copy. Raphe had practically grown up there. He had Bobby planning a SEAL team insertion that had to be improvable and plausibly deniable. They were working well together. Mary was just observing. John was sending messages to the president about what he needed to accomplish on this mission. The list so far included three SEAL teams with enough explosives to blow the entire place and leave a twenty-foot crater. The main problem was that they couldn't kill a lot of dignitaries or powerful people without starting World War III. John was coming up with a plan to clear the place of those kinds of people. They probably needed to be killed, but he had to take it one step at a time. John had satellite pictures coming in. Since everyone else was busy, John asked Mary if she could look them over.

Mary took them and spread them out on a big table. "Incredible. You can see people's faces!" She thought it was amazing to see photographs of people taken from space. She wondered how many secret technologies there were, that she had no idea existed.

"General? Bobby?" said Raphe. There are some places I have been to that are not on this print, but they didn't seem secret. I marked them off anyway, and I'll keep trying General."

"Thank you, men…and women." John nodded at Mary.

Mary sensed he was having a problem. "John, is something wrong? I'm good at solving problems."

"Yes, there is Mary. I need to clear this building out without arousing suspicion. There are foreign dignitaries and royal visitors, not counting the powerful billionaires. If even one of these people gets killed, it could literally start a war."

Bobby said, "That's a tough one General." Raphe nodded in agreement.

"Tell me about it. I've been racking my brain for hours thinking about it."

Mary thought for a minute. "I might have a plan for that General."

"I'm listening, Mary." John smiled. How cute.

"Doctor Black told me about a device she was building called an electromagnetic pulse bomb. It doesn't hurt people. It kills all electrical controls and electronic circuits. The amount of area affected depends on the size of the magnetic pulse bomb, and the electrical components that are in its magnetic pulse's field and blast radius at the time it is set off. My idea is to set off some kind of gas that smells like rotten eggs and is non-lethal, inside the castle. Then, at the same time blow the magnetic pulse bomb. The alarms won't work, so you can have some of our people fake that they are firemen and police, and clear the building, telling them they have to go away because there is a major gas leak. They need to be least a half-mile away. If they need a ride, have a bus pick them up to give your team time. Call in a terrorist threat and create a huge explosion at the other side of town so the real cops and firemen are busy elsewhere. The people will think there are major gas leaks, and it'll be hysteria, and confusion with everyone but our guys. Go in, get it done, blow the place, and get out while everyone is looking the other way."

Mary was pacing back and forth, looking down and concentrating like she was visualizing it in her head. She stopped and looked up at John. "That's all I could think of John. Too much drama?"

Everyone was staring at her like she was an alien. This was a far cry from the soft-spoken, quaint Mary everyone had come to know and love.

"What?" she asked.

John ran over and hugged her. "You are a genius Mary."

Bobby was the most surprised. "Mary, that was amazing! How did you come up with that?"

Raphe joked, "You better never get her mad at you Bobby."

Mary scoffed. "Are you guys making fun of me?"

John told her, "Mary, I would never do that, and they wouldn't either."

"You really think it's a good plan?" Mary asked, surprised.

Everyone agreed it was a fantastic plan. John announced, "I'm going to start getting it set up right now."

"I told you John, I'm good at solving problems." Mary said, "I'll walk down and see Ivory to make sure she has enough of the pulse bombs for the plan. I know: Top-secret. Only our team knows." She walked up to Bobby and said with a smirk, "So, who's the badass now, buddy?" She kissed him on the lips, slapped his butt, and sauntered out the door.

Bobby's face was so funny in a twisted way that Raphe and John keeled over laughing. She had to tell Bobby later how exciting that was, but she wanted to play it cool. On the way to Ivory's lab, she ran into Jane. Simultaneously, they both said, "You won't believe what just happened."

Mary said, "You first."

"All right. Ivory thinks I may have saved us all." Jane told her what happened at the meeting and about Susan.

"Wow. Well you're not going to believe this, but almost the same thing happened to me." Mary told Jane how she came up with the plan and blew their minds. Then she told her what she did to Bobby on her way out.

Jane laughing said, "No, you didn't!"

"Yes! I felt like I was better than them... Wait. That's not good. Your mom told me nobody is better or worse than anyone else. Jane, did I just sin?"

"I think we both did, Mary, we can't handle the glory, that's why it goes back to the Father. Let's tell Jesus we are sorry, and that we are going to try really hard not think like that anymore."

The girls prayed, and right away they felt better. They agreed to tell the team at dinner they were sorry. They hugged and then continued doing what they were doing. Mary walked into Ivory's office and closed the door behind her.

"Hi Ivory, I'm sorry to interrupt, but it's important."

"Mary, you're not an interruption, you're a beautiful breath of fresh air."

"Someone is in a good mood!" Mary answered.

"You won't believe what we have done here; it's a miracle."

Mary said, "I know all about it. I bumped into Jane on the way here, Incredible! Blessing after blessing. Kind of the same thing happened to me with the guys today." She told Ivory the entire story and Ivory couldn't stop laughing. "Ivory, we both thought we were better than others today, and we asked for forgiveness. Tonight, at dinner, we are going to apologize to the team."

Ivory was still getting her laughter under control. "Oh, I wish I was there."

The door opened and Susan walked in with a tray full of plastic vials, with one glass vial. She saw Mary and greeted her, then tilted the wrong way and spilled something in front of her. When she tried to correct her balance, her feet slipped out from under her and she fell flat on her back. Ivory and Mary immediately went to her.

Susan started screaming, "I can't see! My eyes and face are burning!"

Ivory ran to her lab table and came back with an isotonic saline solution to neutralize the acid that spilled on Susan. She poured it all over Susan's eyes and face. Six people came rushing in when they heard Susan scream. She was moaning in pain.

Tina came in and got down beside her. "I'm here Susan!" She squeezed her hand. "I'll take care of you."

Everyone there could see how Susan's eyes were singed and there were scars already forming on her face from the acid. Mary walked toward Susan. Ivory noticed that Mary looked like she wasn't fully in control. She gently moved the crowd out of the way.

Mary knelt down. Very calmly, she asked, "Susan, do you want to be healed?"

"Yes! Please!" Susan was desperate. Everyone around her was afraid to speak. A breeze blew into the room and Mary's hair flew back a little. Ivory noticed that Mary seemed filled with a kind of power. Everyone else felt it too.

Tina begged, "Please, if you can help her..."

Mary cut her off. "I can, Tina." When Mary looked into her eyes, Tina knew it was the Lord God that spoke through her. Mary placed her hands over Susan's eyes and said, "Susan, you have been healed, and your sins have been forgiven. Jesus Christ has paid for your sins." Mary looked at Tina. "Jesus loves you Tina. He loves all his children. If you choose to knock, the door will be opened." Mary took her hands away and Susan was completely healed. Not even a blemish. Tina was also filled with the Holy Spirit, and Susan was overwhelmed with relief and joy.

"Thank you Mary!" She cried.

"It wasn't me Susan. I am just a servant. You know who you should thank."

Susan gave a brief account of her interaction with Jane earlier. She believed now. "Thank you, Jesus!" she proclaimed.

Tina was also overcome with a newfound faith. "I ask you, Jesus, to forgive my sins and come into my heart." Tina's eyes filled with tears. She held Susan as they embraced each other and rocked back and forth.

Ivory said, "Let's give them some room, people!"

Mary felt happy for them. "I'm going to help prepare some dinner, I'm starving. Ivory, it's dinnertime, would you walk with me?"

Ivory looked at her watch. "All right, everyone. Take an hour and a half for dinner tonight. I'll see you all in the meeting room at 7:30 p.m."

Mary waited until everyone left. She looked at Susan and Tina. "Would you like to join us for dinner, ladies?" We would love to they said, and the four of them headed for John's side of the bunker.

"You and Jane have had quite a day," Ivory said.

"That's for sure, I cannot wait to get some food in me! I feel kind of shaky." Ivory put her arm around her. Mary said, "Let me rest here for a little while." She faded out and started to slump to the floor.

Susan and Tina picked Mary up, and then turned to Ivory. "We got this Doctor Black," Tina said.

They carried her to the dining room. Bobby was there asking if his wife was going to be okay before they could even explain what happened. Helen said, "Bobby, she is fine. The glory of God is tiring for our mortal bodies. She just needs to rest a while. Girls, could you put her over here next to Bobby? Come sit here Bobby, so you can make sure she doesn't fall."

Chapter Eighteen: Taking Care of Business

Antonio knew he had to totally concentrate on security for Mr. Grey. He put Raphe out of his mind. He then went through every detail of Mr. Grey's itinerary. This was going to take all night. He got on his phone and called his most trusted security agent, Michael, and had his team go over the jet. Antonio wanted it checked for any kind of foreign electronic devices and explosives.

"Use the dogs," he ordered. "Also, I want it mechanically checked, completely. It has to be done at the very latest by 7:30 a.m. tomorrow. This is a top priority; so don't bother me with asking permission for anything you need. You are in charge, Michael. Do whatever is necessary."

"Yes Sir," Michael replied.

Antonio had to call over twenty security personnel that he secretly positioned on the island. He thought when he finally finished that it was the best he could do with such short notice. By then it was 6:22 a.m. He had just enough time to shower and shave. He planned to sleep on the three-hour flight over to the island. Antonio learned sleep was vital in battle – sleep was a weapon, just like many other things that people overlook. When you are in an exhausted state, your mind can play tricks on you. He had learned to sleep, if at all possible, on a long mission. Even a short nap could make the difference between life and death. Antonio had also learned not to allow the enemy to sleep, if at all possible.

He was waiting outside Mr. Grey's door five minutes before arrival time. He had brought three of his best men with him so they could shield Mr. Grey from the rear and both sides. Antonio would be the front shield and the eyes for the group. Mr. Grey told one of his servants to open his door. The door opened and a small, older woman, who was Mr. Grey's cleaning lady said, "Lord Grey has invited you to come in please, Antonio." She then opened the door fully and Antonio walked in. The first thing he noticed was Mr. Grey standing, dressed impeccably, and grinning at him.

"Lord, you look fantastic," Antonio, said. He was wondering what was going on.

"Antonio I have two things to tell you, and they are both good news. The first is: You are now my second-in-command, not only for security, but also for all of Globocorp. A memo will be sent out this afternoon announcing it."

Antonio was visibly shocked. "My Lord, I surely don't deserve it. It means more to me than you could know. I'm truly touched that a man of your vision and greatness has such faith in me. I thank you from the bottom of my heart, Lord. The honor that you have just bestowed upon me is incredible, but please don't take this the wrong way. I would rather spend my life protecting you than have all the fame and fortune in the world. I wouldn't be able to do that with all the responsibilities

I would have. I just don't trust anyone else to protect you, my Lord."

"Antonio, you are my best and brightest." He smiled slyly. "You will still run security full-time. Now, when you need to go somewhere, all my power goes with you. I have also thought about this, Antonio. I have no living heir, and you and I are like brothers. If I die from any-thing, a sudden aneurysm, or any other way a man can die, you, Antonio Corvino, are my sole heir."

"My Lord," Antonio gasped, and fell to his knees in front of him.

"Antonio you must be of royal blood or a knight to accept this, so we will do this now. A small and quick ceremony for the time being, but when we get back I will throw a fabulous celebration ball in your honor."

A man dressed in a Constantinian-era Roman Commander's uniform walked in from the other room. He handed Mr. Grey a beautiful ancient, ceremonial, jewel-encrusted sword.

Admiring the sword, Mr. Grey said, "Constantine himself once held this sword. I, Lucifer Judas Santi-no, the last living direct descendant of Constantine the Great, hereby knight you as Sir Antonio Corvino. An-tonio, do you swear to uphold my plans to continue to fight for a one-world government?"

"I do, my Lord."

"Antonio, do you swear to fight to help me rule the world for the greater good of the planet, and its people?"

"I do, my Lord."

"Antonio, do you swear to help destroy one-third of the undesirable human population so that the planet can sustain life?"

"I do, my Lord."

"Rise, Sir Antonio Corvino, now the adopted heir of Lucifer Judas Santino and Constantine the Great."

Antonio stood up and another man walked in and stood in front of him. "Lord, may I now present, Sir Antonio Corvino, Constantinian knight, legal heir of Lucifer Judas Santino, with his sword, and his royal seal?"

"You may," allowed Mr. Grey. Then he said with a devious smile, "Antonio, hand those back to your servant. They will be placed in your suite. We have a plane to catch, Sir Antonio." He embraced him. "You have just taken a very stressful worry off my mind."

Mr. Grey was in his private quarters in his luxury jet. Antonio was sleeping in his private quarters, with orders to wake him fifteen minutes before landing. Mr. Grey's personal assistant handed him a phone. The call was from one of the men who were watching Captain Joseph Mills. The message said, "The package has been delivered." Mr. Grey relayed that message to Doctor Spears. He thought sometimes the good doctor was quite motivated. Doctor Spears had come up with the idea of moving everything closer to the target, which meant he could get started in one day instead of four. He really enjoys his work, Mr. Grey laughed.

Things were working perfectly. The American president's pain-in-the-ass pit bull, General John White, and his team would be dead in two days. He would then show Antonio that Raphe was killed in that jet explosion. He had Raphe's DNA. Mr. Grey's plan was that he would lie and say he had some of his men check the crash site. When the test results came back, it would be a positive match to Raphe. There would be no question.

The Americans had killed Antonio's only son and living relative.

He would feign sadness and then be able to tell Antonio that he had been so mad he found the bastard and his entire team. He would say he paid ten million dollars cash to a corrupt congressman who was able to give him the location of the team. He would tell Antonio that he had men on the ground to confirm it. Mr. Grey would say, as a personal favor to Antonio and himself, that he paid the corrupt American politicians one hundred million dollars to have their own men blow the bunker with twice the explosives necessary.

The only thing that remained of Raphe's murderer, General John White, and his team would be tiny microscopic pieces. The corrupt politicians would use the media owned by Mr. Grey and some of his allies to cover it up. They could pretty much say it was a volcano and the stupid-ass Americans would believe it. Then he would have his Antonio back with nothing to live for but hate, and his loyalty to him.

In the meantime, he had to get Antonio away from headquarters. Antonio was a workaholic. There was a slight chance Antonio could intercept a message and figure out his plan. They could let off some steam on his private sex-slave island paradise. He had to replace the vice president, who ran the place. It turned out he was a thief. He didn't mind a thief, but nobody took what was his! Lord Grey would make quite an example out of him. He was getting excited. Finally, a little adventure; he couldn't wait.

One of the flight attendants woke Sir Antonio. He got up and splashed some cold water on his face and looked at the time. Antonio sent some coded messages to his men on the island. He told them his ETA was ten minutes. Their arrival was not scheduled on the private airport's flight plan list. Antonio had control of the airport. He had his security men make sure the air traffic control had cleared the time slot and runway for their landing under a different name.

The vice president of Globocorps' entertainment division was James Robert Roland III, a spoiled-rotten, silver-spoon pedophile, and the grandson of one of the billionaires in Mr. Grey's globalization alliance group. James apparently thought he was above the law because his family was very rich and powerful. Mr. Grey had already contacted the head of his family and told him what was about to happen to measly James III. Mr. Grey also told him if he found out that any warning had reached little James that he was coming to punish him for his crimes... "Well," Mr. Grey said, "To put it simply, your entire family will cease to exist, James Robert Roland Sr. Did I make myself clear enough for you to understand?"

"Yes, Lord Grey. I am dreadfully sorry the boy has been a disappointment to you, Lord. If there is any way I can make this up to you, please let me know."

"I will James, and I am truly sorry for any pain this has caused you, but as you know discipline must be maintained. I am going to have to make an example out of him so that others stay in line with our plans."

"I understand, my Lord. A king must be respected."

"Good answer, James. I will not hold this against you or your family this time, but there are no second chances."

"Thank you, my Lord," James Sr. said.

Mr. Grey smirked; a man just thanked me for torturing and killing his grandson before I even do it. He found that exhilarating. His power had grown so much he could do anything to almost anyone without any consequences. He found out that James III had a fear of rats. Mr. Grey thought that was just perfect. He had Doctor Spears construct and supply him with a small portable Nano cell kit, complete with a signal sender built into his large Rolex watch. He had sent the enhanced pheromone ahead, to have one of his people make sure that little James III would be exposed to the synthetic pheromone the day before their arrival. Mr. Grey had brought James' replacement along to show him what happens when someone steals from him.

Antonio informed him that they were landing. "Please buckle up, my Lord."

"Antonio, come here, sit next to me, and buckle up. You are now the second most important person in the world."

Antonio smiled and shook his head affirmatively at Mr. Grey.

"I know you are worried, but we don't take unnecessary chances with our most important assets. You will have to learn to delegate some minor things. You can't do it all by yourself, Antonio."

"It's hard for me to trust anyone else when it comes to your security, Lord."

"I know, Antonio, but you must be professional and push your feelings for me away when we are on a mission together."

"Lord, you are absolutely right. My feelings, they have made your safety less efficient. You are a genius. Thank you for pointing out what I should have already known."

Antonio led the security detail from the airport to the main building, almost in the center of the island. The island was about ten miles from north to south and six miles from east to west. It was a small island, but beautiful. Top architects designed the landscape and buildings. Money was no object. Mr. Grey always had the best money could buy. This particular island more than paid for itself through sex trafficking and slavery. The most popular sex slaves were between twelve and eighteen years of age. If a customer preferred babies or toddlers, they were also available. Of course, they were quite pricey.

Here anything goes, from torture and murder, to cannibalizing babies and toddlers, made into a soup by a spirit-cooker witch. It was a sexual fantasy island with privacy guaranteed. Lifestyles of the rich and shameless, Antonio called it. Whenever there was a natural disaster, like an earthquake or a hurricane in any country around the world, the vultures would swoop in like they were there to help. Children or young teenagers were taken to the training facility. Their spirits were broken before being re-trained, and conditioned. There were also young adults available. The business was spreading on a global level, just like most other evils in the world today. There was even a fishing charter that went out daily. They would chum for fish, mostly sharks. The chum that was used was the ground-up fish; mixed with ground up body parts of any sex slave who had died the day before. It was the perfect setup to destroy evidence, although it was more of a convenience than a necessity. Mr. Grey had more power than the presidents and rulers of most other countries. Who would dare try to stop him out in the open? He was untouchable!

Antonio's men were waiting in the lobby of the main building when Mr. Grey's entourage pulled up. Antonio led the detail with Mr. Grey in the middle of a human shield wall. Their detail entered the lobby and Antonio sent a message to his snipers that they were headed to the vice president's office. The vice president's security cameras were not working. They had stopped working right before Mr. Grey's jet had landed. Antonio and three security men opened the door to the office and walked right in.

James III looked up. "How *dare* you walk in here unannounced!" he snarled. He had just been on the phone screaming at the security about the cameras not working.

Antonio said, "Am I addressing James Robert Roland, III?"

James said, "Yes, you are. Who are you?"

"I would like to announce the arrival of Lord Grey. He has come to discuss some business matters with you! James, before His Lordship enters this room, my men are going to make sure there are no weapons of any kind."

James stood up and slammed his fists on his desk. "What the hell is this? Do you know to whom you are speaking? I'll have you whipped for this intrusion! Lord Grey would never take time from his busy schedule to come here and visit me personally."

Antonio stunned him. When James came to, he was sitting in his chair at his desk. Sitting across from him was Mr. Grey himself. A look of shock crossed his face. James panicked. "Your Lordship! What an honor, my Lord."

Lord Grey smiled. "Sorry we had to stun you James. Sir Antonio is my second in command and the best security money can buy. He was following security protocol."

"I understand," said James. "They just caught me off guard."

"Yes," Mr. Grey sneered. "He is quite good at that."

Antonio was standing on his right side, and three others were standing at attention near the door. A covered box was on the ground to the left of Mr. Grey. "I'm a very busy man, James. I don't like it when people make me waste precious time…time that I could be using to better the world for mankind." James started to look very nervous. "I have talked to your grandfather and he has told me that you have been a disappointment to him."

"Lord, you know how family can be," he said, terrified.

Mr. Grey laughed, "Oh yes, James, I certainly do. My brother Antonio, that would be Sir Antonio to you, asked you politely to allow his men to clear the room for me. You, James, then said you would have him whipped. Did you not?"

"Lord! I had no idea who he was. My security cameras are down. I… I am very sorry, Sir Antonio."

"Well, see now, that's a start, James. You *do* have some manners after all. Let me get to the point of my visit. I have come to replace you, James. I don't mind a thief as long as he doesn't steal from me! *For* me is okay." Mr. Grey laughed at his joke. "*From* me is an absolute no-no, James."

"Lord, I have not stolen from you! This is all just some kind of mistake."

"Antonio, show James the evidence, please." One of the men handed Antonio a covered box with a handle on the top. Antonio placed the box on the desk and uncovered it. When he did, it revealed the decapitated head of George Sanchez through a clear plastic box. James shrieked. Mr. Grey asked James, "Do you recognize this man?"

"N-, n-, no, Lord." James replied shaking with fear.

"Are you sure James?" Lord Grey spun the box so James could see the face better.

"Y-, yes, Lord. I have never seen this man in my life."

Mr. Grey smirked at Antonio. "A thief and a liar. They both seem to always go together, don't they Antonio?"

"Yes Lord, they certainly do." Antonio nodded in confirmation

Lord Grey turned and glared at James, "This is George Sanchez, the head of one of my Cayman banks. Pardon the pun, James," he laughed. "George, your partner in embezzlement, told us the entire setup before he lost his head." He laughed at that one and so did Antonio. "James, you come from one of the most powerful families in the world. Don't worry James, I'm not going to kill you like your old buddy George here." Antonio covered up the box and handed it to one of the men. "No James, I'm here to replace you with a more trustworthy person; A person who would never be stupid enough to steal money from me, and then put it into a bank that I own. I want you to meet your replacement." A man walked in from the hall. "This is your replacement, Mr. Terry Dickinson. I have regained the funds that you and George stole from me. What do you think I should do with you, James? Your family has been disgraced by your actions and disloyalty. You have risked all of their lives for money. That, James, shows a complete lack of honor. Shall I have you whipped and sent back to the USA in disgrace?"

"Lord, please forgive me and let me make it up somehow!" James panicked.

"I'm sorry, James. I can forgive you, but I don't allow untrustworthy people to work for me. I have come up with a plan." Mr. Grey nodded at Antonio's men, and they grabbed James and cuffed his hands behind his chair.

James screamed, "Please, Lord, mercy! I'm sorry! I couldn't control myself!"

One of the men placed a pair of tight-fitting goggles on James. Then, Mr. Grey picked up the crate that they had brought in with them. He placed it in front of James and said, "I have heard you have a fear of rodents. If you do not scream as my pets crawl on you, I will let you go. If you do scream, I will let them tear you to pieces." He removed the canvas so James could see four full-grown rats in the cage. He moaned, and his eyes widened with fear at the sight of them. "Do we have a deal?"

James whimpered, "Please Lord. Please have mercy."

"Sorry James, these are your choices: pass the test of your fear of rats and go free, or join your friend George Sanchez. The two of you put your heads together to steal from me. In return, I will make sure your heads stay together, in the same box. Antonio does that seem fair to you?"

Antonio, controlling his laughter, said. "Yes Lord it's a stroke of genius. My Lord, may I say, you have a good head on your shoulders." Lord Grey and Antonio burst out laughing.

When their laughter died down, Lord Grey said, "Okay James, what is your choice?"

"Rats," George moaned, whimpering in fear.

Mr. Grey said, "Remember George just one scream and my pets will destroy you!" He looked at his Rolex. "Look at the time." The rats went totally, insanely, savage for a few seconds, and then he stopped the signal with his watch. James screamed his lungs out and was shaking. "James, it seems you still can't keep your word, buddy. I told you I wasn't going to kill you…"

James nodded.

"Like George," Mr. Grey said. "I'm going to kill you in a much different and more exciting way than George was killed. Ready James?" He asked his men if they were filming. One of the men said he was.

"Let them loose," he ordered.

Antonio opened the cage. The rats came out - sniffing and staring at James. He was screaming. Then, Mr. Grey turned on the signal. They all backed away as the rats attacked James so savagely, they tore his lips and face to the bone. One rat was halfway into his throat, and then it got all the way through, and it started coming out the other side of his neck. The goggles had fallen off and one of the rodents was digging James' eyes out. They continued to destroy him for a little over nine minutes before they died.

Mr. Grey looked down at his $7,800 suit. "Rats!" he said jokingly, "I've ruined my suit."

Antonio and Mr. Grey broke out laughing. They were both used to this kind of carnage. James' replacement, Terry, was unable to control his vomiting.

"Who feels hungry? How about some lunch? I'll buy." Both Antonio and Mr. Grey couldn't stop laughing. "Terry, go get cleaned up and get to work. Remember, this is what happens when you are disloyal."

"Yes, Lord," he cried out with one hand over his mouth, as he ran out and down the hall.

"Boy, he shows initiative." Mr. Grey was on a roll.

"Please stop, Lord! I may die laughing," Antonio sputtered out. They went out into the hall and calmed down.

"Good times, Antonio."

"I couldn't stand that traitor from the first day I met him until the last. Lord, why the goggles?"

"The animals seem to go for the eyes first, Antonio. I wanted James to see his fear devour him. Sir Antonio, are we secure?"

"Yes, Lord."

"Let's get a steam bath and a rubdown. Then, we can eat and take a walk. We can visit my harem of beautiful women I picked for myself. They're the cream of the crop. I have a special guard group that protects them. The guards have volunteered to be neutered. I'm the only one who can go there, but you have just been added to the list since the ceremony this morning. Antonio, these are the privileges of being royalty. After all the sacrifices we make, we deserve more than the ordinary men. We are smarter and better than others, and we are going to save this planet. Some inconsequential toys to play with are not too much to ask for. These ladies are lucky. Without us to use them for relaxation, they would be homeless filth or junkies. I make sure they are kept healthy and are not allowed out, except when I need to release some tension. It's okay to be as rough as you want. There are plenty if you need to replace one. Anything goes. Let's enjoy it."

Chapter Nineteen: Miracles and Blessings

John walked into the dining room and saw that dinner was already on the table. Ivory told him about the miracle that she just witnessed, and what Helen said about why Mary was sleeping. John walked over to Mary and put his hands on her shoulders, without explanation; it was almost like he had a supernatural urge to do so. He felt an energy that flowed out of him and into Mary. Mary lifted her arms and head off the table. She turned and looked at John.

"Thank you, John," she smiled.

John looked down at her and thought, Sweetheart, I would suffer and die for anyone on my team. I've never loved any group of people more. Jane and Mary, you have both shown me the love a father has for a daughter.

He told her, "Mary, I've done nothing. You know whom we should thank. He looked at her, Jane, Bobby, and Raphe. These four young beautiful children, well, young adults, are my gift from The Father to know a father's unconditional love. He said, "Mary, I love all you kids like you were my own. The choices I have made in my life have never allowed me to have a full-time family. Our Father has brought us together. I now know how it feels to belong to a real family. Blessing after blessing. Thank you, Jesus."

Jane ran up to John and hugged him. She said, "I love you too John. Like a dad."

Mary got up and hugged him. "Me too."

Helen walked over and joined the group hug, reminiscing about her own John. Ivory was standing near Susan and Tina. "Come on, group hug," she said. The three of them walked over and joined in. Then came Bobby and Raphe. They all felt an unconditional love so powerful, sweet, and peaceful.

They finally sat down to eat. Helen said, "Could I say grace tonight?"

"That would be nice," John said. "I love the way you say it, Helen."

"Thank you John." Helen smiled, and everyone noticed again how really beautiful she was.

Tina said, "Helen, you could have been a super model."

Helen laughed. "I'm not laughing at you, Tina. I was just imagining myself walking down a runway dressed in a crazy-looking outfit." She guffawed at the idea. "Give me a moment."

Jane said, "Sometimes mom has a funny sense of humor."

Tina asked, "Helen is your mom?"

"Yes," Jane said proudly.

"Wow! She looks too young to have a child your age."

Helen said, "Thank you Tina. Could we all hold hands, please? Thank you Father, for all Your wonderful blessings today, and for our two dinner guests. Thank you Jesus, for uncovering their eyes so they could see the truth. Thank you for healing Susan and saving Tina. Thank you for teaching Mary and Jane to be humble and giving them the wisdom to know that all good things come from you. In Jesus' name, we thank you. Amen."

Ivory's phone alarm went off. She took it out. It said 7:15 pm. She shut it off. "That's impossible," she gasped.

"What is it, Ivory?" asked John.

"My phone is reading that it's 7:15 p.m."

"It must be broken." He checked his phone, and it said the same thing. Everyone else checked the time on their devices and each of them also said 7:15 p.m.

Raphe said, "Have our electronic devices been hacked?"

Helen sighed. "It's okay people. God's time is not our time. Let's just relax and eat."

When they started eating, Bobby said, "Be careful! The food is just as hot as when we brought it out."

Helen said, "Blessings after blessings. Thank You Father."

Ivory said, "I have to go. I have set up a meeting for 7:30 tonight."

"Could you call up one of your techs and postpone it until 8:30?" John asked. "I would like to go with you and see how it's progressing."

Ivory winked, "That's a great idea." She called the group and left them a message saying she rescheduled the meeting to 8:30 p.m. She normally wouldn't do that, but she felt that God wanted them there for some reason.

Susan said, "Wow Ivory, I'm surprised, we're so close to figuring this out. You wanted to work all night!"

"I'm surprised too, Susan, but I have this feeling I'm supposed to be here."

John asked, "You're close to figuring out how they have been using the Nano cell tech to control these mammals?"

"No John. It's even better than that. We have already figured that out. We just have to figure out how to stop it." She smiled at him.

"You guys are fantastic. That is what I call a miracle."

"Yes, it is," said Helen. "Jane and Mary helped by obeying the Lord. I'm proud of both you girls today. Jane and Mary, do you know what makes me the happiest?"

"What?" They both asked.

"You both realized by yourself without anyone having to tell you. You are no better or worse than any of God's children. That's called wisdom, my beautiful, darling daughters."

Tina said, "I don't understand. How can Mary not be better than other people? I have never seen or felt anything like what she did in that lab for Susan, and for me."

Helen said, "Tina, do you think Mary actually was able to heal Susan, and to open your eyes to the truth?"

Tina hesitated, "But she did, Helen, I saw it and felt it."

"Tina, when you talked to Mary at that time, who did it feel like was talking through Mary?"

Tina tearfully exclaimed. "It was God, and it felt like pure love actually, better than pure love. Like, something I can't explain."

"It was the Holy Spirit sharing the glory and grace of our Savior, Jesus Christ."

Tina, still with tears in her eyes, asked Helen, "Why would the God of the universe take time to talk to me, Helen?"

"Didn't he tell you why Tina?"

Tina let the tears flow. She asked Susan for a tissue. "Helen, He told me He loved me and that He loved all his children. I am a child of God. I'm not evil; Helen, but I don't deserve Him. I have even told people that God hates," and she cried more.

"Tina, that's called the grace of God. Not one person on this planet deserves God's love. We all are sinners – every single one of us. The Lord loved us so much, that even after we wanted our own way and pushed Him away. He decided to allow His only son to become a man, and suffer more than anyone has ever suffered or will ever suffer. His son chose to suffer for us so that if we wanted to come back to Him of our own free will, we could. I mean, anyone who sincerely asks to be forgiven, and accepts Jesus Christ into his or her heart is forever with the Lord God in paradise. The problem that most people have is that when you have accepted Jesus into your heart, people think you instantly change into a non-sinning person who thinks that they are better than other people, because other people are sinners and we no longer are. That is not true. In fact, it's quite the opposite. Your eyes are opened to truth. You realize you needed to be forgiven just as much or more than all the people who have sinned against you. Tina, let me ask you a question. When Jesus forgave you, what was more of a relief... that you were able to forgive other people, or that you forgave yourself?"

Tina instantly knew the answer. "It was that I was able to forgive myself. I felt free to move forward."

Susan said the same. "Me too Tina. It was amazing."

"We try harder to not sin," Helen explained. "But we will all fall short. Little by little, we become convicted of our sin, which means God helps us to see it, and to try harder to stop it. God the Father sees us sinless because we are covered in the blood of His Son's sacrifice. We have not wasted His Son's sacrifice. The Father God views us as pure. We are part of His Son. When we enter the kingdom, we will be made pure in mind, soul, spirit, and body forever. The Son of God suffered for every single person, even the ones that He knew would not accept Him. Deep in every person, there is a part that knows the truth. You can say Buddha, or Allah, pretty much any other god's name in other religions, and people are fine with it. When you say the name of the true God, Jesus Christ, people freak out. Tina, the world is sin, and has persecuted our Savior. It will also persecute us. The persecution will steadily become worse until, when you mention the name Jesus Christ in a good and loving way. It will mean your execution. It has actually already happened to countless Muslims who have converted from Islam to Christianity."

Ivory told Susan and Tina that they could take some time if they wanted to stay and talk to the others. "John, Opt, and I are going to the meeting."

They both hugged Ivory and thanked her.

"Take your time. I'm so happy for you guys," Ivory said.

"Me, too!" John said. He hugged them. They had a hard time letting go of him.

Susan said, "General, you are giving off some serious love and peace vibes."

"It's amazing!" squealed Tina. Everyone else agreed.

Helen said, "You guys had better go. We can discuss this more later."

John and Ivory were walking toward her lab's meeting area with Opt. The dog stopped, lifted his head, and sniffed. Then he shook his head like his ears were bothering him.

"That's strange," John muttered.

"I'll examine him after the meeting," Ivory said.

"Thanks, my beautiful lady." Then he smacked her bottom. Ivory jumped and gave him a sexy smile. Opt barked and they both laughed at him.

Ivory turned. "Oh! John, I forgot to tell you, I've already loaded the bullet sled with the electromagnetic pulse emitters. I'm hoping to be able to load it tonight with the equipment that can stop any more Nano cell attacks."

"Ivory, are you serious?" He looked at her like she was the most amazing thing he had ever seen.

Ivory was excited, "John, you know I would do anything I could possibly do for you. I love you so much, sometimes it's hard to bear. I want to hug you so badly right now, but after what just happened at dinner, I'm afraid we will lose track of time."

"I know," John replied. "I feel the same, so let's get our work done, and have another mind-blowing night together."

Ivory gave him a hungry look and confirmed. "You have a deal, Mr. White. Why can't you be Mr. Black?" Ivory joked.

"If that's what you want, I'll do it," John said.

"Wait John, you really would?"

"Ivory, if it makes you happy, sure I would."

"I was just trying to make a joke; I love my new name. I can't believe you didn't even flinch before you said you would change it."

"Happy wife, happy life!" They both laughed.

"John, you are the sweetest, most amazing man in the world."

"Remember that the next time I act like an ass."

She said, "I'll try. All right, let's hurry before I can't resist your charm, and start tearing your clothes off right here in the hall." Ivory started to jog.

John jogged after her. "You're serious?"

"Yes!" Ivory said. "You have me wanting you so bad it's insane. Let's move." She started to run faster, and Opt ran on her left side.

"Opt! You little traitor!" John said.

Ivory looked down and smiled at Opt. "Good boy!"

John and Ivory walked into the meeting room with Opt. Ivory sat at the head of the table and John sat on her right side. Opt found a spot to lie down under the table, between the two of them. They were a few minutes early, mostly because they ran. Ivory was telling John about what they had come up with so far. She explained to him that one Nano cell was the main receiver, and when it received a signal, it turned on the other Nano cell that made the animals attack. She asked John if he knew anything about frequencies. He said he did, but very little. Ivory told him that they had figured out the frequency of the Nano cells' main receiver, which was the one they needed to stop. Anton had discovered that it was a low frequency, electric combination sonic, algorithmic ionic code. He was able to analyze the ionic algorithm on the supercomputer.

"The last time I talked to him, he was working on a device that would be able to track that exact signal from anywhere in space that it came from, and then block it."

John was baffled. "I kind of lost you when you said anywhere in space."

"Sorry. I mean any satellite in space," Ivory corrected.

"Fantastic! That's incredible. How do you think he's coming along with it?"

"We will know in a few minutes!" Ivory exclaimed with excitement.

People were coming in. Ivory received a text on her phone. It was from Anton. He said he was almost done and didn't want to stop. "If you absolutely want me there, text me. If you come see me after your meeting, it should be ready for testing."

She texted back, "Keep going, I'll see you after the meeting. Thanks." She showed the message to John, He smiled, looking surprised.

"Hello everyone! I have invited General White to the meeting. He has brought his dog, Opt, with him if anyone has any objections to being near a dog." She hesitated for a second. "You're welcome to leave if he makes you uncomfortable. However, I know from your files that none of you have any dog allergies or else I wouldn't have him here. Okay, that being said, the last time we were together you all witnessed an amazing miracle with your own eyes, ears, and feelings. I know you must have questions about that. I will say right now that Susan and Tina are resting up a bit, and are both in perfect health."

One of her techs spoke up. "That was the most amazing thing I've ever seen! I am a believer now. What do I have to do?"

Ivory didn't expect this sudden revival, although she was happy about it. She looked at John and he winked at her and said, "I got this Ivory."

He stood up and everyone quieted down. He said, "People, even though the world is at stake and we may be bombed at any given moment, I will take the time to help any one of you who wants to accept Jesus Christ in your hearts, and be forgiven for your sins. All you have to do is humble yourself. In other words, truly want it. I'm going to show you how I did it. If you want to, just do what I do and say what I say."

John got on his knees and said, "Jesus, please forgive me of my sins. Please, Jesus, forgive those who have sinned against me. Jesus, please come into my heart, and soul to be with me forever and ever. In your name I pray, Jesus. Amen."

All five people in that room besides Ivory and John accepted Jesus right then and there. Everyone could feel the Holy Spirit, and there was a flood of emotions and rejoicing. Ivory and John had already accepted Jesus, but still felt excited for their team. John let them hug and celebrate their new life, in Christ.

He stood up. "I know how you feel, and I'm sorry that we need to get down to business so quickly after your salvation."

They all sat down. "We understand, General," said some of the assistants.

"Thank you, Jesus," John proclaimed.

They all shouted, "Amen!"

Ivory stood up, wiping away a tear. "Its crunch time everyone. Now, tell me what we have." From what John gleaned from all the science jargon, they had done it. They had performed a miracle.

John said, "Through you few gifted people, God might have just saved the planet. If you don't mind working for me again or working steady with Doctor Black, I'm sure there are going to be more times like these coming up."

One of the techs, the body-builder John kicked out of the gym, said, "I can't wait," sarcastically, "But I'm in, General."

The rest of the team laughed. "We're in too."

Ivory stood up and said, "The General and I have to check up on Anton. Meeting adjourned."

General White left instructions with his two Green berets to load all intelligence and materials onto the bullet train.

When John and Ivory arrived at Anton's section of the lab, Ivory had never seen him so happy and less timid. Anton seemed like a different person. He approached them when he noticed them coming.

"Hello, Ivory. Hello, General. It's good to see you both."

"Who are you, and what have you done with Anton?" Ivory joked.

Anton paused for a moment before letting out a hearty belly laugh. "I get it, Ivory! You may not believe this, but I never understood joking before. You may not believe this either, after what I witnessed with Susan and Mary yesterday. I went to my room and asked Jesus into my life, and asked Him to forgive me and He did. I'm different now. I feel brave and happy. It's wonderful!"

John said, "Anton, I am so happy for you. You know, the rest of your team has just accepted Jesus into their lives, as well."

"Really? That is fantastic!"

"Is there anything we can help you with Anton?" Ivory asked.

"No," Anton said proudly. He smiled and said, "She's all done and tested Ivory. If a signal that operates those Nano cells comes from any satellite orbiting this planet, we will know and be able to block it within seconds."

"Anton, are we absolutely sure the signal comes from satellites?" John inquired.

"Yes General. The nature of the frequencies and the way the last horrific murder occurred, there is no doubt that the signal was from a satellite. The first murder scene signal could have come from a speaker outside somewhere. The difference was very minor. I discovered a very slight difference in the receiving Nano cells. The second murder scene, Nano cells had received the exact same power signature at the exact same millisecond. In the first scene, they were more random in signature power. It doesn't affect the second Nano chip that controls the animals' aggression; both reactions were identical at both scenes. General, it is also possible to make a smaller device to destroy the receiving Nano cell and stop an animal at a close range. Ivory already has a device I made to stop that, on her person."

John looked at her quizzically.

"Yes General, it's true, I do have it on me. Anton, I have offered a job to your team full-time. I now am offering you the same. General, I would like Anton to be the team leader in my absence, if he accepts."

Anton tried to contain himself, "Really guys? It's a dream come true for me! What an adventure! I accept!"

"Fantastic, Anton," John said. "Does Ivory know how to work this?"

"General, I don't believe there is much of anything Ivory doesn't know."

Ivory smiled warmly. "Blessing after blessing."

Anton and John said, "Amen," and laughed.

Ivory turned to Anton. "Could you make sure this is loaded safely in the bullet train A-SAP?"

"I'll do it myself right now."

John said, "We'll help you, Anton."

When they were done at the west tunnel where the bullet train was, Ivory said, "Tomorrow, we are having a late breakfast party at 10:00 a.m. at the other part of the compound. Tomorrow is the day we all leave. We want to give thanks to God."

Anton said, "Great! I'll be there."

John shook his hand, "Thank you, Anton."

"General, you may not believe this, but there is a positive energy flowing from you."

John chuckled. "I believe it Anton. It's a gift from God."

"Incredible, really? That is so cool!" Anton replied.

Chapter Twenty: Timing

"We are actually ready!" John said to Ivory. "It has been amazing, this whole crazy ride."

Ivory nodded, "Yes, it has Husband. Thank you for loving me through it."

"Ivory my whole life has changed since God put you in it. I'm so happy whenever I see or think of you; it feels like a dream, it's surreal. If time stopped flowing, my love for you would continue to flow - it's that strong, my genius, beautiful wife. Ivory write that down it was very profound, it should be recorded for future generations!" They laughed together.

They checked and double-checked the load on the bullet train. They were almost back to their meeting room when John said, "When we get back, I want to hold you and kiss you. We can have our team make sure we don't lose track of time."

"Great, let's hurry, it has been a while since I touched you, and I don't like not holding you when we are alone," Ivory pouted.

When Ivory and John walked in, it was around 10:00 p.m. everyone was still sitting around the table. Ivory said, "John and I are going to hug each other. Would you guys make sure we don't lose track of time?" She winked.

Helen said, "Okay people. Get the crowbars ready." She laughed, "Sorry, I'm tired. Go ahead guys," she giggled.

John hugged Ivory and kissed her. Finally, Bobby came up and shook them after ten minutes. "Sorry General, but it didn't look like you guys had any intention of stopping."

Ivory said, "It seemed like just a minute. How much time has passed?"

"Ten minutes," Raphe said with a smirk.

John was amazed. "Unbelievable. That is so strange. It really only felt like a minute or less passed. Helen, what do you think is going on?"

"John, it is that blessing you received from Jesus Himself. You said the grain of sand felt so powerful when you held it between your fingers that it could explode and start a universe. Then it melted into your soul and Jesus hugged you and wiped away your tears."

"Yes. That's right Helen."

"I'm sorry John. I have been thinking about it, but can't imagine anything except it comes in handy to cheer people up. God's ways are not our ways. The only thing I truly believe is that it's huge, and when the time is right, you will know what it's for. Until then, John, just have faith that God knows what He is doing."

"Thank you again, Helen, for your advice. We are hosting a breakfast at 10:00 a.m. tomorrow with everyone from the tech lab."

Ivory and John filled them in on everything that went on during the meeting. They also gave them the great news about the miraculous results that had been achieved, and how they were now able to stop the animal attacks.

"God is great!" Helen praised. "Let's all give thanks and go to bed. We have a big day tomorrow. Thank you; Lord, for blessing after blessing. We love you with all our hearts, minds, and souls. Keep us safe, and help us to know your will. In Jesus' name, Amen."

John asked Bobby and Mary to check on him and Ivory if they didn't see them up by 8:00 a.m.

"Sure," Bobby said.

Mary giggled. "I hope you're decent when we do!"

Helen asked, "By the way, how many guests are we expecting?"

"Eight, besides us," Ivory said.

The next morning, Bobby and Mary were banging on John and Ivory's bedroom door at 8:02 a.m. After a couple of minutes, John opened the door.

"Good morning, and thanks. If Ivory ever gets out of the shower, we will be right down."

"Really, John?" Mary asked. Her arms were folded across her chest and she was tapping her foot.

"No," he sighed. "It's a good thing you guys came. I was just thinking it's so amazing, you know, with the world crashing down all around us, I've never been happier."

Bobby and Mary shared a look, and then glanced back at John. Bobby said, "I've thought about it and yes! It really is amazing."

Mary said, "You know, I've always been in a place in my life where I had to be tough. I was always scared and worried, and I'm not scared anymore." Mary gave John a serious look and scolded, "I hope you two love-birds are finished, because you don't want me to have to come back here." John's face turned slightly red. Mary and Bobby started laughing.

As they left, Bobby said, "See you in a little bit, General."

Ivory and John entered the dining room with Opt. Ivory said, "John, Opt seems to be acting like something is bothering his ears. I forgot to check him out last night."

Chapter Twenty-One: What a Rush

Ivory said, "Good morning everyone! We are going to go to John's office so I can check out the dog. I don't think he's feeling well. It might be an ear infection. We won't be long, and we will come right back to help out."

"Take your time, we got this covered," said Helen. "We will say a prayer for Opt."

"Thanks Helen," John said gratefully.

When they went into John's office, they both started looking for a small flashlight that John had. "It's on one of those tables. I was using it yesterday."

"There it is!" exclaimed Ivory. "It's on the table with all those photographs." She walked over to get it. When she looked down, she froze. "I...don't believe it."

"What is it Ivory?" John asked.

"This man, right here," she pointed at a man escorting a beautiful young lady. They were both dressed for a formal affair.

"Yes? What about him, Honey?"

"John, this guy is Doctor Robert Jennings, I'm sure of it. He and I were both considered the two top people in our fields of Nano cell technology. I worked with him for close to six months in the past. I am a good judge of character, and I can tell you this man is a good man.

He has not been heard from or seen by anyone in over seven years. I don't know if he's been declared legally dead, but most people assume he is dead. This is a good picture. Do you see that squiggly, reddish mark on his nose? It's not very big, but it's visible and he was born with it. That is a birthmark, and it's exactly the same shape and size of the birthmark Doctor Jennings has. He has aged some and looks pale. What are the odds that he has an identical twin with the same birthmark?"

"That would explain a lot, Ivory. Do you think this guy would willingly work for Mr. Grey to get rich?"

"No! He is already wealthy. His drive and main ambition were to help sick children, and to help cure sickness, and disease. Doctor Jennings is a genius and slightly nerdish. Oh, my goodness!" Ivory said.

"What, Ivory? You're making me nervous."

"What if Mr. Grey lied to him, and funded his research in a hidden facility for the last seven years? That's the same amount of time Doctor Jennings has been missing. Then Doctor Jennings comes through and is flown to Grey's castle to celebrate. Meanwhile, they destroy all evidence of his accomplishments, and anyone who knows about it. They don't want him dead yet, unless he doesn't agree to keep researching to adapt his technology to humans." Ivory took a minute to rationalize her own hypothesis. "He won't do it John. He has very stubborn ethics. He may be gullible, but he won't do that because he knows that is too much power for any human being to have. We had even talked about scenarios like this when we worked together. That is one of the reasons we were partnered. Usually, two established scientists in the same field won't work together. Egos or arrogance get in the way. I was suspicious when I learned he wanted to work with me. When we met and talked a while, I knew all he really cared about was helping people."

"Just like you!"

"Yes. But I also needed money to live on. He didn't. Do you think we can save him too? If we don't, Mr. Grey will kill him."

"He has just been put on the list of people to be saved."

"Thank you John. Ivory picked up the small flashlight, and called the dog to her. "Now, let's see what's going on with you, Opt." Ivory looked in his ears, but they looked fine. Opt shook his head again. He seemed to be doing it a lot more.

"I've never seen him act this way before, Ivory," John said. "It's like he's got a different personality, and he gets less excited about things."

Ivory looked at John and was very concerned." John...what time is Joe due to get here?"

"1:00 p.m. Why?"

"Did you send the pilot our coordinates yet?"

"Yes, they took off ten minutes ago. It's a three-hour flight."

Opt started growling at them. John ordered, "Down!" Opt didn't listen. He leaped to attack Ivory. John grabbed him around the neck in an arm-lock; he was having a hard time holding Opt back. His dog was incredibly savage, so John took out his knife.

"Wait!" Ivory said. She got as close as she could to Opt's head. She pushed a button on a small device in her hand and the dog passed out.

Just then, Mary and Bobby burst in. Bobby said, "We have to go, now!"

Mary saw Opt and put her hand on his head. "This good beast is healed and immune, in Jesus' name."

Opt woke up, and John put him down. He started barking and running toward the door, almost as if to say, "Let's move people!"

"Does anyone else know?" John asked Bobby.

"No. You were the closest to where we were." They ran to the dining room.

John shouted in his command voice, "Let's go, everyone! As quickly as possible! It is emergency protocol! You Green Berets, take charge of your team! Evacuate! My team, to the bullet train, now!" The tech team's exit was closer than the bullet train.

John was pushing his team to go faster because he knew it would be close. He silently thanked God that they all could run and were in fairly good condition for civilians. They were almost there. Just then, he thought he heard animal noises coming from the main eastern tunnel. Opt was barking in that direction. John opened the doors on the bullet train, and ordered everyone to get in. He called for Opt, but the dog was trying to guard them and didn't listen. Ivory called Opt to her and he came. John closed the steel door just in time. He was hearing smashing and clawing noises seconds after the door shut. He got in and checked that all systems were going, and then pushed the launch button.

They started off a little slow, but picked up speed as they went. They were traveling about sixty-five miles per hour. They slowed and came to a stop. John opened the doors and got out quickly. He closed the two-inch thick, steel doors to the tunnel they had just come through. He then pushed a button that blew up and caved in a forty-foot section of the tunnel. Everyone else got out and started to unload the gear and tech equipment that Ivory needed to stop these attacks. The problem was that she needed it installed in a facility that could boost the signal, and reach a satellite.

"Wait here," John said. "I'll be right back."

All of a sudden, more lights came on and the team noticed how huge this place really was. The room they were in was the size of a ten-car garage, and there were doors leading to more rooms. A big piece of the wall slid sideways, and they could see another bigger area. They could also see what looked like John walking toward them with at least fifteen or more other people. When they got closer, it looked like John was walking and talking to the president of the United States. There were also two generals and an admiral, plus every other conceivable ranking officer running around doing their respective duties, given the situation.

"You *have* been busy, General White," Ivory said with amazement.

"Yes, I have, Doctor Black." He smiled, "But we are a little early. I was able to get a message to Joe telling him to abort, that it was a trap, and I was in the process of a rescue mission with a high probability of success. I used our code, so he'd be sure it was from me. I received confirmation from him. Joe can handle himself. Now it is up to us to save his family. I told the president to be on the watch for any kind of aircraft flying over our location. Unfortunately, they were able to accomplish part of their mission before; supersonic ground-to-air missiles shot down their drones. Our Air Force was able to track a signal that was controlling a spy drone to an underground bunker. A SEAL team raided it, killing some people, and capturing some very nasty people. After the animal attack, they were going to launch a bombing drone to erase the Nano cell evidence, and kill Joe while he was in our compound observing all the carnage. One of the people captured was our enemy's head researcher, Doctor Spears. The rest of them were mostly mercenary types."

Helen started walking toward the president. One of his Secret Service agents was just about to stop her when the president said, "Helen McClain! Is that really you?"

"Yes Ronald. It is."

"Come over here please Helen, and give me a hug."

Helen ran over and hugged him. "I have missed you Uncle Ronald," she said with joy.

"You have made my day. Wait until Evelyn hears I saw you," the President said lovingly.

"Give her my love Ronald."

"General White, this is unbelievable! How did Helen wind up on a mission with you?"

"Sir, that is a long story and would take hours to tell."

"Well when you get back, you're all coming to dinner, and telling the whole incredible story," ordered the president.

"Time is our enemy Mr. President," John said. "There is a device that can stop these attacks. Doctor Black will need to show our people how to operate it."

Ivory stepped up to the front with the signal-blocking transmitter. "Mr. President, who can I instruct on this device?"

"General Charles and Colonel Carson," said the president.

General Charles was the first female five-star General and the highest-ranking officer in the entire Air Force. She walked up to Ivory and said, "Finally! I get to meet you Doctor. If you had stayed in the Air Force, you would probably have my job."

"Thank you, General, that is a nice compliment coming from such an accomplished person such as yourself."

General Charles nodded, then said, "Doctor Black this is Colonel Carson. He is our best scientist and researcher."

"It's a pleasure Doctor Black," he said, shaking her hand. "I have studied some of your theories and experiments. You are an amazing person. I'm a huge fan, Doctor."

"Thank you, Colonel Carson. Let me show you how this works and give you all the schematics. This device may save millions, or even billions of people, so be very careful with it, and make more of them as soon as possible. We need to boost this signal and have it adapted to our satellite systems; to be able to block the signal that starts these animal attacks A-SAP. This is the only one, and it is a miracle we were able to make it in the time frame we had."

"Yes Doctor Black. We will start right now." Colonel Carson called a group of technicians and engineers over and handed them the device and the schematics. "Be careful with this!" he ordered them. "This is a prototype. Start building at least two more right now and don't stop until they are done."

"Yes Sir." They left and went into an enormous plane equipped with a high-tech lab.

Colonel Carson said, "Doctor, perhaps someday we could discuss some science and bounce ideas off each other."

"Colonel, I love doing that. Could I bring my husband along? He's taken an interest as well."

"Sure. That would be fantastic. You would get along with my wife. She loves your work, also. We'll do it when you get back, Doctor." He saluted her, and she saluted right back.

General Charles turned to Ivory. "If you ever want to get back in, even as a consultant, here is my personal cell number. Just give me a call." She handed Ivory her card with her number on it. "Goodbye Doctor, and good luck."

The president wanted to meet Bobby and Raphe. As he was walking toward them, a Secret Service agent whispered something in his ear. The president gave him a funny look and said, "Really?"

Helen knew what his agent had told him by the look on the president's face. "Raphe is now family, Ronald. He is married to my Jane. Bobby is married to Mary."

Bobby and Mary were closest to him. The president shook Bobby's hand first. "Son, I'm proud to know you. General White told me your story. I promise you Bobby I will never let you down. If I weren't so old, I would go with you."

"Thank you Mr. President," Bobby said. "That really means a lot Sir."

Then, President Ronald Jefferson looked at Mary and said, "Mary, you are a very beautiful young lady, and Helen has told me you're her daughter now. So you can call me Uncle Ronald." He hugged her much like her father used to.

She gave him her best smile and said, "Thank you Uncle Ronald."

He shook Raphe's hand. "The famous Raphe Corvino. The General has given me a report on you, and Helen has told me she loves you. My niece Jane loves you. We are family now. I am very happy about one thing, Raphe."

"What's that, Mr. President?" Raphe asked nervously.

"I'm happy you're on our side now." They both laughed. The President hugged Jane. It was the first time he'd seen her since she was a toddler. "You're as beautiful as your mother, and that is saying something. Your dad was one of my dearest friends. When you all come back to the White House for dinner, we will have so many stories to talk about. Much doesn't usually excite me, but there is a feeling of profound love and peace around you people." They all looked at John. The president said, "More stories for when you get back? Helen, are you sure you have to go?"

"Ronald, it's God's will," Helen asserted.

"All right. Be careful please, all of you. Helen can you lead us in prayer?"

Helen closed her eyes and bowed her head. "Father, give us the wisdom to follow your path, even when we want to do the opposite. Help John, our leader, to be wise and victorious. Thank you Lord, for all your blessings, and thank You for this meeting with my dear Uncle Ronald. In Jesus' name we pray. Amen."

The President went up to John and hugged him. When he let go he said, "This is God's mission son, we are just lucky to be called to serve. John, if God is with us no matter what, we have already won. I am proud to serve with you, General White."

John said, "Thank you Sir," then he stood at attention and saluted the President, and the President did the same.

The President then said, "Godspeed to all of you."

Chapter Twenty-Two: The Mission

The group was ready for takeoff. They were on a slightly larger phantom jet with stealth technology. The jet would fly at supersonic speed with two fuel stops on Navy aircraft carriers. The closest carrier to their target had four large helicopters for their support teams. Three were for Navy SEALs. The fourth one was for rescue and medevac.

When Mary heard John explain this, she said, "You didn't forget about the distraction, did you?"

John put his hand on her shoulder and said, "Mary, don't worry. I hope your plan works. It sounds good, but a lot of lives are riding on it."

"General, it was just a suggestion. It's not my plan! I'm only a college student for goodness sake."

John started laughing. "Mary, it was an excellent plan, and a lot of precision and timing went into your fantastic idea." The rest of the team laughed because they saw how nervous Mary was.

"Whew! I don't know how you do it?"

"Mary, God is in charge of the mission. He is responsible. His will shall be done."

"Thanks General. That just took a huge weight off my shoulders."

"I know exactly what you mean, Mary."

They were making their approach for their first landing, and it went smoothly. Everyone was able to get out, use the bathroom, and stretch their legs. John got out to talk to the Commanding Officer. He knocked on his door and the Captain's lieutenant answered.

"Tell the Commanding Officer I need to speak with him A-SAP," John said.

"Who may I say you are, Sir?"

"General John White, FCIC."

"The General of what service or agency, Sir?"

"The General of NET. Tell him that if he doesn't speak to me in one minute, I'll have him court-marshaled and thrown in the brig." John used his command voice. He was thinking time is an enemy.

The Commanding Officer appeared. "Finally, the Captain himself!" John said.

The Captain said, "How would you like-"

John interrupted him with his command voice, "Quiet. Sit at your desk and read this, then have your lieutenant escort me to the proper area. Captain, this is a priority 1-A emergency. Time is an enemy, Captain. I need to send an encrypted message A-SAP."

"Lieutenant, escort the General to the communications center. He needs to send an encrypted message, double-time son!"

"Yes Sir. Follow me General." They moved swiftly to the message center. "General, this is our encryptions officer."

"Thank you Lieutenant, you're dismissed." General White addressed the encryptions officer, "Lieutenant Stark I need this sent now, exactly how it is written. I will wait for confirmation." John had about five minutes before the jet would be ready for takeoff. He watched Lieutenant Stark send the message, and in thirty seconds he received a confirmation.

Lieutenant Stark looked at John and said, "Your confirmation, General White, from the President of the United States of America, in thirty seconds. Sir, that's amazing."

John looked at the Lieutenant. Using his command voice, he said, "Son, this never happened."

"Yes Sir," Lieutenant Stark answered.

John hurried back to the jet. He called down to see if it was fueled up yet, but was told he had to wait five more minutes. Perfect, he thought. John needed to use the bathroom, and just as everyone was boarding, he returned, Perfect timing-so far, so good.

The phantom jet took off and made good time to the next aircraft carrier. This time, the Commander Officer was waiting for them and personally escorted him to the message center. When they entered the message room, they were ready for him. General White told them to send it exactly as it was written.

"I will wait for confirmation," Commanded General White. This time, it only took twenty-eight seconds for confirmation from the president. The lieutenant said, "Amazing, Sir."

"This never happened, son," General White said again, using his command voice.

"Yes Sir!"

The General headed directly for the jet. He ordered the Captain to follow him. General White had a job for the Captain. They were still fueling up and said it would be close to five more minutes. He figured to hurry up and wait was fine with him. They were on time so far.

The Captain asked John, "What does FCIC and NET stand for?"

"Field Commander In Chief. NET stands for National Emergency Team. It is a necessity when we are in a national or worldwide priority 1-A emergency. Believe me Commander; it is not a title I am happy to use. It's always connected to scary shit. Captain, our President tells me you're a good man."

"Really?"

"Yes," John said. "I cannot stress this enough. This *never* happened. Captain, our country has been infiltrated by enemies. I want you and other people that you are sure you can absolutely trust to personally watch and monitor all communications. Make sure your ship sends out no communications for the next twenty-four hours unless it's absolutely necessary, then you must personally do it. Captain, my presence here and my mission are above top secret, you will not mention it or allow anyone else to. I know that you have told your communications officer not to tell anyone about myself, and the message he sent and received. I would like you to let him know if he does, he will be arrested for high treason in a time of national emergency. Those are your orders Captain!"

General White handed him a sealed envelope, and told him to read it then hand it back to him. The Captain opened it and read the following: The United States is in a national state of emergency! General John White has complete authority as Commander in Chief, second only to me. His orders will be obeyed immediately as if they were mine. General John White is my Commander in Chief in the field. Failure to obey his orders in a time of emergency is high treason! Signed... President Ronald Jefferson. The Captain saw his personal code on the message that only the President, Vice President, and very few others would know.

"Yes Sir, General White!" The Captain stood at attention and said, "I won't let you down, Sir.

"At ease Captain. The fate of our country, and even the world, might depend on it."

"I won't let our country down General."

John put his hand on the captain's shoulder, and he knew that the commander meant what he said. "I know you won't, Captain."

As John was leaving, the Captain said, "Good luck Sir," and saluted.

John saluted, then headed for the jet. He was just in time, as they were boarding. Ivory looked at him and smiled. He thought, each time that she looks at me like that makes me thank God that she is my wife.

They were on approach to their mission control aircraft carrier. John's entire being started to transform from a regular person to a warrior, focusing on the mission. Every thought, every sense, was about this mission. The timing and execution of every aspect were ingrained in his mind. He pictured every move he would make and every order he was to give. Timing and contingency plans were the keys to success on every mission. He looked at his team and went over the plan again.

"Ivory and Helen?"

"We go with you, General."

"Raphe?"

"I lead a twelve-man SEAL team to the main area that controls electrical power, alarms and communications. We plant the E.M.P. devices then fall back until they go off. After they go off we move in and secure the area. Then we search the outer buildings for the people on our rescue list."

"Bobby?"

"I lead a ten-man team to plant our demolition charges for two gas-like explosive diversions, then make our way back to the castle to help out the other teams."

"Jane and Mary?"

"We stay with the medical chopper."

John said, "Ivory, Helen and I will lead a twelve man team to search the castle. We will secure the area and rescue any prisoners we find. All teams will confront the enemy with extreme prejudice. We take no enemy prisoners. The only people we take are people that are on our list. Any questions?" Nobody spoke.

"Fantastic," John said. He felt confident in his team, even his rookies. "Check your gear," he told them. They all checked their gear. "Confirm with your list." They all confirmed. "I have to go check with the other teams. Before I go, I have one bit of advice. Be the mission. Think of nothing else except contingency plans if needed. Do not daydream; remain alert. Watch your stress levels. Try to remain as calm as you can."

Helen asked, "John? Can I say a quick prayer?"

"Please, Helen. Go ahead."

They all held hands. Helen closed her eyes and said, "Lord God, we are entering an evil realm, but You are with us and there is nothing that can stand against us. Your will be done in our mighty king's name, Jesus Christ, the King of Kings."

"Amen," they all said.

"Great job Helen. I'll be back in an hour. Try to rest if you can. When I come back, I'm going to take you to meet the other teams. Ivory, you're going to make sure the team that plants the electromagnetic pulse emitters knows how to operate them. Bobby and Raphe, your job will be to coordinate the exact timing sequence of every move we have planned for this mission."

They both looked at him skeptically.

"Don't worry, I have already done it. I just want you to check it for me and make sure I didn't screw it up."

The ladies giggled. The General stopped them with a stare and continued. "The rest of you, just make sure you know your part and study the whole plan. We have eight hours before we start this mission and it has to look like we were never there."

Chapter Twenty-Three: Old Friends

Colonel Alex Barns and three SEAL team Captains were waiting for him. He smiled at Colonel Barns and he smiled back. John believed, once you've gone to battle with someone, they are forever ingrained in your mind for good... or, sometimes, for bad. Alex had been John's commanding officer years ago. John was in his late twenties and Alex had been close to forty back then. John walked up to the Colonel and his SEALs. They were standing at attention.

He saluted them. "At ease. Colonel Barns, I was thinking about you the other day. I thought my old Captain is probably retired, sitting at home knitting finger puppets for his great-grandchildren."

"Excuse me General, but will your husband be joining you?" Colonel Barns replied. They both laughed and grabbed each other in a bear hug.

"It's great to see you Alex. It gives me some relief that someone with a brain will be in charge of home base."

"John, you don't know how many times I've talked about you in training and to the men for morale. It is an honor for me just to have served with you."

"All right. Enough bullshit Alex."

"John, I'm serious! Do you know that half the training manuals and tactical maneuvers have been rewritten because of you? You are a legend with the Navy SEAL teams."

"I only did the best I could with the gifts I was given. Are the men ready for briefing? Time is an enemy, Alex. You taught me that."

The Colonel smiled and saluted. "Yes, General White. Your men are ready, prepped, and waiting Sir."

"Lead the way Alex. We have a lot to do in a short amount of time." John addressed the Captains on their walk to the meeting room. "Captains, have your teams and the rooms been checked out and secured?"

"Yes Sir, General," they answered. Colonel Barns said, "the rooms and the perimeter have been swept for any spyware or any kind of electronic or sonic devices, General. We have Navy SEALs guarding the perimeter Sir!"

"You *do* get it done, Colonel." John smiled about some memories from past missions with him. "Colonel Barns, I am personally proud to be able to work with the best commanding officer I ever had. When you see how vital this mission is to the security of our country, you will realize that having the best men available is a necessity, and not a luxury."

They headed for the door. Colonel Barns opened it. The Master Sergeant shouted, "Attention on deck!"

The men all stood at attention. John walked up to the podium. He looked around the room, sizing up his men.

"At ease," he ordered.

The men relaxed a little. The rumors and theories had been spreading around since these men had arrived. They had been kept in isolation from the rest of the crew, and were not allowed to communicate with anyone but each other.

"Men, my name is General John White."

The room all of a sudden became noisy. John looked around at the team. He had been in the same position many times. He knew these men were thinking that this was something big. He could feel their excitement. John knew that every man in this room had heard of him, and of his record. He *had* become famous, a legend. He thought about it, I'm just like these guys – no better or worse. It is a man's choices that make him what he becomes. John decided to tell these brave men who were willing to put their lives on the line for God and country, the truth. He shouted for them to stand at attention: the men immediately did as they were told. There was complete silence.

"Men, you are Navy SEALs and the cream of the crop. Many different people, including myself, have handpicked you. I have decided to ignore precedence today. I have decided to let you know exactly what this mission is all about. I have never done this before; as a matter of fact there are very few missions where a SEAL gets to know all the facts. What are we going to accomplish during this mission? What is so important about this mission? I am going to tell you men everything. This is labeled above top-secret level. The reason is that failure is not an option. I believe you all need to know what it is you will be fighting for." He looked at them and smiled. "At ease. Be seated."

The men relaxed and sat down.

"Some of you may have heard of me."

He heard most of them give a short laugh, as if to say, "Who hasn't?"

"Most of you are intelligent." He heard some chuckles. "Men, you know about legends. Most times, they are exaggerated. In my case, they were not. As a matter of fact, they were underrated. I am not saying I am better than anyone else in this room. I am not saying I have never failed at anything. I *am* saying that everyone in this room is as good as me. You may ask yourself, why do I think this? The plain, simple truth is, we are Navy SEALs, and we kick some serious ass! We have been secretly saving our country for generations. We don't back down! We can't be beat, and only very stupid people piss us off!"

Every single man in that room cheered, "HOO-YAH!"

"My wife has a sticker on her laptop that says, 'I have fought with a Navy SEAL and survived.'" Everyone laughed.

"My brothers, she is the only one that can say that. You, my warrior brothers in arms, you have been hand-picked by the president of the United States of America. The United States of America is in trouble men. This mission is the most important mission I have ever been on. I am not exaggerating. If anyone else besides the best of the best Navy SEALs were not chosen for this mission and it failed, it would mean the end of our country, and possibly the Third World War." He used his command voice. "Do you understand me brothers?"

Every man in the room stood up and yelled, "Sir! Yes Sir!"

"Warrior SEALs, your country needs you. This is where we have drawn our line in the sand. Before I get down to business and fill you in on this mission, I have to say one thing that is extremely important: If we leave any evidence that can prove we were there, we lose. That, my brothers, is the tricky part. Being a badass Navy SEAL is not only kicking ass but also doing it with extreme intelligence. We are lions with IQs off the charts. We are invisible. We go in, get it done, and get out before most people can blink. One more thing, this is strictly a volunteer mission. John raised his voice and shouted! Do I have any volunteers?"

The room went crazy. Every man in that room was on his feet yelling, "I'm in, General White!"

He said, "Sign in, and I'll be back with my training team and the plan. Thank you, my fellow SEALs."

Everyone was signing in. John was a good speaker, and his words felt like they were dripping with truth.

John and Colonel Barns were walking back to the jet to bring all the equipment and plans back to the meeting room.

The Colonel said, "John, that was the best speech I have ever heard in my life. I have goose bumps on my arms. I'm telling you Son, I want to go with you myself. I know you were the best I've ever trained, but you're different. I can't explain it, but it's like you're leaking bravery and confidence and everyone is catching it."

"Alex, buddy, I'm the same guy you knew."

"In some ways John, but you looked like some ancient super warrior up there. I can honestly say I don't believe that any other man in the world could have gotten those men so gung-ho. Those are some of the smartest and toughest men in the world. Every one of them was looking at you like you were Samson and Einstein put together as one man. General, you're their hero. Those guys love you. I think I just witnessed a miracle."

"Me too Alex. Come on. You won't believe what kind of miracle we will need tonight, or the evil we're fighting against."

When they got back to the jet, men were already loading small transport trucks with the equipment they brought for their plan. Ivory and Bobby were organizing and supervising.

John and Colonel Barns walked up to Ivory. "Alex, I would like you to meet my beautiful wife, Doctor Ivory Black."

"Hello Mrs. White, it's my extreme pleasure to meet you." Alex shook her hand.

"Hello Alex, the pleasure is mine," she replied with a smile.

"Alex is the officer in charge of home base while we're out there. He was my commanding officer when I was younger."

"John, is *this* Alex - the one you told me was the best officer you ever had?"

"Yes. He is now Colonel Alex Barns."

"Mrs. White, I never thought I would hear those words. General, I thought you were married to your country. It warms my heart to see you were lucky enough to find such a breath-taking, beautiful lady."

"Call me Ivory, Alex."

"Ivory, call me Alex when we're not in front of the men. John is the best and most loyal man I know, but I still think he got the better deal. John, how did you get this sweet young lady to say yes? Tell me you didn't use the voice."

Ivory laughed, "No, he didn't! And so far, he has only done it once, and it was an emergency."

John blushed. "I don't know what you guys are talking about."

Ivory and Alex both laughed.

"Alex, I need to have Ivory explain the operational details of the toys she has brought for our men. I also need to bring in Bobby and Raphe to help explain in detail our entire plan and its timing. I'm bringing in my entire team to help our men learn it."

"John, where is your team?"

"You're looking at them, Alex."

"You're bringing your wife and three women with you?"

"Yes Alex, just trust me, it is absolutely necessary."

"Hello Colonel Barns," Helen said as she smiled.

"Ma'am, please call me Alex." They both stared at each other.

John couldn't believe it. "Helen," John said. She didn't answer. He looked at Ivory, and she looked at him and shrugged.

Ivory said, "The Lord works in mysterious ways, John."

"I guess so, but time is an enemy. Alex," John said a little louder. Alex looked over.

"Yes John? What do you need?"

Before John could answer, Helen asked the colonel, "When we get back, Alex, how about you and I have dinner...and maybe some dancing?"

Colonel Barns said, "Helen, I don't think I could possibly be rude enough to say no to such a lovely lady." They both smiled as he took her hand, and helped her down.

"Thank you, Alex. You are quite a gentleman."

"It's my pleasure, young lady."

Helen giggled.

John rolled his eyes. *"This* is Raphe Corvino."

Colonel Barns said, *"The* Raphe Corvino? One of the deadliest assassins in the world?"

"Yes," Helen chirped. "But now he's a good guy!"

Jane said, "Paul the Apostle killed Jews before our Lord Jesus opened his eyes."

Astonished, the colonel said, "Yes, that's true, young lady."

Helen introduced Jane. "Alex, this is Jane, my daughter, and Raphe's wife."

"Young lady, you certainly are beautiful like your mother."

Jane blushed, "Thank you Alex. I also think she is the most beautiful woman in the world."

Colonel Barns was shocked, "Did I say that out loud?"

"No Alex," said Helen. "Jane just needs to mind her manners."

Jane whispered, "I think he's handsome too mom."

John cleared his throat. "Alex, this is Lieutenant Bobby James. He is married to Mary, Helen's adopted daughter."

"Wait a minute. Were you with the team that was compromised by a treasonous politician? You accomplished your mission and made it back wounded? You received the Silver Star?"

"Yes Sir, I am."

"I'm sorry, son. My nephew, Peter, was on your team."

"I'm sorry Colonel. I threw the Silver Star in a garbage can somewhere in Virginia. Peter was a good man. I still pray for him every day."

"Thank you, son. Bobby, I want you to know the corrupt politician has been punished with extreme prejudice."

"Thank you for telling me Sir. At least I know he won't be able to sell patriotic lives to fatten his wallet anymore."

"Bobby, you never re-enlisted. We had big plans for you. You remind me of this big lug when he was younger." He pointed at John.

"Thank you Sir, that's quite a compliment."

"Bobby, if you want back in, just say the word."

John said, "Alex, he *is* back in. When we get back, both these lieutenants will be promoted to captain."

"I don't know why Helen or any of the civilians are going with you, but I have faith that you know what you're doing."

Helen straightened up. "It's God's will, Alex," she said proudly.

"Well then, If God is with us, who can stand against us Helen?"

"Nobody Alex. Would you mind escorting me?"

"I would be delighted, Helen."

She placed her arm in his. Alex smirked, "General, I am so glad you're back with such a kick-ass team." Helen and Alex laughed with each other and started heading toward the secret meeting room with the supplies and plans.

John just shook his head. "Ivory, I would never have imagined or dreamed of having a team like ours. It goes against a soldier's instincts to bring civilian women and children into battle. The SEAL teams are going to think I'm crazy."

"John, after we work with them and get the plan down, I have a feeling we will fit right in. Don't you worry about a thing General White!"

"I know it's God's plan that we all go, but some of these guys don't have the faith that I do. At least maybe not yet."

"Remember," Ivory said, "God brought us here, not you. Have faith that He will handle it. He has to this point, and will continue to do so."

"I'm not worried about them not following orders. I just want them at their peak performance rates."

"You sound like you're talking about machines, John!" Ivory exclaimed.

"These men are like machines - high-performance, technologically advanced, high-speed machines. They are handpicked Navy SEALs; the best and most intelligent elite group of fighting men on the planet."

Ivory stopped him and looked into his eyes, then kissed him hard and fast. "Can they do that, General?"

He smiled at her and said, "No, Ivory."

She smiled back. "Chill out, stud. Remember, blessing after blessing. We now have an army of mighty men like King David had."

"Yes, we do Ivory, thank you."

"You are most welcome. It's a calming technique my husband taught me, my sweet General," and they both laughed.

Colonel Barns was leading the way arm-in-arm with Helen. When they approached the door to the secret meeting room, two guards saluted the colonel. Helen stepped to the side while he instructed the men. John told Ivory to stay with him, while the other members of his team were going to enter the room through a larger garage-sized door that would make it easier to offload their equipment. The SEAL teams were assembled and being briefed before training on any special equipment that they were unfamiliar with.

The master sergeant yelled, "Attention on deck!"

The men all stood at attention. John entered the room with Ivory. He walked near the podium with Ivory following him. John was waiting for Colonel Alex Barns to finish instructing his men. Earlier, John had asked Ivory to put on an Air Force Colonel's uniform.

Ivory asked, "John, I was a captain in the Air Force when I left. How did I all of a sudden become a colonel?"

John told her. "Ivory, I have the authority to make you the top general of the entire Armed Forces if I want to. I am the commander in chief of all government agencies, second only to the president. I have this authority at all times, but only use it in times of national emergency. I made you a colonel because you won't have to waste time with any politics from captains or anyone else. Time is an enemy, so we save it any way we can."

"Okay. That makes sense. I just didn't want to impersonate an officer. General, am I legally a colonel in the Air Force?"

"Yes. I wanted to make you a general, but a colonel is the one who is known for operating and organizing the missions. Ivory, I am going to introduce you after I explain the mission to the men. Then you can get everyone split up into their individual specific jobs."

Ivory stood at attention and saluted. "Yes Sir, General. With the general's permission, I would like to ask a question."

John stood at attention and saluted back. "Yes, Colonel, you may speak freely."

"General, do you think this uniform makes me look sexy? Because, I'm feeling it, and Sir, when we get back, would you help me take it off?" She winked.

John laughed because he wasn't expecting her to say something like that. Ivory laughed also. They both knew they had only seconds to get it together before they were in front of an entire room of Navy SEALs.

"Okay Ivory, thanks for the laugh. We may not get another chance until the mission is over." They composed themselves and focused on their task at hand.

"You're welcome General," Ivory said seriously.

They heard the master sergeant call the men to attention.

"That's my queue, Colonel," John said.

John walked up to the podium. "At ease, men. Be seated. I am going to give you a summary of recent events that have led up to the reason we are here. Corporal, you may begin."

The corporal started a digital recording of the pictures of the animal attacks at the Globotech research lab. The pictures of the carnage of mutilated men and women were showing on the screen. In some cases, there were just skeletal remains of people covered in gore and blood. There were photos of animals, mammals of every kind in the area. They were lying dead with their eyes bulged out, and blood spray from their eyes, nose and ears was visible. Pictures of the carnage at the church ten miles away from Globotech came up on the screen. There were pictures of men, women, and children torn to shreds...even babies. These were American people, families on a beautiful Sunday morning at church. The dead animals were mostly lying on top of whom they were tearing to pieces when they died from what looked like a small explosion in their brains.

John told the corporal to turn it off. He then told them about Mr. Grey and his alliance with most of the richest billionaires in the world. Their goal was to take over the United States of America from within because our military was too powerful to destroy in an open battle. He told them the reason these corporations want to do this is because they want a one-world government and our military stands in their way. If the President had lost this election, the country would already be lost. The silent majority came through because they knew what would have happened if a lying, corrupt, communist would have won.

Globocorp has invented this technology to wipe out thirty-three to fifty percent of the world's population. They want to be able to choose which percent of the people will be horribly massacred. John went on to say that the planet is facing a population problem, every forty years, the population doubles. He explained how in about fifteen to thirty years, the natural resources won't be able to sustain the population.

"This is not the way to handle that problem. This man, Mr. Grey, runs the largest global sex trafficking ring in the world. He is the richest man in the world and considers himself a god. He owns Globocorp and has developed this technology to wipe out the opposition. That, gentlemen, is not even the worst part. He has tricked one of the best Nano cell research scientists in the world into developing this technology, thinking he was helping mankind to cure disease and help the world. This man is Doctor Robert Jennings."

A picture of Doctor Jennings appeared on the screen. John said, "This man must be rescued within two days. Mr. Grey will be back and asking Doctor Jennings to expand his technology to control humans. He has already learned how to control mammals."

"Oh, shit," someone in the audience, whispered.

"Men, we are mammals too. I have reliable intelligence that Doctor Jennings will refuse, and also that Doctor Jennings is suspicious about what is going on. Why can't he talk to his colleagues at the research facility he lived in for over seven years? It's the laboratory he was flown out of right before his technology was tested on co-researchers and friends. These people had devoted years of their lives to it for the good it could do for mankind. You saw their reward. The only reason Doctor Jennings was spared is because the enemy wanted to see if they could convince him to join their side for money and power. I have it on good authority that he will not take part in any human mind control. He will be tortured and then killed…unless we save him. I have a personal interest in this also." A picture of Joe in his Navy Seal uniform was on the screen, along with his wife and two sons.

"This SEAL is my brother; we have been in more battles than I can remember. Mr. Grey has kidnapped his wife and two boys. The youngest one is named after me. These people are family to me. The boys call me Uncle John. I spend the holidays with them when off duty. Mr. Grey has high-ranking, corrupt, treasonous officials in our government agencies, and paid them for my sealed top-secret records. He then tried to have my brother in arms air jump into an animal attack that was supposed to kill us both. Well, let me tell you something. Mister Grey forgot one thing: Don't piss off a Navy SEAL. Captain Joe Mills was smart enough to figure out I was being set up and he secretly sent me a coded message warning me. I sent one back telling him to abort, and he confirmed. I also sent him a message that I would save his family or die trying. Men, some of you may have heard of Captain Mills. He and I have saved each other's lives and kept each other mentally stable on countless missions for God and country. I cannot let him down."

John looked around. He could see these warriors were very pissed off. America was under attack, and one of their own brother's wife and children were taken. That breaks all honor and justice codes. This could not be allowed. John almost felt what they were thinking.

"That's enough for me right there. How about you warriors?"

"HOO-YAH!" the men said. It was so loud that Ivory actually jumped.

"This is a very tricky mission, men. As much as I want to go in there and waste every enemy in the place, we cannot do that. We have been trained to outsmart our enemies. My team and I have devised a way to have all the visiting dignitaries, diplomats, and any other powerful billionaires in the compound moved out safely. Men, this is a precise mission. Rescue the people on the list. We get the powerful people out of the way. Then we blow up the place, so it looks like a huge gas explosion. The only thing left behind is a crater twenty-feet deep where Mr. Grey's entire headquarters and compound used to be. I gave the President my word we wouldn't start World War Three. The cost of failure is losing our country, and having a one-world government ruled by Mr. Grey who, in my opinion, is pure evil dressed in a human body. My people will soon split you up and give you what you need. Timing is important as usual."

John then looked out among his men. "I thought you should know what you are fighting for, my brothers in arms." Louder than anyone had heard a human being yell before, he shouted, "Are you with me?"

Ivory looked at him. He looked like a mighty warrior that couldn't possibly be defeated. Everyone, even her, yelled "HOO-YAH!"

"Thank you, men. I would like to introduce Air Force Colonel Doctor Ivory Black. She has come up with a way to stop this technology in two weeks, when it took billions of dollars and ten years for some of the greatest scientists in the field to invent it. Show her respect. I had to marry her to get her to show me any."

Ivory was just about to walk up to the podium when everyone in the room started laughing because she smacked him with her folder. They all stood up and clapped for Ivory.

"Congratulations, Colonel Black!" someone yelled.

John went around checking on all his different teams and meeting all his new men. Whether they knew it or not, he was going to keep them. They were going to keep pressure on Mr. Grey and Globocorp. They had to agree and volunteer to stay with him. John didn't want anyone doing something against their will. It could be counterproductive. The men seemed in awe of him and his team.

Chapter Twenty-Four: Pulling the Weeds

Ivory was right. It really didn't matter that his team weren't tough Navy SEALs, or even civilians. They had some serious skills and the men were smart enough to know that was what won battles. John got a good feeling from almost everyone except three of the men. He went through their records: two highly intelligent men and one who showed bravery in battle. Mr. Grey has people infiltrated in the government and the Armed Forces. John decided he could not take a chance that any one of these men was on Mr. Grey's payroll. Colonel Barns had given him his office so he could do his work. He called Helen and Colonel Barns into the office and told them his problem.

"Helen, if it is all right with you, I would like to ask Jane to use her gift to help me find out if any of these three men are traitors." John showed them the files he had on the men.

"Thank you for asking John, but Jane is a grown and married woman now, it's up to her."

"Ok Helen, I also wanted to get both of your opinions."

"I think it must be done, if that's what you feel," Helen replied.

Colonel Barns said, "I have no idea how Jane can help, John."

"Alex, Jane has a gift from God," Helen said. "She can know what a person is thinking when she is looking at them."

"That would sound insane to most people, Helen, but after watching John use that voice thing he has, I believe it. Now that I think about it, she did read what was on my mind when she said, 'I think she's the most beautiful woman in the world, also. I thought I might have said it out loud because I haven't ever felt that way," Alex replied.

"What way is that, Alex?"

He turned red, embarrassed. "In love with a woman," he mumbled.

"Which woman, Alex?" She smiled at him.

"You, Helen, I'm in love with you. From the first second I saw you. I loved you at first sight. I thought that was just a romantic myth."

"No, it's not, Alex. I never imagined it could happen twice in one lifetime." Then Helen kissed him.

John smiled. He was happy for them. He cleared his throat. "Time is an enemy, guys."

Helen and Alex continued kissing. John shook them, "Guys, we have a set time to accomplish a large number of things."

Colonel Barns said, "Sorry General, I feel like a teenager, you're right John. Let's get it done."

John smiled at Colonel Barnes. The Colonel said, "What?"

"Colonel, you are one lucky guy."

He looked at Helen and said, "You got that right, John."

"Blessing after blessing," Helen beamed.

John then said, "I want you guys to stay here while Jane and I question them one at a time. The first man,

Harold Brown, should be here in ten minutes. Jane is due now."

There was a knock on the door. "Come in, Jane."

The door opened. Jane walked in and hugged Helen and Alex. She hugged John and had trouble letting him go. He held her at arm's length. She knew something was about to happen.

He told Jane what this was all about. He explained that if any one of their men was a traitor and got word to the enemy, things could get very bad, very fast. John told her to write down what they were thinking, and not to say anything about their thoughts. He didn't want her gift known to anyone, especially an enemy. He said, "Jane, if any one of them is a traitor, say General is this how you want it written?"

"Okay John, I promise I'll keep quiet. I'm glad you warned me because I sometimes blurt stuff out when I'm angry. I'll float like a butterfly."

John smiled. She has been talking to Ivory, he thought.

"You're right John, and I really have been practicing 'floating like a butterfly and stinging like a bee.'"

There was a knock at the door. "Come in," John said.

Harold walked in at attention and saluted. The General ordered him at ease, and to take a seat. Harold looked nervous. "What's this about General?"

"I am interviewing random men to see if they would like to stay on the new team I have put together."

"Oh! All right, that would be a yes from me Sir." Harold replied.

"Great Harold. I just have a few questions to ask and we can wrap it up," the General said convincingly.

"Yes Sir." Harold answered enthusiastically.

Jane chimed in. "Excuse me General, but is this how you wanted it written?" She showed John what she had written. Apparently, Harold was willing to die if he could kill General White for his lord, Mr. Grey.

John used his command voice, "Attention, Harold!" He stood at attention. "Turn around, Harold." He turned around, and John came up behind him, and handcuffed him. John got on his communication device and called his guards. When the guards arrived, he told them to gag him and place Harold in the cell that was right down the hall from his office. The cell was built so nobody could see in or out of it without a handheld monitor or the security monitor in Colonel Barns' office. John said, "Search him thoroughly. Leave him gagged and cuffed. Chain him to the steel rings on the wall with enough slack so he can sit down. If he tries to escape, shoot him. Dismissed,"

John and the others watched the security camera monitor as Harold was escorted to the cell. John showed Helen and Colonel Barns what Jane had written down.

"Thank You Lord Jesus, for Jane's gift," sighed Colonel Barns.

Helen and John nodded and said, "Amen."

John had given orders that nobody was to be armed until they were ready to leave for the mission. Ivory had made sure that any kind of electronic communication device didn't work but theirs. He asked her how she could do that, and have their stuff still work. Ivory explained how it was the same principle as a Faraday Cage. They were inside one, and the only communication possible was inside it. If someone leaves the area and goes outside through the magnetic field wall that surrounds them, any device they have would be burned out. "The reason you can call out, John, is that I blocked our phones with enough shielding that they are able to go through the magnetic field without any damage. Once you get to Colonel Barns' office, you're outside the shield wall and can call whoever you need to."

What a smart woman Ivory is, John thought. He caught Jane looking at him, smiling. He knew she had read his thoughts.

"She sure is," said Jane.

"All right, Larry Marshal is next. My guards are bringing him through metal detectors, but we are talking about Navy SEALs, so I need Helen to stand behind Alex. Jane, stand next to your mom in case I have to move fast." Alex unsnapped his side arm. "My command voice has never failed me, but we take no chances."

"Agreed," said Colonel Barns.

There was a knock on the door. "Come in," John said. The door opened and Larry Marshal walked in. He stood at attention and saluted.

John saluted back. "At ease. Take a seat, Larry."

He sat down and waited patiently. John waited a minute to see if Larry got nervous. He seemed calm and relaxed.

"Okay, Larry. I have brought you here to see if you would like to remain on my team permanently after this mission is over."

Larry took a few minutes to think about it. "General, Sir, what would my duties include?"

"Unknown at this time, as usual Larry. I don't even know what will be coming up next."

"General, do you need my answer right away, or could we wait until after this mission?"

"I need it right now, Larry," the General ordered.

"Then it is a yes from me Sir," Larry stated.

Jane said, "General, did I write this correctly?"

John walked over and looked at her notes, "Yes, that's the way I want it."

He then ordered Larry to stand at attention. He commanded him to turn around and put his hands behind his back. Larry obeyed, and John cuffed him. John called the guards in. Again, he told them to search him thoroughly, gag him, and chain him up next to Harold. He showed Alex and Helen what Jane had written about Larry's thoughts.

Larry thought, I wonder what this asshole wants from me. I wonder how the mission will go, when as soon as I get on land, I call in Lord Grey's reinforcements. I should probably say yes in case somehow, this jackass pulls it off. His Lordship will want somebody on the inside.

John said, "Thank You Lord, for the warning,"

Colonel Barns said, "Man, I can't believe even the teams have been infiltrated. I hope we didn't miss anyone."

Helen asked, "John, did you shake everyone's hand that has or will have any knowledge of our mission?"

"I did Helen, and I checked the list three times."

"Wow John," exclaimed Jane. "You're more efficient than Santa Claus." They all had a short laugh.

"You know John, since you all got here, I feel like I'm in some kind of twilight zone," Colonel Barns said. "I love it though." He looked at Helen.

John said, "Yes Alex, it's different. It takes a little while to get used to. We have to get back to business. The last contestant is William Means. His record shows that he has quite a few confirmed kills and he has the nickname 'Mean Willy Means'. He likes to fight and has been in more than a few bar brawls. I think the only reason he was picked is because he has more missions and kills under his belt than anyone else. Otherwise, he doesn't have much else to offer seeing as he scored one of the lowest on the IQ tests. He scored just above minimum to be allowed into the SEAL training program. Jane, if you know he is a traitor just say, 'Excuse me General'. Don't come any closer to me or Willy!"

When William knocked, John said he could enter. William walked in and saluted. He was big for a SEAL. He looked about six-feet, two-inches tall and weighed about two hundred and thirty pounds. John could see how he had gotten his nickname. 'Mean Willy Means' looked like a mean person.

"At ease, William, and take a seat."

Willy sat down and looked around. It seemed like he was filled with hate. He had a permanent nasty look on his face. John didn't know if it was intentional or if he couldn't help it.

"William, you probably know why you're here."

"Yes, I do General." Before John could get another word out, Willy had lunged at him.

Willy caught him good with a right hook to John's left ear. Willy threw a left, but John was able to duck and counterpunch him in his ribs. Then he hit him with a left jab that dazed him. He finished him off with a four-punch combo, ending with his left, which wasn't really necessary because Willy was out cold from the first three punches of the combo. The guards came in. Alex had called them. They flipped Willy over and cuffed him, then looked at their General with awe and respect. Willy was known to be one tough SEAL.

"Don't forget to gag him," John panted.

Jane came over and looked at John's left ear. There was blood coming out of it. "I'm sorry John, it happened so fast, I didn't have time to warn you. Let's go see if Mary can fix you up. That guy is an evil man John." She showed him what she had written about his thoughts. John read it and it turned out Willy had joined the service so he could kill people without getting into trouble. It also turned out that when he was off duty, he had killed a few people and gotten away with it so far.

"You still got it, John! That was a great combo buddy; you still have the speed, man! That was exciting," gleamed Colonel Barns.

"I hate to admit it, but that was amazing," Helen said.

Jane said, "General, you can kick some butt."

John smiled, holding his ear. "Helen, do you think we're good to go as far as enemies in our ranks are concerned?"

"Yes John. I do. I feel it. Thank you, Father, for weeding out the evil in our army of mighty men, in Jesus' name. Amen."

John went to the bathroom to clean up his ear. Then they all headed out of his office. He told the guards that the men in the cell were to be kept there and guarded until the mission was over. If, for any reason, he didn't return, the men were to be shot for treason and dumped into the ocean, without any identification on their person at all.

They saluted. "Yes Sir, General."

"Ladies, I know that sounds wrong, but we really have no choice. A lot of innocent people will die if those men get loose."

Helen and Jane looked at him with understanding. Helen said, "We know John. We are starting to understand the choices you guys face." She looked at Colonel Barns.

Jane looked at John. She was concerned. "No way John. We are going to see Mary. We need you at your best tonight. I know your ear is ringing. Don't try to be a tough guy. Lives may depend upon your hearing tonight."

John smiled at her. "Blessing after blessing."

Jane smiled back. "I'm proud of you too John."

They found Mary. Jane asked her if she could spare a minute. Jane, Mary, and John went into the bathroom, and locked the door. Jane told Mary about John's ear. Mary put her hand on his ear and said, "In Jesus' name." It healed right away.

"Thank you Mary." John hugged her.

Mary felt energy feeding into her from John, more than she ever felt before.

Jane noticed. "Wow Mary, John gave you some serious juice."

Mary said, "I have a feeling that I might need it tonight."

"Don't worry, Mary, God has been leading us. Can't you feel it?" Jane asked.

Mary said, "Yes Jane, and it's wonderful."

"Mary, you should have seen John kick this big, tough, mean-looking guy's butt. It was incredible! Even the guards thought so."

"Cool! I wish I was there."

"The only reason that creep even got a punch in was because it was a sucker punch. It was unexpected. I learned in science class that action is quicker than reaction."

"Girls, let's go, I've got to talk to Bobby and Raphe to make sure they will be on time. I also want to check that Ivory has her team all set, and I need to get us all together to go over it one more time before we leave."

They both stood at attention and saluted. "Yes General!"

He cracked up. Jane and Mary asked him if they could have uniforms like Ivory.

He said, "Yes! I actually have them in my office. Ivory suggested it. There is one for Helen, too. She is the captain and you two are lieutenants. Why don't you ladies get Helen and go get dressed for the mission? Then meet me in Ivory's area." The girls headed to his office and John headed for Bobby's team.

Chapter Twenty-Five: Battle Plans

Bobby's job was to make sure the diversionary explosions were huge, but controlled, to not actually kill anyone. They were supposed to look like natural gas explosions. There was going to be a second explosion five minutes and twenty seconds after the first one, to make it look more like an underground gas pipe was randomly leaking and exploding. The second explosion would be close to the first one, but far enough away that police and firefighters at the first explosion site wouldn't get hurt. They were coordinating with Raphe's team. At the exact second the first explosion goes off, timers would set off canisters of invisible gas spray, placed in the outdoor fresh-air circulation fans that circulated air to all the main areas of the castle. The gas would travel inside the castle, and smells like rotten eggs, just like a gas leak. At the same exact time, magnetic pulse bombs would go off and disable all electrical and electronics inside and outside of the entire compound, including the alarms, cell phones, and all communication devices. The insertion team: three snipers and three spotters. They would drop magnetic pulse emitters before the first explosion. They would drop them from small stealth electrical flying drones to expose any guards using stealth technology suits, like the one Raphe wore to get into John's first bunker. They would do this in the landing zone and all along their approach route. Then they would eliminate any enemy lookouts. This would allow the teams to land unseen by the enemy. Raphe's team would have to deal with any enemies in the target area. The plan was to sneak in, place the pulse emitters and the gas canisters, then sneak out. The timers would set them off at the right time. Raphe's team had 90 minutes to complete this phase of the mission and get out of range of the pulse bombs. Then they would wait for the diversionary explosion, and the timed magnetic pulse to go off. Once the pulse destroyed the enemy's electronics, they would use the same stealth technology to take out any guards. They would have night vision goggles with stealth suits and their enemies would be blind and helpless. As Raphe's team was taking out the enemy, they would also be placing a high-tech explosive ordinance on the outside of the castle walls and its outer buildings.

SEAL Team Three's job was to dress like police, firemen, and other first responders. They would make sure all important dignitaries and royalty were escorted out safely, while at the same time placing explosive munitions inside the castle. The people they were evacuating would be told to hurry onto buses, and that they had to get far enough away in case the place exploded. General White's command team, Ivory, Helen, and seven Navy SEALs, would search the castle for Joe's wife and sons. When Team One and Team Two were finished with the first or second phase of their mission, they were to head back to the target area and help search.

Raphe and his team would check out all the places that he knew about that were not drawn on the blueprint of the castle. All SEALs were instructed to take out enemies with precision and stealth, and inform the other teams if they found any innocent slaves or anyone on the rescue list. All explosive munitions, ammunition and weaponry, had Italian-made parts so they couldn't be traced to America.

John was done checking out the total plan. "It looks great. I couldn't have done it better myself. We have one hour. Call everyone to the meeting room."

Once they were all assembled, John asked Helen if she was sure she wanted to go.

"Want has nothing to do with it John. I'm supposed to go. The Lord God wants me there. For what, I don't know, but I'm sure I will find out."

"Good enough for me, Helen," John said.

He walked up to the podium. "Men, in less than one hour, we have a go. If you were a person of faith now would be the time to pray. I would like to ask a dear friend of mine to send us off with a prayer. Helen, would you mind?"

She stepped up to the podium. "Not at all General. Whether you believe in God or not, it doesn't matter to me. That is between you and God. That is your choice. That's what America is all about, freedom to worship God without violence. I am exercising my right as an American to ask God to bless us and be with us on this mission. Father, we know that You will be with us and watch over us. We know that we will be victorious because if You are with us, nothing can stand against us. In Jesus' name, I pray. Amen."

his men, with every weapon or device they would be using in battle, so that on the next mission they would all be experts'. Raphe breathed a sigh of relief when they finally reached their target area. They began placing the EMP devices. He noticed a lot of blurring imagery around him, as he spoke quietly through his COM link to his men, "Fluid movements men." A moment later his second-in-command said, "Mission accomplished."

"Copy, move out," Raphe ordered. One of his men moved very abruptly and was brought down with automatic rifle fire. Raphe saw where the muzzle flash came from and shot at it and the general area it came from. The place exploded into a gun battle, which was bad because these men knew where they were stationed and Raphe's team could be anywhere. They were not sure where to shoot because they didn't want to hit their own guys. Raphe ordered, "ceasefire" then he manually set off all EMPs from a remote detonator in his pocket. Raphe had it in case they needed to improvise. He had to use it so the enemy wouldn't be able to send out an alarm. When the EMPs went off, there was a static-like wind that felt like it went through you, along with a crackling noise. Everyone was instantly visible. Raphe yelled, Fire! His team, and the enemy's team were in a face-off firefight. Both sides were dropping fast. Finally, all the enemies were down. Raphe was assessing the situation, when suddenly he took a round to the chest from a wounded enemy, lying on the ground. He was able to kill the man before he fell about ten feet from him. He ordered his men to return to the choppers and report to General White. His two remaining men came over and checked him out. Raphe's wound was mortal.

He was bleeding into his lungs fast. Five enemy guards were heading over to see why their men hadn't checked in. Raphe ordered, "Move out," and waved them away. The remaining two men double-timed it back to the choppers. Raphe asked, "Lord take care of Jane." He whispered, "Please tell her I'm sorry for dying on her. That I love her and will be waiting for her." His last thought was of Jane, he was picturing her in his mind as he stopped breathing, and died.

Jane and Mary were busy organizing supplies. Jane started to feel strange. "Raphe is in trouble," she said to Mary. A voice in Jane's mind told her to run like the wind, do not be afraid, I am with you. Jane felt like she was in a waking dream. She could see Raphe and the path to get to him. She started to run as fast as she could. Mary turned to say something to her, but she was gone, and nowhere in sight. Mary shouted for Jane, but she was already out of hearing range. Jane felt powerful and as fast as a strong wind. She had already run a mile at her top speed, and she wasn't even out of breath. Jane was approaching Raphe. She could see him. She also saw five men standing around Raphe with rifles. Jane knew nothing could stop her. She ran into the target area with a powerful wind at her back. She jumped eight feet into the air and landed on the ground next to Raphe at the same time she put her right hand on Raphe's chest, the hand with the small light of God's Glory on its index finger. Jane didn't know why she was doing this, but she felt she was being guided to do so. At the exact second she put her hand on Raphe, he shook like he was being shocked, and the ground shook also. A powerful wind blew through the area and was gone in a matter of seconds. Every enemy on the entire exterior grounds fell dead, like rag dolls.

"Raphe, are you okay?" Raphe opened his eyes to see Jane standing over him. She looked like a fearless warrior scanning the area for anymore enemies that would dare to hurt her man. Jane looked so beautiful and powerful standing over him, back straight and fists clenched, protecting him.

Raphe was filled with love and amazement. "Jane, my love, you were amazing." Jane looked down and smiled; then she helped him up.

She stared into his eyes and said, "My poor husband you have been seeing things like this horror scene we are in since you were a little boy." Jane lost it and started crying, as if inconsolable. He hugged her tight. Raphe knew that combat, especially the first time, was a shock, and an adrenaline rush.

Raphe changed the subject. "I believe I was dead for a minute or so." Jane squeezed him tight. "Then I felt a wind, and when I opened my eyes I saw a mighty lion leaping down on me. Somehow I knew it was God. Then I healed and was breathing again. I heard a voice asking me if I was okay. When I looked up, I saw a beautiful warrior woman protecting me. I didn't know where I was and felt disoriented. Then it all came back to me and I realized it was my beautiful, loving wife standing over me. I am so in love and amazed by you." Jane looked up at Raphe and wiped her face on her sleeve. She smiled and kissed him. "I feel that way every time I see you, Raphe." Raphe looked at her in awe.

"Raphe, remember it was Jesus working through me. I just accepted His Blessing."

"I know Jane, but you sure make one beautiful warrior woman."

Raphe realized they were standing in a battlefield having a conversation. "Jane we better get back." they headed toward the choppers.

Jane walked about twenty feet and said, "Raphe I need a rest." Without warning, she lay down and went into a dead sleep.

Two of the twelve men Raphe was in command of made it back. Ten were killed in action. They would be found and brought back to the states. The two men had reported that Raphe went down, mortally wounded. General White was still at the landing zone with the choppers. Mary was standing next to him, crying. She had just finishing telling the story about Jane disappearing. A voice reported over their coms, "Friendly coming in, carrying wounded." When they noticed Raphe carrying Jane coming toward them, they looked at each other, and then ran to them. Raphe needed time to catch his breath before he could say a word. Jane had passed out. Raphe carried her as fast as he could run. He had never before pushed himself to that limit; his heart was pounding harder, and his breathing was heavier than at any other time in his life. General White said, "its okay Raphe, let me hold her for a couple of minutes so you can calm down, and catch your breath."

Mary was already checking out Jane and found nothing physically wrong with her. Jane's pulse was good and she was breathing okay, and then she remembered what had happened to her. Mary put her hand on Raphe's shoulder and said, "Let General White hold her; it will help Jane, Raphe, I promise."

The General moved in and gently took Jane. The moment he held her, he felt power go from him into Jane, and she started to stretch and yawn. When Jane opened her eyes, she saw the General holding her.

Jane hugged him and said, "Thank you Pops."

General White smiled and said, "Don't thank me." Jane smiled and said, "Thank you, Jesus." When he put her down, she noticed Raphe down on all fours, still catching his breath.

"General, could you touch Raphe?" General White wasn't sure if it would work because so far it had only worked for people who God had used His power through to perform a miracle.

The General then said, "Sure I'll try." He bent down and put his hands on Raphe. Immediately. He felt power go out of him into Raphe. When it stopped, General White took his hands off of Raphes' shoulders, and Raphe jumped up fully awake, and breathing normally. He saluted General White and gave him a brief summary of what happened. He then added, "I'm sorry about the men, Sir." General White knew from experience that when men you are in charge of go down, it is very hard.

"Raphe I know how you feel, but it is not your fault. Missions don't always go as planned. We are all sorry about our brothers who lost their lives today. Now is not the time to mourn them; now is the time to honor them. Those brave warriors sacrificed their lives to protect others. Those men chose to go to battle for justice, and doing what is right. They didn't want to die Raphe, but were willing to if need be. These men had a gift. They were experts on the battlefield. They all knew someone had to fight for others who couldn't fight for themselves;

they all knew how important their jobs were. These mighty warriors died with honor. They gave the most anyone could give for their people and their country. There is no greater gift anyone can give than to lay down their lives for others. These brave men fought and died for God and country. We who are left living will proudly continue their mission. Whether we live or die, we will complete this mission! Remember that these men gave their lives for this mission, let's remember them and finish it in their honor! There will be a time to mourn them, but that time is not now, now we honor them!"

The General looked at his watch, then at his team. All of them had heard what General White had said through their communication links. They were all standing at attention, and when they noticed he was looking at them, they all saluted. General White stood at attention, looking at them for a moment, then saluted back - crisp and hard, letting them know he was proud to serve with them. He then looked at his watch and said, "We move out in five minutes."

General White ordered Raphe to get suited back up, and he smiled as he said, "We're not done yet Son." He contacted Ivory and Helen and told them that they were all moving out in four minutes, but he saw them approach a minute later. Ivory sensed something wasn't right.

She asked, "John what's wrong?"

He looked at her and said, "team one was in a fire-fight. Raphe and two others survived. Ten men are down in the field. They were still able to complete their mission, so get your combat faces on ladies, it is Go-Time!"

Looking at his watch he said, "Move out!" They all turned on their stealth suits and vanished, almost at the same time. They headed for their target area where the firefight was and waited for the diversion-explosion and gas canisters to go off. The EMPs had to be set off earlier than planned, so there was no power or communications for the enemy. General White's teams had everything, including infrared night vision. General White knew they had a great advantage over the enemy, now they waited and watched. They had to wait for the evacuation team to finish. The General asked Helen and Ivory how they were doing and they both said okay. He ordered the men to locate their fallen brothers and place them together along the path. He knew keeping busy was better than waiting, and it needed to be done.

Mary and Jane were waiting at the LZ. (Landing Zone) with the flight team and the perimeter guards. They were both leaning against one of the helicopters. General White had told them to "Stay with the choppers, unless someone with higher authority tells you different," then he winked at Jane.

Mary turned to Jane. "What happened to you Jane? You said Raphe's in trouble and when I turned to look, you vanished."

"Mary, it was incredible, I heard a voice in my head say, Raphe's in trouble, run like the wind, do not be afraid, I am with you. Then everything felt like a dream, Mary. I can't really explain exactly how I felt. I do remember that I felt powerful - like nothing could harm me, and I could accomplish anything. I started to run super-fast to Raphe. I could see him and the path that led to him, kind of like I could see everything I needed to see, even in the dark. I felt like I was running on a fast wind, the wind all around me felt alive with enormous power. I saw five armed men coming toward Raphe. I had just passed two of our men and they didn't even notice me. The men were starting to point their guns at Raphe. I moved even faster, and then I jumped into the air, and came down right in the middle of the five men who were now surrounding Raphe. I placed my hand on Raphe's chest, the hand with God's glory in the index finger. Raphe shook like he was being shocked and the ground trembled like an earthquake." Jane took a breath and continued, "then every person on the outside grounds fell dead. I could see it all, even though it would not normally be visible to me because of trees and buildings. I asked Raphe if he was okay, even though I somehow knew he was. Then I stood guard over him until he was able to stand. When Raphe got up and hugged me, all of a sudden I was back to the normal Jane. I looked around and saw all the dead bodies, and Raphe had come back to life."

Mary said, "What do you mean Raphe had come back to life?"

"Raphe was dead, Mary. He died right before I told you he was in trouble, and I felt it." Jane hugged Mary and started to cry. "Mary, it's hard to even think about that part," Jane sobbed.

"It's okay, tell me the whole story later. You have gone through a lot."

Jane stopped crying and said, "Don't worry Mary. The rest of the story is not scary. Raphe and I started heading here. I walked about twenty feet then lay down and went to sleep. I woke up in John's arms feeling great; you know the rest."

"Wow, Jane that is amazing. When we get back, you should write that down so we all remember how great God is."

"You know what Mary? We should write our whole story down so we never forget. We can read it and get closer to God. We can remember the miracles."

The team that was to evacuate all visiting personnel was up. Angelo Sicinolfi was the leader of Team Three. Angelo was fluent in Italian, English, Spanish and some Arabic. He was a perfect fit for the job of liaison between his men and the castle's security team. Angelo's men were dressed as six police, four firemen, and two paramedics. Earlier, four of his men were able to procure two big city buses and one fire truck. They reported it was fairly easy due to the diversionary explosion, plus the fact that they had the proper uniforms for both the buses and the fire truck.

Angelo laughed. "Just to tell yourself, I really am a firefighter or a bus driver, with confidence, and you project an air of reality." Angelo loved this kind of stuff; snickering he thought, I could have been an actor. He laughed as he approached the castle's main entrance. Angelo spotted two armed security men coming out of the front entrance. He took out his badge and identification and said, "Hello my name is Lieutenant Angelo Sicinolfi. We need to evacuate this building, there is a gas leak in the area and we believe it's coming from here."

The security guard looked at him suspiciously, and took his identification. The guard took out a penlight from his pocket and it didn't work. Angelo offered him a flashlight that worked, and the guard used it to check out the identification.

"Officer Sicinolfi," the guard began. "Isn't it strange that not only is our electricity down, but even our cell phones and radios are dead?"

Angelo said, "Yes, it is very strange. We have gotten similar calls from other crews. Sir this is an emergency, what is your name?"

The guard said, "You can call me Sir for now." Just then the second diversionary explosion went off.

Angelo said loudly, "Who is in charge? We are wasting time! These people have to evacuate these premises immediately, it could explode at any time!"

The guard said, "I am going to have to clear this with my superior. Do you have a cell phone I can borrow, Officer?"

Angelo was getting worried that he would have to use the contingency plan, and just execute these guards, and drag them inside. Just then another guard came out and said, "Sir, people smell gas all over the building."

Angelo then said, "Sir security guard, we are evacuating this building, either you help us, get out of our way, or be placed under arrest. What is it going to be?"

The guard said, "All right, Angelo. You will call me Captain Romano and I will be in charge here!"

"That is fine, Captain. Do you think we can get going here?" The security and Angelo's team went in; it was pitch black. Angelo's men handed out flashlights to the guards. Captain Romano told his men to get the guests out as quickly as possible. He told his second-in-command that he had to leave for ten minutes to make a call, and that he was in charge until then. Angelo walked over to a dark corner to talk on his phone. Captain Romano saw him talking, and walked over to him.

When he was close, he said, "Angelo I need that phone. Get off it and hand it over." Angelo said goodbye to who ever he was fake-talking to and put the phone in his pocket, then he shined his flashlight in Captain Romano's eyes. In the next two seconds Angelo had his combat knife under Captain Romano's chin stuck all the way to the inside top of his scull bone. He pulled out his knife and stuffed the Captain in a closet, what a dick that guy was.

His men called him one by one until the building was clear of all the guests on the list; they were all accounted for and driven away on the buses. He ordered his men to clear out all enemies with extreme prejudice. Time to contact the General.

The General had to wait for the go-ahead signal from Team Three. He took an educated guess that it would take anywhere from thirty minutes to one hour. They were waiting in the same area Raphe had planted the EMPs. He hoped that the people Team three were clearing out would be scared enough to move quickly. The General hoped that their personal security would help them move faster. Forty minutes had gone by, and he was starting to get nervous when he received the signal from the evacuation team.

"All accounted for, and cleared out. You're a go Sir."

"All teams move out!" General White ordered.

They were close. They had stealth suits and 9mm pistols with fifteen-round clips, and silencers. Thank you, Mr. President. The General had sent Raphe's stealth suit to the president. He had surprised John with fifty suits, and fifty new high-tech silencers, fit for 9mm semi-automatic pistols, which were pretty damn quiet.

When they had met at John's command center after their bullet train ride, the president told him, "You're not the only one who knows how to get things done, General," after he saw the look on John's face.

General White ordered, "In two hours, we are on the choppers heading for base! If any surprises come up, message me, "Confirm."

They all confirmed.

Chapter Twenty-Seven: The Witch

They all went through the castle's main entrance to their separate missions. John and his team went to the lower levels where most likely any prisoners would be kept. On their way, John, Ivory, and their SEAL escort took out quite a few guards. With the confusion and the stealth suits, plus the fantastic silencers, it was going smoothly. They headed down to the lowest level. The underground part of the castle was decorated with satanic emblems and it reeked of death and decay. John led the way down the staircase. He had memorized the blueprint of the castle. They came to a long, wide hallway with many doorways to other rooms, Great, more time-consuming crap, and not on the blueprint. He communicated to four of his men that they had to clear each room one at a time as quietly as possible.

The door was not locked, and they went in carefully. They had to turn off their stealth suits when they were working close to one another. What they saw sickened them. There were six children chained to the walls sitting in their own feces and urine. Ivory and Helen found that two of them were still alive. It looked like a five-year-old boy and a ten-year-old girl. Helen realized she had seen them in her vision. John called in their position and ordered ten men to give them a hand to take these poor children to the medevac chopper. He wanted enough men here to take more, because he felt like there would be more of these children to rescue. Time was an enemy, so they would have to move faster. One of the SEALs signaled to the General that there was no key and the chain manacles were very thick.

John felt led by God. He walked up to the first child's manacles and pulled them apart like they were made out of cheap Styrofoam. Then he did the same with the other child's restraints. The two SEALs looked at each other with amazement because they had both tried to take them off and failed. It went faster than John thought because there were only prisoners and no guards in these torturous cells. In total, they had found eleven children still alive. One of the children was a one-year-old, barely alive. They also found a room full of dead corpses, mostly children. It looked like there were at least twenty-six corpses. John heard Ivory and Helen crying, but he knew they were also extremely angry.

The assistance they needed arrived. They wrapped the kids in blankets and took them as quickly as possible to the medevac chopper. The team continued down the end of the hallway and entered a large Satanic worshipping room with a sacrificial altar. All of a sudden, they heard a voice, or many voices-coming out of one mouth. It was the evil, satanic witch that Helen had described in her vision. She was praising Satan and her arms were raised. She was holding a strange curved knife over her head, ready to plunge it into the crying baby girl on the altar. The witch was seconds away from sacrificing the same baby girl that Helen had seen die in her vision.

Helen felt immensely powerful hands on her shoulders and heard a voice bellow, "Be still evil one!" The voice was coming from her position.

A light lit up the room like the sun.

The evil witch said, "This one is for my Lord, Satan. Not for you, Bitch."

"You have harmed my children and kept them from me!"

The witch was screaming in pain and could not move.

"It would have been better for you if you had never been born!" The Voice roared.

The Voice seemed like it came from where Helen was standing. It shook the room like an earthquake.

"From dust, you have come, and to dust you shall return!"

The witch turned to dust in a split second and was a pile on the floor in front of the baby. Ivory ran to the baby and picked her up.

"She has been saved. Your prayer has been answered, Helen!"

They all heard It. Helen started to fall to the ground and John caught her. He felt a power surge from him into Helen.

She stood up, dazed. "What happened? I passed out after I remember hearing, 'Be still, evil one.'"

John said, "It was amazing, Helen, but it will have to wait. Let's get the baby out of here!" Ivory was carrying the baby; and the baby was visible.

John still felt full of energy, even though Mary and Helen had drained him. He suddenly received two very good messages. The first one was that Joe's family had been found alive and healthy. They were heading to the chopper. The second message was that Doctor Robert Jennings had been found with a woman he refused to leave without, so they took them both to the helicopter as well.

"Let's move, everyone! Back to the choppers!" John was looking to the left checking for enemies. He felt he should look right and he did. He saw a man sighting in Ivory with a rifle. John fired four shots into him, right before he could pull the trigger. John said, "Thank you, Lord." General White ordered his men to find their brothers that were killed and get them to the choppers.

They arrived at the medevac at the same time as Bobby. Mary, Raphe, and Jane were already there, waiting for the doctor to let them know about the children.

The doctor in the medevac chopper came out and said, "I'm sorry, but it's too late for some of these children. They have been damaged beyond healing. The others will live, but most with some permanent damage."

Mary frowned, "Not on *my* watch," she said, determined. A pure wholesome wind blew into the medevac chopper as Mary entered it. Her hair was flying every which way with the strange wind. She hugged each child, and said, "Jesus sent me to tell you that he has healed you. She told them, "Jesus loves you so much." She cried softly, smiling at the beautiful children. The children got up off their beds and hugged her. She asked them if they were thirsty and hungry. They all said yes, and she laughed and smiled while she hugged them. She told the doctor, "Give these children all they can drink and eat, please." Then she turned to the children and said, "I'll come see you on the ship. Don't be afraid. Jesus sent us to help you." They all started to cheer, and Mary left with the team.

John ordered the doctor to do as Mary said. He took his hand and pushed the doctor's chin up to close his mouth. "Doctor?"

"Yes General?"

"Did you hear my orders?"

"No. Sorry, Sir, I think I was in shock. Did you see that, Sir?"

John laughed. "I said, do as the young lady asked. Give these children all they can drink and eat."

The doctor said, "Yes Sir!" with a big smile.

"Evacuate," John ordered.

Chapter Twenty-eight: Mission Accomplished

General White contacted Colonel Barns with the message, "Mission accomplished!"

Halfway back to the aircraft carrier, John pushed a button on a small electronic device. An enormous explosion occurred right where they were, no more than fifteen minutes prior. He made sure the areas where the helicopters landed on were blown up as well, so there were no tracks. Ivory took care of any satellites that could record their mission; how she did that, he didn't know. John was sure she would tell him later on.

"Take that you, evil bastard," John muttered. "It may not be the end of you, but we sure put a dent in your plans."

John also had two of his men, trained experts in anything to do with computers, confiscate the main hard drives from Mr. Grey's office, and the office of Antonio Corvino. He sent a message to the president, and he knew Joe was there waiting. "Mission accomplished. HOO-YAH!"

They landed on the carrier and filed into the secret meeting room. All the men went to their seats and stood at attention.

Colonel Barns said, "General, Captain Joe Mills' family have already left for the States."

They both smiled at each other. John said he would see them soon, thanks to God. The General had flown back in the chopper with his men that were KIA. He wanted to honor them when he blew up their target. General White saluted them and said, "Mission accomplished, my brave heroes."

Mary and Bobby took the children to get baths and clothing. The children didn't want to leave Mary's side. She couldn't stop looking at them with love in her eyes, full of happiness.

Bobby said to her, "Mary, I can actually feel the love you have for these kids. You are going to make a great mom."

"Bobby, I won't be able to rest until I know for sure that these children will be loved and cared for." She turned and looked at Bobby with a different kind of look, a motherly one. She said, "Bobby, for a second, Jesus let me feel the love He feels for these children, and all of us. It was just a tiny fraction of the amount of love he has, because it was so powerful it would have consumed my mortal body. Jesus gave me that gift tonight, and it is so amazing. I just can't believe how great I feel. Then I look at you and feel like I hit the jackpot." She smiled at him, full of peace, and she melted into his loving arms.

Bobby hugged her tightly. "Do you know – I forgot. I have something to show you in our quarters."

"Let me guess. Gun safety again?" She laughed. "You know Bobby, I don't think I can ever get enough gun safety lessons. As long as you don't stop them, I really don't care if I ever learn to shoot."

"Mary, we have to do double safety lessons when we actually shoot. One before, and then one after."

"Oh, my goodness Bobby, I might get to be as good a shot as Ivory. I love the safety lessons so much! I think we will be shooting a lot." They both laughed and headed for their quarters.

Colonel Barns was holding Helen's hand, and Ivory was standing beside him when John walked up to the podium to address his team.

John said, "Men, I would like to say a prayer for the mighty warriors we lost today. Father let these mighty warriors find the peace and happiness they deserve, they have given their very lives to protect their fellow man from a very dark evil, in Jesus' name, I ask Father, Amen. Men, we will have a memorial for these heroes when we get back home. I can honestly say that besides the grievous losses of our brothers in arms, this mission - a complicated and precise mission - has gone as smoothly as it possibly could. I have never worked with a group of warriors such as yourselves who have exceeded my expectations so much that I have to ask you all a question. Will you men work for me as my team full-time?"

The whole place went crazy, cheering.

When they calmed down, John said, "From the bottom of my heart, I thank you. You men not only made this mission a success, but you made it look easy. On a personal note, you helped save my family, our country, and quite possibly the world." John yelled, "HOO-YAH, my mighty men!"

Ivory saw the warrior that her husband was; God had chosen him for this. He was a hero to every man in this room. The things that some of his soldiers saw happened tonight were miraculous: John breaking the manacles with his bare hands; John knocking out the toughest SEAL in the group without breaking a sweat. These things are going to be added to his already famous reputation. I hope his head doesn't get too big, she laughed. He can be so gentle, and he is always so kind.

John said, "I have to say this, and you all have heard it before. We were never here, and this never happened. Men, one more question: When the mission seems impossible, who you going to call?" He yelled out again, "HOO-YAH!" The team went crazy.

He walked over to Ivory and gave her a big, juicy kiss in front of all his men. They started to whistle and clap. Ivory was surprised he did that in front of everyone; and surprised again that she was disappointed when he stopped.

She said, "General, was I part of your show?"

"Ivory, my sweet, sweet love, you *are* the show." She smiled and he kissed her again.

When they stopped, Ivory saw Helen and Colonel Barns were joining in. She thought they were a handsome couple.

Ivory softly spoke. "General?"

"Yes," he said.

"I'm not sure if your hat will fit anymore. Your head might be getting too big."

"My head is the same size, honey. I know all glory goes to the Father. That is an old trick to boost morale. The General told her, "Ivory, I do have a peculiar injury that seems to be swollen, and it's not my head. I might need you to take a look at it for me."

"If I do, General, do I have doctor-patient confidentiality?"

"Ivory, anything you want from me is yours. Your happiness is what I live for."

"If that's true, General, I would be very happy if you would take me to our quarters. I have a few ideas how we can deal with your peculiar injury problem."

They were both laughing when they headed for their quarters.

They had to stay an extra day because Mary would not leave the children behind. The president's daughter agreed. The president sent another jet so that all the children could come to the White House with them. Colonel Alex Barns also tagged along.

Finally, they all made it to the White House dinner party that the president had promised them. They were telling their entire story from beginning to end. They left nothing out. President Ronald Jefferson and the First Lady were fascinated. They would stop them at times and ask to hear the story again. Helen showed everyone her engagement ring, and announced she was engaged to Colonel Alex Barns. She asked President Jefferson if he could legally marry them.

"Yes, I can, and it would be an honor. When would you like to do it?"

"Right now," Alex and Helen both said. Helen asked, "Could we spend our wedding night in the Lincoln bedroom?" Then added, "We just want it simple and blessed by God."

The President said, "It would be one of the greatest honors in my life to perform the ceremony."

Jane was the maid of honor and Mary and Ivory were bridesmaids. John was Colonel Barns' best man, and Raphe and Bobby were groomsmen. It was quick and simple. They all danced to the band for a while, and stayed on as guests for three days. They had dinner together every night. John and the President had many meetings.

President Jefferson said, "All of you are now on Mr. Grey's hit list. John, Captain Mills and his family are already living at the beautiful place I have prepared for all of you, with everything you will need. I have prepared a safe place for you and you are all welcome to stay here whenever you would like. We really enjoy your company. I am truly sorry that your lives have changed and you need to remain in hiding."

Helen said, "Oh, but Uncle Ronald! We have never been happier!" They all agreed.

"Well, you all had better come back and visit often."

Evelyn said, "Helen, every year we will have an anniversary party for you here."

"Thank you, Evelyn." Helen walked over and embraced her. She thought, what a beautiful woman Evelyn is, inside and out.

Evelyn said, "I wish you all could stay. I already miss you. You are a very exciting and fun group!"

The next morning, they were flown to a new home. It was a partially converted military base with a courtyard and Olympic-sized swimming pool. It had a private airport with two runways and a weapons room with an indoor-outdoor shooting range. Every known weapon and all the latest technological weapons were available. They all had their own suites with large master bedrooms, small kitchens, dining rooms, and a living room. There was a large commercial kitchen and dining area in a big, open space. It also had a fantastic gymnasium and spa. After all they went through, it felt like paradise.

John, Alex, Joe, Bobby and Raphe had plenty of work to do collecting intelligence and keeping an eye on Globocorp. John had plans on interviewing Doctor Spears with his special note-taking secretary, Jane. He was keeping his new SEAL team busy by sending them on missions collecting intelligence, and other things pertinent to staying ahead of the bad guys. Ivory and Helen were teaching the girls college-grade courses. Ivory was still doing research. The President made sure she had a high-tech laboratory with a static free, clean room.

Her team from the mountains all made it out safely. They were working full-time in the lab. Doctor Jennings and his new wife, Annette, had their own suite. They were on the other side of the laboratory. Doctor Jennings and Ivory worked together on new and exciting projects. Their first project was to improve the stealth suits. It was a big problem on the mission, not being able to see or know where your own people were. They were all still on active duty and on-call at any time if an emergency came up. For now, they just lived life to the fullest. Blessing after blessing.

About the Author

Mr. Keiser is a retired construction contractor. He resides in the southern United States where he spends time with his family. He is currently working on a sequel to *A Time For The Wicked*.

H. T. Keiser's loyalties are to God, family and country. Mr. Keiser's dream is to leave a healthy, stable place for his children and grandchildren to live. This dream requires all good people to step out and get involved.

People of our nation need to stop corruption and evil by voting it out. Take a stand against evil. If we don't do it now, evil will win because good men and women did nothing!

Made in the USA
Monee, IL
15 April 2021